Praise for Wendy Delaney's

TRUDY, MADLY, DEEPLY

Trudy, Madly, Deeply is hysterical and riveting! Wendy Delaney had me at Page 1.

~ NYT bestseller Vicki Lewis Thompson

"Full of twists, turns, and laughs! *Trudy, Madly, Deeply* is a great mix of mystery and romance peppered with plenty of wonderful small town charm. I can't wait for the next one in this series!"

~ Ann Charles, award-winning author of the *Deadwood Mystery Series*

"Wendy Delaney's *Trudy, Madly, Deeply* is delicious, and that's no lie! Her fun human lie detector sleuth, quaint small town, fabulous descriptions, and mystery that will leave you guessing until the end make this debut a real page turner, and I predict this author's future will be bright."

~ Kari Lee Townsend, national bestselling author of the *Fortune Teller Mysteries*

"Wendy Delaney's witty style delights the reader and her engaging characters captivate. *Trudy, Madly, Deeply* is simply irresistible."

~ Kylie Brant, bestselling author of the *Mindhunters Series*

TRUDY, MADLY, DEEPLY

A Working Stiffs Mystery
Book 1

Wendy Delaney

TRUDY, MADLY, DEEPLY

Copyright © 2013 by Wendy Delaney

This book is a work of fiction. Names, characters, places, and incidents are the product of the author's imagination or are used fictitiously. Any resemblance to actual persons, living or dead, business establishments, events, or locales is coincidental.

Cover design by Lewellen Designs
Editing by Mimi (The Grammar Chick)

Second Edition 2016

Printed in the United States of America

ISBN-13: 978-0-9969800-1-2
ISBN-10: 0996980016

Wendy Delaney LLC, Publisher

To Jeff, my partner and soul mate.

Acknowledgments

I am indebted to a small army of friends and advisors who helped me breathe life into this story.

First of all, I must offer my gratitude to my critique partners and friends, Jacquie Rogers, Ann Charles, and Sherry Walker. You who truly are This Side of Deranged helped me find my way on this writing journey and never failed to cheer me on when times got tough. Thanks for all the years of unfailing support.

Thank you to former Jefferson County Prosecutor/ Coroner Juelie Dalzell and Funeral Director Real Robles for generously sharing their time and expertise with this mystery writer. Because of you, I knew I had a story.

To Lee Lofland, I so appreciate you helping me get my facts straight and for not reporting me to the police when I asked about how I could get away with murder.

Thank you, Renee (aka Eyes for Lies). Charmaine wouldn't be nearly as interesting a character if not for you.

Mary Buckham, a wonderful writer and teacher, will always have a special place in my heart because of the time and attention she gave my book. Mary, I count myself lucky to call you friend.

Many, many thanks to my readers and critiquers: Ann Charles, Jacquie Rogers, Kathy Coatney, Chassily Wakefield, Sabrina York, Celeste Deveney, Polly Iyer, Linda Lovely, Kari Townsend, Jim Vavra, Merry Parisotto, Pamela

Hiestand, Karen Linstad, June Linstad, Odette Tanner-Holmyard, Karen Haverkate, and Bryan Tretheway. I'm so grateful for your invaluable feedback.

To the Goal Girls—Gerri Russell, Joleen James, and Ann Charles—thanks for the years of unfailing encouragement. Achieving this goal is one I'm happy to celebrate with you.

A special thank you goes to the fabulous Vicki Lewis Thompson. How lucky I am to have met such a generous spirit.

Finally, to Jeff, thank you for your love and support (and for making dinner more times than I can count). You're my guy in every sense of the word, my rock, and the one I most want in my corner. I'm thrilled to share this next chapter of my life with you.

Chapter One

My life of crime began at seven twenty-eight this morning.

Nothing hard-core. But judging from the steely-eyed gaze Chimacam County Prosecutor, Francine "Frankie" Rickard, was leveling at me, I knew some hard time could be in my immediate future.

"What the hell are you doing?" she asked as I entered her third floor office in the stately courthouse overlooking the Port Merritt waterfront.

She'd asked the question du jour—what I'd been asking myself ever since I hijacked her Friday morning doughnut order.

I'd been a good girl, never before prone to vigilante acts against pastry. But after a year without a regular paycheck, I was done with playing it safe.

I needed to make the most of this golden opportunity for some one-on-one time with my potential employer, so I shot Frankie my best smile and set the Duke's Cafe bakery box on the corner of her oak desk. "Special delivery!"

Leaning back in her desk chair, she squinted at me over her wireframe bifocals. "Duke has you making deliveries now?" she asked, a wary glint in her slate-blue eyes.

In the last two decades, the population of the former mill boom town of Port Merritt, Washington, had dwindled to a tight-knit community of just over five thousand. Like Frankie, most everyone who frequented the waterfront was well-acquainted with my great-uncle, *the Duke*—Darrell Duquette, owner of Duke's Cafe, the best breakfast and burger joint in town.

The fact that Duke had me around this summer for cheap, temporary labor was supposed to be working in this delivery girl's favor. Instead, I felt like I'd been caught with a sticky-fingered hand in the tip jar.

"Deliveries, waiting tables. I'm just filling in wherever I'm needed until I can find something full-time," I said, hoping she'd take the bait I was dangling in front of her.

Despite the August sunshine filtering through the arched window behind her, haloing her upswept auburn-gray hair, sixty-year-old Frankie didn't look the least bit angelic as she crossed her arms. "Well, I have to admit I'm disappointed, Charmaine. Since I could use someone with your *ability* in this office, I'd hoped to entice you to work for me."

My *ability* had earned me a local reputation that had been following me around like a chain-rattling ghost ever since Heather Beckett labeled me as a freak back in sixth grade. If it could also pay off in the form of a steady salary, I wasn't too proud to do a little rattling of my own.

"You did. I submitted an application for the open position you told me about last week," I said, trying to ignore the telltale quirk of irritation pulling at Frankie's lips.

After completing the online application process, I'd spent the next ten days jumping at every ring of my cell phone like I was once again a teenager in need of a prom date. Much like seventeen years earlier, when Frankie called to ask me to babysit that Saturday night, my phone had rung just once about a job.

The offer had come from an old classmate who managed the Roadkill Grill, home of the *You kill it – We grill it* t-shirt that all the line cooks wore.

"Free t-shirts!" he said as if this were a coveted job perk that every thirty-four-year-old woman should have her sights set on.

Seriously, if I'm ever that desperate to save money on my wardrobe, I want someone to shoot me.

I met Frankie's gaze, my heart pounding with anticipation. "But since I never heard anything back about the job…"

She puckered, accentuating the fine lines surrounding her frosted strawberry lips. "No one called you for an interview?"

I shook my head.

Frankie pushed back from her desk, rising to a height almost eye level to my five foot six with the aid of the two-inch heels on her taupe pumps. "Come with me."

I followed her past the cluttered desks of two watchful assistants clicking on computer keyboards to a smaller office four doors down a threadbare hallway, where Ben Santiago sat in front of a laptop dwarfed by his massive mahogany desk.

"Ben," Frankie said as she and I stood in the doorway. "May we interrupt you?"

It was obvious from the cordial smile that didn't reach his hooded walnut brown eyes that the Deputy Criminal Prosecuting Attorney thought we already had.

Ben Santiago's gaze tightened when it landed on me, making me regret opting for the ponytail instead of taking an extra ten minutes with my blow dryer to tame my raggedy brown mop of curls. At least my white chambray shirt was clean. If you didn't count the smear of egg yolk on my right sleeve.

He removed his horn-rimmed glasses and pointed with them at the two black leather captain's chairs facing his desk. "Please."

The leather chairs appeared to be cheap and utilitarian, like they'd been ordered out of a discount office supply catalog along with the bank of black file cabinets to his right. Aside from the red tones in his desk, the worn rust-brown carpet, and the windowless eggshell-white wall featuring two sepia-tinted street scenes of Port Merritt in its late nineteenth century heyday, the monochrome office looked as warm and inviting as a loaf of five-day-old white bread.

And that included an unsmiling, fiftyish Ben Santiago—a burly, onyx-haired fireplug in an off-the-rack charcoal gray suit.

Frankie sat in the chair to my left. "Have you met Charmaine Digby?"

Standing a couple of inches taller than me, he reached across his desk and shook my hand with a firm, warm grip, projecting professionalism blended with a dollop of guarded disinterest. "Not officially."

I'd served this guy lunch at Duke's at least a dozen

times in the last couple of months while I filled in for one of the waitresses on maternity leave. He took his coffee black, preferred ranch dressing with his fries, and wanted his double beef bacon cheeseburgers served without a side order of conversation, so I wasn't surprised to hear I hadn't made the grade of official acquaintance.

"Charmaine is interested in the level one assistant position we have open," Frankie said.

Especially since it was the only employment nibble I'd had in the last nine weeks that didn't require me to have Rocky Raccoon roadkill stretched over my C-cups.

Unfortunately, although Ben Santiago smiled and nodded, the crinkle of annoyance etched between his thick eyebrows suggested that I should ring my buddy to give him my shirt size.

"She's the one I was telling you about, but it appears she was never called for an interview." Frankie dismissively flicked a wrist. "Probably because of some clerical error."

Ben's mouth flatlined for a fraction of a second.

Clerical error, my ass. Clearly, some barrel-chested prosecuting attorney with a receding hairline hadn't deemed me worthy of a phone call.

"Since you've been conducting the interviews, I thought you could take this opportunity to chat with her," Frankie stated, making it abundantly apparent that an answer of *no* wasn't advisable.

"Sure. I'd be happy to." Ben sounded as enthusiastic as my then-husband the last time I suggested we head up to the Pacific Northwest and spend the holidays with my grandmother.

"I'll sit in on this if you don't mind." Frankie smiled,

folding her slender arms and sending her deputy prosecutor the none-too-subtle message that she didn't care what he thought. "Just to expedite the process."

With the tug of displeasure at the edge of his tan lips betraying his emotion like a tell in a poker game, Ben turned his attention to me, his pinstriped tie rising and falling with each deep breath he took.

"Charmaine, I'm sure you're busy and need to get back to work, so what do you say we get right to it?"

Obviously, Frankie wasn't the only one who wanted to do some expediting.

"Since I haven't seen your resume...." He glanced at Frankie like he wanted to convince her of that fact, making it ring less true. "Tell me about your work history, Charmaine, aside from being a waitress."

"Most recently I worked as a process server for a private investigator in San Mateo, California."

The PI was the father of a friend I met at culinary school. She and I had both worked in four-star restaurant pressure cookers—probably why she thought I could handle the door-to-door verbal abuse, usually inflicted by irate soon-to-be-ex-spouses, pissed at being served with notices to appear. But it had its upside. I got to exchange being yelled at by the resident kitchen czar for a daily dose of California sunshine while I waited for my divorce to become final.

"I did research and ran background checks," I said, making sure that I hit some of the key duties of the level one assistant job description, "and I served as the assistant office manager." Which meant that I was the low man on the totem pole in charge of picking up the PI's dry-cleaning, but at least I had a title.

"And before that?" Ben asked, sounding like a food critic with zippo interest in the menu I'd just offered him.

"I co-managed an Italian bistro in San Francisco. Supervised the kitchen, handled the payroll."

Actually, I collected the staff's timecards and handed them over to my former mother-in-law, who wouldn't let me touch her computer. But to get myself into an office at the courthouse, I figured a sprig of creative garnish could only help my cause.

A flicker of disdain at the corner of his pursed mouth signaled that I was wasting his time. No doubt because I'd served him a double beef bacon cheeseburger last week.

"Before that, I was a pastry chef for ten years," I volunteered to cut to the chase.

Blowing out a breath, he stared at his boss as if she were forcing him to eat his vegetables.

"She has other skills, Ben," Frankie stated. "One in particular that could come in very handy around here."

The Criminal Prosecuting Attorney shot me a fake smile. "I'm sure you do."

I hadn't had this kind of confidence boost since my husband won a top chef contest on TV, then came home to announce that he was trimming the fat in his life— namely me.

Frankie peered at me over her bifocals. "You'd better show him."

"Okay." It wasn't the first time someone had trotted me out as if I were their trick poodle, but I could guarantee this guy wasn't going to like the show.

I scooted my chair closer to sit directly across from

Ben Santiago, and he scowled like I was invading his space.

"Is this going to take long?" he asked Frankie. "I'm due in court in ten minutes."

Doubtful. Until now he'd shown no indication that he was in a hurry. No surreptitious glances at his wristwatch. Nothing.

"Sorry, Mr. Santiago, but I think the truth is that you just want me out of here."

Getting into a man's face and calling him a liar is a lot like poking a bear—often not good for the one doing the poking. Since I didn't want the grizzly behind the desk to toss me out of his office, I thought it best not to use too sharp a stick.

His tie slowly rose and fell while a crease between his thick black brows punctuated his thoughts.

"I see that I'm right about when you're needed in court," I said.

"I'll mention that to the judge when I see him."

"When? In an hour or two?" I was guessing, taking a wild swing with my stick.

His eyes narrowed into a squint worthy of Dirty Harry. Bingo. "Right again, huh?"

"I see what you're trying to do, but trust me, I don't have time for games."

"Really? You seemed to be playing one earlier when you said that you hadn't seen my resume."

His tie stopped moving. "I—"

"Lied to me. You saw that I lacked the depth of experience you're looking for, and you didn't want to waste any more time on me. Would you like to tell me I'm wrong?"

His lips thinned. "You're awfully sure of yourself, aren't you?"

Not lately. But I still had faith in my bullshit barometer. "I'm only telling you how I'm reading you."

He tapped a thick index finger several beats against the surface of his desk. "Listen, I appreciate that you have...some skills," he said with a headshake that told me otherwise. "And this is nothing personal, but—"

"Nope. Sorry. I think it's very personal and has a lot to do with the fact that I'm the one who's been taking your lunch orders at Duke's."

"That has nothing to do with this."

"Sure."

His mouth quirked. "Okay, maybe it has a little bit to do with it. A waitress isn't exactly a natural fit for someone working in this office."

I couldn't disagree with him. "But I'm a natural at identifying deceit. I've sat through hundreds of interviews and correctly interpreted thousands of flashes of expression in two university studies to prove it."

I'd participated in the deception detection studies as a favor to my former sister-in-law, who was working on her doctoral thesis in clinical psychology, but the results validated Heather Beckett's claim. Compared to the perceptive abilities of the average person, I really was a bit of a freak.

Ben's eyebrows arched with interest. "That may be true," he said, "but—"

"I'm a hard worker and a quick study." I would have added that only one percent of the population had my level of deception detection accuracy, but I didn't want to sound like a used car salesman trying to make a hard sell. "I might fit in better than you think."

The look he gave his boss told me that he still wasn't sold.

"You already know how I feel about this," Frankie said. "But as head of the Criminal Division, your team would also work with her, so it needs to be a joint decision."

He leaned back, his desk chair creaking under his weight as his gaze swept over me.

I placed my hand over the yolk stain on my sleeve. "I'm good at what I do, Mr. Santiago." Despite all appearances to the contrary.

The pinstripes on his chest rose and fell. "Call me Ben. And we'll see about how good you are."

Not the most enthusiastic job offer I'd ever received, but every fiber in my being was singing a hallelujah chorus.

He looked at Frankie. "Thirty-day trial?"

"Fine," she agreed without hesitation.

Ben shrugged. "Then it looks like you just found yourself a new assistant."

Chapter Two

Three days later, energized to start my new job, I bounded up the well-worn marble stairs of the Chimacam County Courthouse. By the time I made it to the third-floor landing, I had a stitch in my side and I needed oxygen. Pitiful. Since when couldn't I handle a few stairs?

I only had to look down for the answer. Since I had eaten my way through a divorce.

The patty melts and pie happy hour at Duke's had to go. And no more double helpings of mashed potatoes and gravy at my grandmother's house.

"Stairs. Every day," I huffed. It was barely eight o'clock and I already had a diet and exercise program. Sort of. My hips and thighs would thank me later, after they stopped screaming.

Gold and black tile spanned the third-floor hallway, the geometric pattern interrupted by a wooden bench and three yellow vinyl upholstered chairs that looked like refugees from a garage sale. Gleaming wainscoting accented walls the color of vanilla pudding.

Breathing in the slightly musty scent of the nineteenth century courthouse, I noticed a sheriff's deputy watching me from a desk opposite the stairs.

I smiled.

He didn't.

Maybe Chimacam County's version of a security system wasn't supposed to fraternize with the help.

Heavy oak doors with department names etched in the glass identified each county office in the four-story, red brick building. The Prosecutor's office was no exception.

Inside, two mismatched vintage desks littered with paper and stacks of file folders stood side by side. An African violet with electric blue blooms, catching filtered sunshine from a narrow window, sat atop a tan metal file cabinet with two drawers open and chock-full like an over-stuffed cannoli. Apparently, no one around here believed in going paperless.

Using her shoulder to press the telephone receiver to her ear, the middle-aged, honey-haired receptionist waved me in after I told her my name. "See Patsy," she whispered.

I figured Frankie had arranged for me to get the fifty-cent tour of the courthouse. It was probably best to be polite and not mention that I had toured the historical landmark back in the fifth grade.

I made a left and headed down a short hallway, where Patsy Faraday, Frankie's legal assistant, stood by her desk with her gaze set on me like a sentry training her rifle on an approaching enemy.

Her black polyester-blend slacks hugged a pair of tree trunk thighs, emphasizing a panty line that her plus-sized paisley print tunic couldn't disguise. I knew from the gossip pipeline at Duke's that Patsy's husband had cheated on her for most of their twenty-year marriage. Like me, she appeared to have landed on her feet after her recent divorce, holding a fork in her hand.

Patsy flashed me a tepid smile. "Good morning. Frankie's going to be a little late, but she asked me to show you around."

Since we had another hour before the ferry from Seattle arrived and dozens of sun-seeking tourists caravanned toward the historic Old Town district in their RVs, I knew Frankie wouldn't be late because of the usual mid-morning backup on Highway 19. "Is everything okay?"

Patsy jutted her pointy chin at me. "I'm sure I wouldn't know."

She knew plenty. It just wasn't for me to know.

Patsy grabbed a thin red binder from her desk. "If you'll follow me," she said, leading the way down the hall. "Most of the attorneys aren't in yet, so we'll start with the lunchroom."

I watched her plaited hair sweep across her back like a pendulum, keeping rhythm with the sway of her rounded hips. The tawny color had probably come from a bottle she'd purchased at Clark's Pharmacy, but the gray roots were all Patsy's.

At the lunchroom doorway, she flipped a light switch, illuminating a coffee machine cooking the sludge in its pot. "You should check in here periodically. Not everyone thinks to make a fresh pot when they take the last cup. Coffee and filters are in there." Patsy pointed at the metal cabinet next to a dark brown mini-refrigerator, leaving no doubt which assistant she expected to make the coffee.

She switched off the light and I followed her down the hall to an office bullpen of five legal assistants where Patsy systematically introduced me to each woman.

Their ages probably ranged from early thirties to late fifties. I already knew the oldest lady—Karla Tate, a two pack a day smoker who lived on G Street down the hill from my grandmother. The other four I knew by sight from having served them lunch at Duke's. Based on Patsy's speed-dating approach to today's introductions I could only hope there wouldn't be a who's who quiz later.

"And here we are…your desk," Patsy said as she and I made our way to the windowless rear wall, where four black filing cabinets shared the dreary space with a scarred walnut desk, an empty, black plastic pencil cup, and a spindly philodendron languishing in the corner.

If this concluded the tour, my desk certainly looked like it was at the end of the line.

Patsy handed me the red binder. "You'll find your computer login in here, plus a manual on navigating the network. When there's time tomorrow, I'll schedule you for some training."

"I'll probably have time today." Considering that I didn't even have any pencils to sharpen, a lot of time.

Her pale lips disappeared for a split second. "Maybe."

That looked more like a *no way*. Patsy definitely knew something she didn't want to share.

She aimed her chin at me again. "If there's nothing else you need, Frankie will call when she's ready for you."

"What should I do in the meantime?"

"Make coffee."

Swell.

Fifteen minutes later, while the coffee machine gurgled, laboring to spit out its last few drops, I stood at the lunchroom window and considered cleaning out the refrigerator until I saw Frankie's Volvo roll into the parking lot. Happy to give the fridge a reprieve, I found a ceramic mug in the cabinet, filled it with some fresh brew and headed down the hall to find out what was going on.

"Charmaine," Frankie said, standing at the doorway of her office. "What good timing."

For both of us.

I lifted the mug in my hand. "Coffee?"

Her lips curled into a pleasant smile, but the tension in her jaw made it look forced. "You must have been reading my mind." She gestured toward her desk with her briefcase. "Come in. I'd like to talk to you about something."

As I stepped into her office, she asked Patsy, "Do you have Trudy's file ready?"

Trudy? The only Trudy I knew was Trudy Bergeson, the Port Merritt library *Story Lady* of my youth and one of my great-aunt Alice's oldest friends. Since Trudy had been in the county hospital with pneumonia for most of the last week, it couldn't be a good thing if my favorite story teller had a file.

Carrying the blue folder Patsy handed her, Frankie set her briefcase on the two-drawer file cabinet to her right and eased into her desk chair. "Have a seat," she said as I placed the steaming mug in front of her.

I took the closest of the two Georgian high back chairs facing her.

Frankie took a sip of coffee. "I know you've hardly had a chance to settle in, but I have something I'd like you to do."

I was fine with ending this morning's tour of KP duty,

but I had a sinking feeling about the contents of that blue folder.

Setting the mug aside, Frankie folded her hands, her gaze soft as warm butter. "Trudy Bergeson died at the hospital early this morning."

My sinking feeling hit bottom.

Any breaking news of a birth, death, engagement, or divorce always made a beeline to Duke's Cafe. Aunt Alice had to have already heard about Trudy.

"And one of the doctors on duty has some…concerns," Frankie added.

Concerns? About how Trudy died? Most everyone in town knew that she'd been in failing health ever since her stroke last year.

Even though I was well aware that Frankie had recently been elected to a third term as the Prosecutor/Coroner of rural Chimacam County, this made no sense. Why would a doctor contact her about the death of a frail seventy-seven-year-old woman?

"Dr. Cardinale called early this morning." Frankie handed me the folder. "These are my notes. I'd like you to go with Karla and get a statement from him."

I knew Frankie wanted me to sit in on witness interviews and be an emotional barometer for the prosecution, but after we left Ben's office on Friday, she had talked about me shadowing a couple of the legal assistants in the office for the first week. Maybe observe the criminal case that was supposed to start jury selection tomorrow.

Obviously, with the call about Trudy's death, the plan had changed.

"The statement is just a formality," Frankie said as

if she could sense the nervous knots in my gut twisting themselves into pretzel rolls, "but it will be a good chance for you to jump in and get your feet wet. If the two of you leave soon, you can probably catch the doctor before his shift ends."

To avoid embarrassing myself during my first interview, I scanned Frankie's notes. At the bottom of the page, three letters were followed by a question mark. "C-O-D?"

"Cause of death, which will remain unknown until we hear back from the forensic pathologist."

"A pathologist. Like a medical examiner?"

"Exactly, and he'll be doing the autopsy that Dr. Cardinale requested." She leveled her gaze at me. "Of course, nothing about any of this will be shared with anyone outside this office."

Like anything juicy could be kept quiet within earshot of Duke's. I nodded anyway, then started for the door.

"One more thing," Frankie said, stopping me in my tracks. "Go downstairs and get sworn in before you leave."

"Huh?"

Chapter Three

"I'm here to be sworn in," I said to the Julia Child lookalike in the County Clerk's office on the second floor.

She leaned against the counter, the name placard at the bank teller style window identifying her as Gloria. "And what might you need to be sworn in for, honey?"

"It seems that I just became a deputy coroner." I tried to not choke on the words coming out of my mouth.

When I'd handed Frankie's notes over to Karla, she explained that deputizing me simply meant that I could speak with the doctor as an official representative of Frankie's office. No more, no less.

Since my skill set required working with people who were still breathing, I was totally counting on that *no more* part.

Gloria's unpainted lips pulled back into a lopsided grin. "Weren't you the one who sold me a cinnamon roll last Thursday?"

"That would be me."

"Interesting career path."

"Tell me about it." I just prayed that path wouldn't lead to me wearing my breakfast on my shoes before the day was over.

She grabbed a form from behind the counter and slid it toward me. "Fill this out."

Fifteen minutes later, Gloria handed me a laminated badge with the county seal that looked about as official as my library card.

"That's it?"

"That's it, hon." She patted me on the hand. "Try not to lose it or do anything to get the county sued."

Nice. "I'll give it my best shot."

Since I had to make a side trip to the County Clerk's office and Karla needed to get a registered letter out in today's mail, we had agreed to meet up at the hospital. Figuring she had a ten-minute head start on me, I dashed to the parking lot, slid behind the wheel of my ex-husband's Jaguar, and put the pedal to the metal to blast up to Chimacam Memorial at the crest of the hill on 6th.

Don't get the wrong idea about the Jag. I got it as part of the divorce settlement. I needed a car and Chris was motivated to supply the wheels to fast-track me out of his life. Considering how much he'd loved the sleek, silver XJ6 he'd been driving when we met at culinary school, I was more than a little suspicious that he'd been so willing to part with it. Turned out for good reason—it overheated on my way back home to my grandmother's house and cost me over a thousand bucks in repairs before I'd even made it out of California. The mechanic told me that for another grand he could fix the Jag's oil leak and have her purring like a kitten.

As long as the damned thing didn't cough up a hairball, I could live with feeding it a quart of oil every couple of weeks. Especially since that was all I could afford until I saw my first paycheck. Then I was going to unload it before it bled my bank account dry, and buy a car that wouldn't make me feel like my ex had played me for a sucker.

When I entered the hospital lobby, I didn't see Karla so I went to the information desk. "Where can I find Dr. Cardinale?" I asked the twenty-something who'd had her pierced nose buried in a romance novel when I served her a grilled cheese sandwich last Wednesday.

She popped her chewing gum. "Do you have an appointment?"

This seemed like a good opportunity to test drive my newly acquired plastic, so I pulled out my badge. "I just need to speak with him."

She squinted at the badge, an uptick at the corner of her high gloss lips signaling her amusement. "You're a deputy coroner now?"

I might have been given the county stamp of *officialdom*, but that obviously didn't mean squat to anyone who'd seen me at Duke's last week.

I pasted a smile on my face. "Yeah, I got a promotion. So, is Dr. Cardinale around?"

"Maybe. Take the elevator to the second floor and ask at the nurse's station."

When the elevator door opened, my cell phone rang—a local number but I didn't recognize it.

"I have a problem," Karla said without identifying herself. She didn't have to. I'd have known her throaty smoker's voice anywhere.

I also recognized the sounds of street noise and walked to a window overlooking the hospital parking lot. "Where are you?" I asked, looking for her.

"Third and Main. A tourist in the mother of all Winnebagos rear-ended me. I'm waiting for the cops to arrive."

"Are you okay?"

"I'm fine, but my car's not. Are you at the hospital?"

"Yes, do you want—"

"Good. This will take a while, so I want you to meet with Dr. Cardinale and take his statement."

Me? "Are you sure we shouldn't wait and—"

"There's nothing to it," she said over the rumble of a passing truck. "Just ask him the five W's—*who, what, when, where*, and find out *why* he called to report a suspicious death. That should get him talking. Your job is to take good notes, then I'll follow up with him later to fill in any blanks."

"Okay." That sounded easy enough.

"Gotta go. A patrol car is pulling up. I'll catch up with you in a couple of hours." *Click.*

I dropped my cell phone into my tote and then sucked in a shaky breath as I started down the hallway.

A woman in her mid-thirties dressed in a pink Winnie the Pooh tunic looked up at me from a computer monitor at the nurses' station. Her face broke into a smile as I approached. "Char?"

"Hi…" Drawing a blank, I sneaked a glance at her hospital badge. "…Laurel."

"It's Laurel Seeger now," she said, flashing me an emerald cut diamond ring.

I remembered a Laurel from high school. She'd been two years ahead of me, a Goth type with long, stringy black hair and thick glasses. This Laurel's hair complemented her oval face in soft brown curls. "Sorry, I didn't recognize you without your glasses."

"Yeah, I got that a lot when I moved back to town last year." She leaned back in her desk chair, her gaze settling on my hips. "But you haven't changed a bit."

Liar.

After a minute of obligatory chitchat about our families, I brought up the subject of the funeral both our grandmothers would soon be attending. "I heard the sad news about Trudy."

Laurel shook her head, a smile frozen on her lips. A little off, but Laurel had always been half a bubble off plumb, so I didn't make too much out of it. "Such a shame. She was supposed to go home today."

Really. I hadn't seen that tidbit of information in Frankie's notes.

I leaned closer, resting my elbows on the counter. "What happened?"

"You should probably talk to Dr. Cardinale," Laurel said, her gaze fixed on the hunk and a half walking our direction.

Solid with spiky hair the color of espresso and an olive complexion paying homage to his Italian surname, Dr. Cardinale stood a few inches taller than me, making him around five foot ten. He wore black high tops, faded blue jeans, and had dark stubble that could give a girl some serious whisker burn. The front of his white lab coat was stained with dark smears I prayed had nothing to do with Trudy.

"Can I help you?" he asked, the tension in his square jaw betraying his wariness.

"I'm Charmaine Digby." I showed him my badge which drew a nod, then his whiskey brown eyes shifted toward two women in green scrubs waiting for the elevator. I knew I needed to get him out of the hallway for both our sakes. "Is there someplace we could talk privately?"

His chiseled lips drew back, giving me the impression that he'd done all the talking he wanted to today.

"Just for a few minutes," I added with an easy smile.

After a nod, he led me down the hall to the doctor's lounge, where I sank my butt into an aqua blue vinyl chair.

"I've been asked to follow up with you about the call you made to the County Coroner," I said, catching a whiff of deodorant soap as he took the chair opposite me.

He rested his toned, tan forearms on his thighs and steepled his fingers. "I already told her everything I know."

"I'm sure you did." *But now you need to tell me.* "This will just take a few minutes."

I pulled out a notebook and a pen from my tote bag, then noticed a *GQ* magazine on the table between us. I recognized the popular actor on the cover as one of my mother's former boyfriends. Tilting my head I scanned the text to the right of his perfectly straight, bright white teeth. Not that I was interested in anything he had to say—as long as the article didn't mention anyone I knew.

"You can take it home with you if you're a fan," Dr. Cardinale said.

I covered the magazine with my tote. "I'm not."

For the last twenty years, I'd made a point of avoiding my actress mother's boy toys in person and in the media. Really, the less I knew about the guys boinking my mom, the better for all of us.

I opened my notebook to a clean page. "Shall we begin?"

Taking a deep breath, Dr. Cardinale leaned back and crossed his legs.

I mirrored his posture—something that I'd seen my divorce attorney do during our first meeting. When I asked him about it, he sheepishly confessed that it was a technique he used to help establish a rapport with new clients.

Since my first interview could use all the help it could get, I also shot the doctor a friendly smile. Mainly to help me relax, but if it could do the same for him, all the better.

The corners of his lips curled, then he lowered his gaze, lingering at my breasts. I was struck with an immediate sense of curiosity mixed with male awareness, like he wanted to know what I was hiding under my oversized cotton pullover. A nanosecond later, his eyes were fixed back on mine.

The extra zip in my pulse confirmed that rapport had definitely been established, so I diverted my focus to the task at hand and the first of the five W's—*who*.

"What is your full name, Doctor?"

"Kyle Edward Cardinale," he said, spelling his last name.

"Address and phone number?"

I scribbled down the local post office box address and cell phone number he provided.

"And you live in town?"

"On my boat. Slip 51."

That explained the tan. Since he lived at the marina, I'd wager that meant he was single.

"Married?" Probably not a question Karla would have

asked him, but I wanted to know that I was right.

"No."

Knew it. "And your job title here is…"

"It's not much of a title, but I'm an attending."

Which meant he was probably close to my age.

He tried to stifle a yawn and failed.

"Long day?"

"They all are." He swiped at the waist-high brown smear on his lab coat, then glanced up at me. "I was slimed by a four-year-old who decided to finger-paint me with chocolate pudding."

I breathed a sigh of relief and hoped that my gag reflex got the message.

As pleasant as it might be to chat about the artwork on his lab coat, I knew I needed to move on to the next *W—what.*

"So, Doctor, I understand you called the Coroner about Trudy Bergeson's death early this morning," I said, hoping he'd swing at the slow pitch I'd just served up.

He nodded, tight-lipped. "That's right."

Which told me nothing except that he didn't want to play.

"Because she took a sudden turn for the worse?" I asked, prodding for more than a two-word confirmation of what I already knew.

A frown line etched a path between his dark brows as if I had poked a sore spot. "Not exactly. She just coded."

My hospital jargon was limited to old episodes of *ER.* "Which means you get a page and rush to her room, right?"

"Basically."

"Who paged you?" I asked in case Karla needed to

interview one of the nurses or another doctor.

"A nurse. Cindy Tobias."

I knew Cindy from having worked with her at Duke's the summer after my junior year of high school. Smart, warm-hearted, skilled at telling little fibs to make people feel better. I wasn't at all surprised when she became a nurse.

"And what time was this?" I asked, mentally crossing off another *W* from my list.

Dr. Cardinale propped his feet up on the table between us. "Around three forty-five."

"Then what happened?"

"She asphyxiated."

Unblinking, his eyes were fixed on his high tops. By the intensity of his gaze I sensed he'd just replayed the scene in his head.

I'd also played it in my own mind. It wasn't the way I wanted to envision my favorite Story Lady, and I swallowed the lump threatening to clog my throat. "She died?"

He nodded.

"Anyone else there?"

He shook his head. "Just Cindy and me."

"Then what happened?"

"I called her primary care doctor."

Before calling Trudy's husband? That struck me as odd, especially since his words were accompanied with a hard edge of distain. "Who was...?"

"Warren Straitham."

The name came as no surprise, despite the fact that the doctor who had delivered me had to be pushing seventy. Most of the local gray hairs preferred good old

Doc Straitham to the new kids in town, and all the senior citizens in my family were no exception.

"I advised his service to let him know about Mrs. Bergeson and he arrived about ten minutes later," Dr. Cardinale said.

I looked up from my notebook. "That's pretty darn quick."

Folding his arms over his chest, Dr. Cardinale shrugged, a tight, little sneer of contempt dimpling his cheek.

Warren Straitham lived in the hills, a couple miles south of Port Merritt. Once the phone message was relayed to him, there was no way he could have rolled out of bed and driven to the hospital that quickly.

Clearly, the attending doctor had some strong opinions concerning Trudy's primary care physician, but I'd seen nothing to indicate that Dr. Cardinale had lied to me.

I jotted a question mark next to my notes about the ten-minute arrival time. "After Dr. Straitham got here, what happened?"

"I briefed him on the situation and told him he'd better call Norm Bergeson." Shifting in his seat like he wanted to make a break for the nearest exit, Dr. Cardinale scrubbed his face, hiding it from my view. "And that's about it."

I didn't believe that for a minute. He was holding something back.

"Just one more question, Dr. Cardinale." *Maybe two.* "Why did you call the Coroner to ask for an autopsy?"

He blew out a breath. "With Mrs. Bergeson's heart and history of stroke, she didn't have long, maybe a year, but...." He slowly shook his head. "According to her chart the asphyxiation doesn't fit."

I had no idea what that meant, so that made my next question a no-brainer. "For someone in her condition who is also battling pneumonia, would asphyxiation be considered unusual?"

He frowned. "Not necessarily."

Since I'd just met the man, I couldn't tell if the tension I saw in his piercing stare meant that he was pissed off or if he was just concentrating. I suspected some of both.

He raked a hand through his hair, making it look even more perfectly unkempt. "I don't think this is an isolated incident."

"Which means what exactly?"

"It may be part of a pattern."

"A pattern in which other people have died this way?"

He slowly nodded.

I sat at the edge of my seat. "How many people?"

"At least two in the last year."

"Holy cow," I muttered, my hand shaking as I tried to capture his exact words. "Who?"

"I don't know if I should—"

"Dr. Cardinale, I'm here to take your statement as follow-up to the call you made to the County Coroner's office." I may not have known how to act like a deputy coroner, but I could damned well sound like one. "Trust me, you should name names."

He cast a quick glance at the door. "Bernadette Neary and Howard Jeppesen."

Port Merritt was a small town, so I half-expected to recognize the names. But he had just sucker-punched me by naming two friends of my grandmother's.

"They were also Straitham's patients," he said, landing

another punch.

So was I for the first twenty years of my life.

"Are you accusing Dr. Straitham—"

"I'm just saying that it's too coincidental. And I don't believe in coincidences."

Neither did I.

Chapter Four

It was almost ten-thirty when I pulled out of the hospital parking lot. Duke's was sure to be buzzing with the news about Trudy, so I thought I'd stop for some coffee on my way back to the courthouse. Not that I needed the caffeine. My body was already pumping with enough adrenaline to catapult me into next week. But since my great-aunt and uncle lived four blocks from Chimacam Memorial and could have driven past Dr. Straitham coming up the hill on 6th Street early this morning, I wanted to find out if they had seen anything that could confirm the doctor's arrival time.

After I cruised by a new three-story apartment complex for seniors where a block of century-old, clapboard row houses built for the mill workers had stood last year, I turned left onto Main Street and angled into a parking spot in front of the Shabby Apple, an antique store a half block from Duke's Cafe.

The silver bell over the door signaled my arrival at the 50's era diner. If I inched close enough to the wall, the big mouth bass mounted next to Aunt Alice's fish tank would chime in with a tinny rendition of *Don't Worry, Be Happy*—

my great-uncle's idea of cheap entertainment.

Wish I could take advice from a plastic fish, but it wasn't a *Don't Worry* kind of day.

All but two of the eight booths hugging the buttermilk yellow walls sat empty. Occupying the scarred round table in the corner were four Gray Ladies, members of an early morning exercise group decked out in matching heather gray sweatshirts with their first names stitched on the front like pre-Disney Channel Mouseketeers. They always stopped in for pastry and gossip after their class at the senior center up the street. No doubt Trudy's death would be the featured topic of conversation of this morning's coffee klatch.

Ernie and Jayne, a couple in their mid-seventies, sat across from one another in one of the booths next to the front window. Ernie, a widower, looked like he'd gelled his white hair. Judging by the way he was looking at Jayne, it wasn't to impress his fishing buddy, Duke. Bellied up to the lemon yellow Formica counter was ninety-year-old Stanley, reading yesterday's newspaper at his usual barstool.

Looming large in the cut-out window above the grill, six-foot-three-inch Duke squinted at me. "Aren't you supposed to be at work?"

"I'm on a coffee break." Sort of.

Duke, a salty Navy veteran who still sported a military-style crew cut, huffed out a deep breath. "Coffee break, my sweet patoot."

Worry deepened the creases in his forehead as he turned and watched Alice, his wife of fifty-two years, roll out pie dough on the butcher block work table in the middle of the kitchen. "You must have heard about Trudy."

"I heard." I didn't dare mention what else I'd heard this morning.

I pulled out a white porcelain mug from under the counter and filled it with industrial strength, black as crude oil java from a carafe at the coffee station.

"How's Alice doing?" I asked as I dumped some half and half into my cup to make Duke's coffee palatable.

He flipped the two bubbling pancakes on the grill. "Hasn't shed a tear."

That was weird. Like Dr. Cardinale had told me, it didn't fit. Trudy and Alice had been friends since childhood. Shedding some tears would be a normal reaction. This news gave me a very uneasy feeling, and after what I'd heard this morning at the hospital I was already feeling plenty uneasy.

I wasn't going to feel any better until I got some help with the jigsaw puzzle I kept trying to piece together in my head.

Leaning a hip against the counter, I watched Duke through the cut-out window as he scrambled a couple of eggs. "Let me ask you something," I said, keeping my voice low. Stanley, sitting at the end of the counter, might have been a little hard of hearing, but today wasn't the day to push my luck.

My great-uncle shot me a wary glance, the same look he reserved for every restaurant equipment salesman who stepped foot in his diner.

"When did you leave the house this morning?" I asked.

"Around four, like usual. Why?"

"Did you see anyone on the road on your way in?"

"We passed a couple of cars on Main." He furrowed his bushy silver eyebrows. "Why?"

I didn't want to get into why. If I suggested that I had the tiniest concern about where Warren Straitham was when he got the call from Dr. Cardinale, it would spread in the kitchen like a grease fire. "You didn't recognize the cars?"

"No."

Then he didn't pass Dr. Straitham's Cadillac on the way to the hospital, and I'd just hit a dead end.

"So, is there something I was supposed to have seen?" Duke asked, brushing my arm with the strings of his white canvas apron as he reached for a plate.

Yes. "No, nothing like that."

"You're such a bad liar."

Not usually. But I had a bigger problem. If I took everything Dr. Cardinale told me at face value, then how did Trudy's doctor get to the hospital so quickly?

Duke dished up the eggs he'd scrambled, added a wedge of cantaloupe, and set the plate onto the shiny aluminum counter in front of him. "Order up."

Lucille Kressey, a grandmotherly waitress who had worked for Duke ever since she lost her job at the mill in the late seventies, lumbered past me.

"Denver. Bacon. Wheat," she said in rapid staccato, slipping the breakfast order on the aluminum wheel over the grill.

Lucille wore squeaky, white orthopedic shoes, styled her fine platinum hair in a bob that curled into her plump cheeks, and punctuated the breakfast order with a heavy sigh.

It wasn't the sigh that telegraphed her mood. That had more to do with her bunions. The little flicker of disgust at the corner of her puckered mouth, as visible to me as the coral lipstick bleeding into the surrounding fine lines, was what had my attention.

She shook her head. "I really don't see how people can eat at a time like this."

"They're hungry." Duke pushed the plate toward Kim, a perky strawberry blonde college student who swept by me, leaving a trail of patchouli in her wake.

"They won't be when they find out what's going on around here," Lucille said, directing an icy glare at Jayne and Ernie.

I couldn't begin to guess what Jayne Elwood and Ernie Kozarek had to do with any of the events surrounding Trudy's death, but Lucille had evidently made some connection.

Stanley sent a nervous glance our way. So did a couple of the Gray Ladies.

Wide-eyed as a horror movie extra, Kim waited at the counter for the rest of her order. "You're scaring the customers," she said to Lucille in a breathless stage whisper.

Lucille shrugged. "Maybe they should be scared."

Duke passed a plate stacked with pancakes to Kim. "Deliver those, then take Jayne and Ernie's order, and keep an eye on things for a few minutes." He pointed at Lucille. "You. In the kitchen."

Lucille narrowed her watery blue-eyed gaze at my great-uncle. If looks could kill, Trudy wouldn't be the only obituary notice in Wednesday's *Port Merritt Gazette*.

I knew from experience that Lucille's conspiracy theories could take me down a rat hole. But if she actually knew something that could back up Dr. Cardinale's suspicions, I had to jump in with both my size eights.

I grabbed the coffee carafe, three clean cups, and followed Lucille into the kitchen. Rolling pin in hand, seventy-four-year-old Alice looked up at me from her wooden stool. Five unbaked fruit pies sat in a row to her left, awaiting their turn in the oven, the unmistakable aroma of cinnamon and sugar hanging in the air. The news about Trudy obviously hadn't stopped my great-aunt from filling her bakery racks. But her deep-set hazel eyes seemed dull, the apples of her cheeks devoid of their usual glow, like someone had snuffed out the spark in the former fiery redhead.

Lucille pulled up the old desk chair Duke used to tally the register receipts and lowered herself into it, sitting across from Alice.

"What's this?" Alice demanded, scowling at Duke.

He sat on the stool next to Lucille. "We're having a meeting." Extending his long legs, he glared at me as I set the cups on the table and started filling them with coffee. "Don't you have a job to go back to?"

I handed him a cup. "Not done with my break yet."

"Fine," he said. "Just keep your yap shut."

Leaning against a stainless steel refrigerator, I smiled sweetly at the old buzzard. "Yes, sir." I was more interested in listening than talking anyway.

Duke wrapped his meaty hands around his cup like he needed to warm them even though it had to be almost eighty degrees near the oven. He cleared his throat. "Listen, we're all sad about Trudy."

"We wouldn't be if people around here had listened to me," Lucille snapped.

On a typical day I could easily ignore Lucille's editorial opinions. But nothing about today felt like a typical day, so I had to ask. "About what?"

Duke fixed his steely gaze on me like a sharpshooter with an itchy trigger finger.

I know, I was supposed to keep my yap shut.

Lucille reached for a coffee cup. "About Rose."

Rose was Ernie Kozarek's wife, who had passed away almost two years ago after a lengthy stay in the hospital.

"For crissake, Luce." Duke raked a hand through his clipped silver hair. "Give it a rest."

Lucille aimed a laser-like glare at him. "That's what you said when Jesse Elwood died, and now Trudy's gone."

She was connecting the dots between those three deaths?

Kim stood at the door to the kitchen and waved a white order ticket at Duke, who growled an obscenity, then pointed at Lucille. "Enough of this crazy talk. It doesn't help anybody."

I was sure the *anybody* he was most concerned about was Alice. Even before I'd seen the cocoon of pain she was hunkered down in I would have shared his concern.

He stood, flattening his palms on the table. "I don't want to hear it. The customers don't want to hear it, so knock it off. Do I make myself clear?"

Grumbling, Lucille waved him away like he was a pesky fly.

Duke stalked past me. "I give up. Talk some sense into her to make her stop stirring the pot."

That was like telling me to drop ten pounds by midnight. When Lucille had something fixed in her mind, there was no convincing her otherwise.

Once Duke had busied himself at the grill, I scooted his wooden stool over to sit between the two women. "What do you mean people should have listened to you?" I asked Lucille.

She leaned into my shoulder like we were schoolgirls sharing a secret. "All I know is that when I got to the hospital to see Trudy last night, she was sitting up in bed and eating tapioca pudding. After Norm got there, they started talking about how she'd be going home today. I ask you, does that sound like someone who's gonna die in the middle of the night?"

No, but it did confirm what Laurel had told me an hour earlier. Only she hadn't mentioned Norm, Trudy's husband.

"It's just like Rose," Alice said, staring into the depths of her cup.

"It's *exactly* like Rose. She seemed to be doing better, then the next day...bam!" Lucille slapped her palm on the table. "She's gone."

"It wasn't her time," Alice agreed, slowly shaking her head, but I had a feeling it wasn't Rose my great-aunt was referring to.

"Damned straight it wasn't her time." Lucille wiped a tear from her cheek. "And now look what's going on."

She lost me. "What?"

Lucille wrinkled her nose. "Jayne Elwood and Ernie Kozarek, making eyes at one another like a couple of teenagers. I even heard that Ernie showed up at Clark's Pharmacy with a prescription for Viagra."

That was so not the image of Jayne and Ernie that I

wanted in my head.

"Whatever. It's been over a year since Mr. Elwood died." Jesse Elwood had been my junior high school principal. There was no way I could call him anything other than Mr. Elwood. "And almost two years for Rose. It's not like anyone is cheating on their spouse."

Lucille slapped the table top again. "Exactly my point. Damned convenient."

Alice stared at her rolling pin. For someone typically quick to shoot down Lucille's conspiracy theories, she was too quiet.

I touched her hand. "What do you think, Aunt Alice?"

She blinked at me through her wire-rimmed trifocals as if she were having trouble focusing. "I think Trudy was supposed to come home today. I think she should be with Norm—a few more months, even a few more weeks." She hung her head, slowly shaking it, her short reddish-gray tousled hair not budging a millimeter. "It wasn't her time."

Despite the heat radiating from the oven, I shivered.

"I'll tell you what I think," Lucille said, without waiting to be asked, as usual. "There's something going on at that hospital."

If I hadn't known that Kyle Cardinale shared that opinion, I would have reminded Lucille that she also believed that Elvis had faked his death and lived down the street from her sister in Fort Lauderdale.

"And Norm and Ernie are on the same bowling team." Lucille folded her arms under her ample chest. "Some people might call that a coincidence, but I don't think so."

Huh? "Just because they're on the same bowling team doesn't mean—"

"Then what do you call all this?" Lucille demanded.

"It should be a good thing. Ernie's just getting on with his life. So is Jayne."

"Bullshit!" Alice exclaimed.

"Fine!" I clenched my teeth to keep from screaming in frustration. "Then what do *you* call it?"

"Murder."

Chapter Five

Murder? A bowling team connection? And the prime suspect was the doctor who brought me into this world? The butterflies churning in my stomach might be buying into this insanity, but since I didn't want to fricassee my chances to reach day thirty of my thirty-day trial, I couldn't just go with my gut.

I needed more information, and I knew exactly where to find it.

This called for backup, so I filled a large paper cup with coffee, threw a couple of glazed doughnuts into a white to-go bag, and hoofed it two blocks up Main to the Port Merritt Police Station.

Wanda McCormick, sitting at a desk behind the front counter, poked her head out from behind her computer monitor. "Hey, Char."

Wanda had been the chief's secretary for most of the last decade, and she ran the station like a mama bear protecting her cubs. Everyone knew that if you wanted to get past the lobby, you had to get past Wanda.

A sign printed on a wrinkled sheet of plain white paper

was taped to the scarred wooden counter. YOU ARE BEING VIDEO RECORDED. Undaunted, I flashed Wanda and the camera mounted in the corner the to-go bag and my best winning smile. "Is Steve in?"

She looked at me quizzically. "I thought you were working for Frankie now."

News around here traveled fast.

"I was in the neighborhood, so Duke asked me to make the delivery." It was an easy lie to sell. It had plausibility, which was key, and since Duke sent food orders over to the station on a daily basis, I knew Wanda wouldn't think twice about it.

She pressed the button next to her desk that released the security door separating the public from the restricted domain of the fourteen-person police force.

I entered the secure area and headed down the narrow hall to the open door stenciled with the words, *Investigation Division*. Inside the cramped office sat the one and only member of that division, Detective Steve Sixkiller.

He had his telephone receiver to his ear so I gently knocked on his door. We locked gazes, his dark eyes impenetrable, but I could tell Steve wasn't happy to see me.

He pointed at a hardback chair across from his metal desk. Seconds later, he ended the call and leaned back in his black vinyl chair, facing me. "Shouldn't you be at work?"

"I'm on my lunch hour, so stop acting like a cop." I held up the cup and to-go bag. "Especially when I come bearing gifts."

Steve set the paper cup on his desk, away from the short stack of paperwork in front of him. "Then you must want something."

He knew me too well.

"I do have one teensy thing I'd like to ask you," I said, pushing the white sack at him.

Steve pulled out one of the doughnuts. "If you think this is a bribe, think again, Chow Mein."

I smiled at the nickname he gave me back in the third grade. "I just thought you might be hungry."

"You're such a lousy liar," he said with his mouth full.

I was good enough to make my way past Wanda but now wasn't the time to press the point.

"You've heard about Trudy's death."

"Yeah. Nice lady." He took a sip of coffee.

No visible reaction to the news about Trudy, much as I'd expected.

"I was at the hospital this morning, talking to Dr. Cardinale."

Steve's chocolate brown eyes narrowed. "Why?"

"There appear to be some concerns surrounding Trudy's death, and Frankie wanted to get his statement," I said, avoiding the particulars in order to comply with her earlier instructions instead of being my usual full-disclosure self.

"And she sent you? It's your first day for crissake."

"I'm perfectly capable of asking the man a few questions."

Steve's lips curled in amusement. "Okay. So, you *chatted* with Dr. Cardinale."

I didn't appreciate the sarcasm.

"Don't tell me, let me guess." He dropped the rest of the doughnut into the bag. "You *saw* something."

"It wasn't just that. Kyle Cardinale is pretty suspicious

of the way Trudy died." So much for avoiding particulars.

Steve licked some sugary glaze from his thumb. "And your boss is ordering an autopsy, right?"

There was no point in denying it, so I nodded.

"Then your job is done, Deputy."

"How'd you know I was a—"

"Half the staff in the Prosecutor's office are deputy coroners. Welcome to county government on a shoestring budget."

Okay, I admit I felt a little less special about my new job title. At least he didn't warn me to avoid getting the county sued.

"But I've talked to some people who have good reason to think that Trudy could have been murdered," I said, not wanting to mention names.

"Uh-huh. The Story Lady was murdered. And since when do you believe any of Lucille's conspiracy theories?"

I shrugged. Since my great-aunt agreed with her.

I decided to cast out a line to see if he'd bite. "So you don't think there's anything to this, despite the fact that Bernadette Neary, Howard Jeppesen, and maybe even Rose Kozarek died the same way."

No answer. Not even a nibble of a reaction.

"Char?" he finally said.

I studied his face, watching, waiting. "Hmm?"

He leaned closer as if he were daring me to a staring contest. "This conversation is over."

"Come on, Detective. Tell me that you don't find Trudy's death just a little suspicious."

His gaze sharpened, unamused. The tan, lean planes of his face had left hardly a trace of the neighbor boy

I used to play with. Instead, a man wrapped in sinewy muscle inhabited the former Port Merritt High School football star's body, and this guy knew how to intimidate. Fortunately, I was immune, more or less.

After several silent seconds, he blew out a coffee-flavored breath. "Okay, that's enough."

I feigned innocence. "I don't know what you mean."

"Stop it."

"Stop what?"

The hard edge to his eyes softened like a block of bittersweet chocolate over a low flame. "I hate it when you do that."

"No, you don't." We had played this game ever since we were kids. "Besides, you read people's body language just as much as I do."

A fleeting curl of his tan lips answered before he did. "Yeah, but I get paid to do it."

"Now, so do I."

All traces of Steve's smile disappeared. "And if you're not careful, that could get you into a lot of trouble."

"Hey, I'm doing my job, just like you."

He chuckled. "Right. Just like me."

I might have been able to appreciate his finding some amusement in this situation if I hadn't been the one he was laughing at.

He pushed away from the desk and unfolded his long legs. "So, is there anything else I can help you with today?"

I stood, taking the cue that it was time for me to leave. "Am I being dismissed?"

He grinned, showcasing the high cheekbones he'd

inherited from his Cherokee grandfather.

I'd kill for those cheekbones. Gram once told me that I took after my mother in the bone structure department. Personally, I didn't see it, but maybe if I lost thirty pounds and had the right lighting, I might be able to find me some cheekbones.

Steve's eyes scanned my face, making me wish that I'd applied a fresh coat of lip gloss and popped a breath mint before I left Duke's.

"You did your job." Using his index finger, he brushed back a strand of hair that had escaped the tortoiseshell clip at the base of my neck.

My traitorous pulse raced like I'd never been touched by a man before. Pathetic.

"You interviewed the guy. Now, go type up your report and stop trying to make more of this than it is. If the autopsy results warrant an investigation, I'll be all over it."

I took a step back, putting some distance between us. "When will we get the results of the autopsy?" A week? Two?

"Lab results typically take four to six weeks."

"Four to six weeks! What do we do in the meantime?"

"We wait."

Not a chance.

When I returned to the office, I went to my desk to test-drive my computer login and then spent the next hour trying to make Dr. Cardinale's statement look like it hadn't been written by a rookie who got a C in English

Composition. After I emailed the statement to Karla and heard from Patsy that Frankie and Ben were in a meeting for the next hour, I figured I could keep myself busy by making a *Trudy* file for myself.

I typed up everything I'd learned from Aunt Alice and Lucille, and then printed it out along with a copy of the Cardinale statement.

The three pages read like a recipe for disaster. There was more rumor than fact from Aunt Alice and Lucille, but they shared one important truth with Dr. Cardinale—a suddenly dead Trudy.

On the back of the last page I wrote the four names Trudy's death had been linked to: Bernadette Neary, Howard Jeppesen, Rose Kozarek, and Jesse Elwood. I then asked Jan, a petite, curly-haired legal assistant who sat at the desk next to Karla's, to show me how to search the county database so that I could go back to my computer and print out their death certificates for my file.

Supporting what Kyle Cardinale had told me, Dr. Straitham was listed on the death certificate as the attending physician for both Bernadette Neary and Howard Jeppesen. He'd also certified their deaths. In fact, he'd certified all four.

I compared birthdates and did the math. Bernadette Neary had been the youngest, passing at the age of seventy-six. The only other common factor was that they all had died at Chimacam Memorial Hospital between one and four-thirty in the morning. And, according to the death certificates, none of them had been autopsied. At least not yet.

I saw no smoking gun in the database, not that I had

really expected to find one. But if Jesse Elwood and Trudy really died *just like Rose*, someone at the hospital had to know about it. Someone with some suspicions of his own.

Fortunately, I knew just the guy.

∽

Six hours later, my eighty-year-old grandmother looked up at me from the kitchen stove as the back door clicked shut behind me. A stainless steel pot occupied every burner. She didn't have to tell me what she'd cooked for dinner. The aroma of pot roast had my salivary glands on high alert the second I stepped into the kitchen.

I come from a long line of women who believe in the power of braised beef to get through most of life's emergencies. Personally, I think it works best with my grandmother's buttermilk biscuits and lots and lots of gravy.

"Perfect timing. Dinner's ready," Gram announced.

Given the fact Trudy and my grandmother had been friends for almost seventy years, I hadn't expected to be greeted with a cheery *how was your first day at work?* Since Gram wanted to put on the feedbag the second I stepped through the door, something felt out of whack.

Gram cast a nervous glance in the direction of the staircase, and I had a bad feeling that the pot roast had very little to do with Trudy.

I noticed the dining room table had been set for three and with the good china. "Do we have company?"

"Not exactly," she said, staring down at the gravy

she was stirring and accentuating her double chin in the process.

"How not exactly?"

"I talked to your mother this morning, after I heard the news."

I closed my eyes, bracing myself.

Gram pushed back a springy curl that had escaped from her helmet of peach-tinted cotton candy hair. "You know as well as I that she was very fond of Trudy."

No. No. NO. "Where is she?"

"Upstairs."

There were only two rooms upstairs with beds. Gram's and the guest room—my old bedroom.

I met my grandmother's hazel-eyed gaze. "In my room."

"It's only for a few days. Until after the funeral." She bit the inside of her lip. "At the outside, a week."

"A week! Where am I supposed to sleep?"

"I put your pillow and some linens on the hide-a-bed in your grandfather's study."

Swell. That *rack* was older than I was. "I'll need to move my clothes out of the closet." And stock up on aspirin.

"I already took care of everything. You don't need to do anything except go up and say hello to your mother."

I rolled my eyes. It was like I'd entered a time portal and was thirteen again.

Gram shot both barrels of her *do-it-now* look at me. "And tell her it's time for dinner."

"Fine."

Crossing the foyer, I caught a glimpse of a stack of clothes in the study—*my* clothes, folded and neatly laid out on the cocoa brown Naugahyde sleeper sofa like I was packing for summer camp. And Gram's fat tabby cat, Myron, was lying on top of the pile.

Wonderful.

At the top of the steps, I rapped on what had been my bedroom door for the last nine weeks.

My actress mother turned and her cherry red lips stretched into a megawatt, chemically enhanced, white smile. "Chah-maine, sweetie!" she exclaimed, gliding toward me in bare feet. Since I rarely saw her out of high heels, she seemed even shorter than her five foot four.

"Hi, Mom."

She pulled me into her arms, enveloping me in musky jasmine. "It's so wonderful to see you."

She took my hands in hers, and the wattage of her smile dimmed. "Ah just wish it were under happier circumstances," Marietta Moreau added solemnly, acting like she was blinking back tears, which might have been very effective except for the fact that her green eyes were dry.

In her heyday, the former Mary Jo Digby had been a working actress in Hollywood—just not a very good one. Not a very employed one since hitting the big four-oh, either. But she still looked like a show stopper in skin-tight white capris, a scooped neck red and white striped cotton sweater that accentuated her double D's, a white patent leather belt cinched at her tiny waist, blood-red nails, cropped auburn hair, and flawless makeup.

At fifty-six, she didn't look that different from the fascinating beauty I used to watch on the big screen after I moved in with my grandparents. Once I'd realized that

I had more in common with my dark-haired father, the sperm donor she'd only refer to as *that pasty-faced, French bastard*, and accepted the reality that I'd never fill out a C cup, I lost any illusion of reaching anything resembling *fascinating* status. Which was okay. I couldn't afford the upkeep.

Marietta's gaze swept over me, and despite her last Botox injection, a little wrinkle etched between her perfectly arched brows. "Oh, sugah," she said, using the dripping-with-honey accent she'd acquired in her mid-twenties when she got cast in a southern-fried *Charlie's Angels* ripoff. "Ah've been on that divorce diet, too. It'll come off. Trust me."

She should know. She'd been divorced three times.

I forced a smile.

She squeezed my hand. "Ah hope I'm not inconveniencin' you, takin' over your room and all."

"Of course not," I lied, but couldn't bring myself to do it with much conviction.

It didn't matter because she instantly beamed, then we stared in silence at one another.

Criminy, it couldn't have been more than two minutes and we'd already run out of things to say to one another.

She tilted her head and sniffed the air. "What's that heavenly aroma?"

"Pot roast."

"Ooooh, mah favorite! Let's eat!"

Okay, in some ways, I am my mother's daughter.

Chapter Six

"Where do you think you're going?" Gram demanded, staring at me over the rim of her teacup as I headed for the back door. "Your mother wants to give us facials."

Not a chance.

"Sorry," I said, barely breaking stride. "I just remembered; I have a date."

It was a whopper of a lie, but after two hours with my mother grilling me like a patty melt about my divorce, the only way I was going to make it through the evening twitch-free was to vacate the premises.

Heaving a sigh, Gram leaned back in her easy chair. "Sure, abandon me."

I kissed her plump cheek and grabbed my car keys. Ten minutes later, I arrived at Eddie's Place.

Eddie's featured juicy burgers, the best pizza in town, and a couple dozen beers on tap served up in a renovated red brick warehouse too far off the beaten path to benefit from the tourist trade, making it the local watering hole of choice.

Tonight, Jon Bon Jovi belted out a song about living on

a prayer through the speakers bookending the well-polished oak bar, but no one in the room was listening. Everyone, Eddie included, had their attention fixed on the Seattle Mariners game on the fifty-inch flat screen mounted in the far corner—their groans after a strikeout with the bases loaded drowning out the clatter of bowling balls knocking down pins in the adjoining Merritt Lanes.

Roxanne Fiske, Eddie's wife and my best friend since elementary school, grinned at me from behind the bar, looking pretty as always with little more than a coat of mascara on her long dark lashes. "Well, look who's up late on a school night."

After years of working as a pastry chef and getting up before the birds, I didn't have much of a reputation as a night owl.

"My mother's in town."

"Say no more," Rox responded, pouring beer into a frosted glass. "We'll commiserate over that, but first we need to celebrate your first day at the new job."

Ordinarily, I'm not a beer drinker, but since she was buying I made an exception.

Tucking back several chin-length caramel strands that had escaped from behind her ear, she raised her glass. "To Char, our new...what the hell is your title?"

"Among others, Deputy Coroner."

She wrinkled her nose. "Ewwww!"

"It's not like that. I won't have to see any dead bodies." At least I hoped not.

She clinked her glass with mine. "I'll drink to that."

The guys behind me groaned in unison, and a human mountain in greasy denim overalls stepped up to the bar and slid an empty plastic pitcher at Rox.

George Bassett, Jr. was a beefy six-foot-six redhead with a scruffy beard and a ruddy complexion. He'd been called Little Dog ever since he had strapped on his first pair of overalls and gone to work lubing engines and rotating tires for his dad, the Big Dog, at Bassett Motor Works.

"Hey ya, Chow Mein," he said, using the nickname that had come from hanging out with Steve in high school.

I saluted him with my beer glass. "Hey, Georgie."

He edged closer, and I smelled engine grease mixed with sweat. I also got a whiff of the salami and onions he'd had on his pizza.

"You here alone?" he asked.

I froze. George had never come on to me before. I met Rox's brown-eyed gaze to see if she could clue me in.

She shrugged.

I inched back, trying to get a read on him. "Yep."

"Dang! I thought your mom might be with you."

Like she'd want to spend her evening at the local bowling alley. "She was tired and decided to turn in early."

"Too bad. Your mom is *hot*," he said, blasting me with onion breath.

I smiled at Rox. "That just never gets old."

She slid the refilled foamy pitcher of beer toward George. "You're quite the sweet talker, Dog."

"What?" He looked at Rox and then back to me. "She is hot. And if I said any different, you'd know I was lyin'."

Mainly because he'd been saying the same thing ever since I first met him back in the eighth grade. "You never disappoint, Georgie."

He nodded, satisfied. "See?" he said to Rox, as if she

needed convincing.

Sipping my beer, I turned to watch him rejoin his baseball buddies and noticed a willowy woman in her mid-forties entering the bar. She had straight reddish-brown hair that brushed the collar of her dusty rose, linen blouse. Designer jeans hugged her slim hips. The man with her wore chinos and a pressed, white cotton shirt. Casual, yet not completely casual.

They had to be on a date.

"Who's that?" I asked Rox as the couple sat at a table in the far corner.

She followed my gaze. "You don't recognize Nell?"

The only Nell I knew had thick glasses and mousy brown hair pulled back in a long braid and spent her evenings at home taking care of her mother, who had become a shut-in after she'd had a series of heart attacks.

Tonight, nothing about this woman seemed mousy. "That's Nell Neary?"

Rox nodded. "It was a shame about her mom, but maybe that was a blessing in disguise."

With everything I'd learned today, that blessing was feeling more unholy by the minute.

The crowd gathered around the flat screen roared. Something big had just happened. I came to the same conclusion when I saw Bernadette Neary's daughter lean into her date's shoulder, laughing, happy—probably for the first time in years.

Before I'd met Dr. Cardinale, I wouldn't have given this date a second thought. But now, Jayne Elwood, Ernie Kozarek, and Nell Neary appeared to have something in common besides a dearly departed loved one.

ᑐ

After four sleepless hours of cursing the invention of the hide-a-bed, I headed for the upstairs bathroom like a punch-drunk boxer staggering to a neutral corner. One steamy shower, two cups of coffee, and three aspirin later, my back still ached like it had been pummeled by the *Crippler*, but at least I felt capable of stringing together a couple of coherent sentences.

I blasted my hair with my blow dryer, then applied a few swipes of mascara, a dab of concealer to minimize the circles under my eyes, and a swish of my mother's bronzer to add a little glow to my chipmunk cheeks. Not that I should care that much about how I looked this morning.

Although if Kyle Cardinale were to give me another once-over like yesterday, I might care.

After smoothing on a layer of copper glaze lip gloss and checking my look in the mirror, I shrugged into a black and blue plaid tunic, which matched how I felt. Fortunately, I could still zip my black cotton twill fat pants. Barely. All the more reason for me to change into a pair of sweats and go for a jog instead of heading over to the hospital in the middle of the night. Of course, that meant I'd have to do the hair and makeup thing over again in an hour. Not happening. It was enough effort the first time around. Instead, I opted to burn a few calories by going on the hunt for a hot doctor.

Ten minutes later, I found Kyle Cardinale in the hallway outside the ER. No chocolate pudding stains on his white lab coat this time.

The corners of his mouth curled into a charming smile as he watched me approach. "You're up early."

"Couldn't sleep."

"There's a lot of that going around."

I pointed at the deserted ER lobby. "Could we talk for a few minutes?"

"Sure, it's pretty dead right now."

Dark humor? Considering Dr. Cardinale had taken it upon himself to report the suspicious nature of Trudy's death, if he were joking, this whistleblower was one cool cat.

"So to speak," he added sheepishly.

I took a moss green vinyl chair next to a sparsely stocked magazine rack. He sat to my left, facing the ER desk. His knee grazed mine as he stretched out his legs.

He didn't say anything about the knee contact, and I shifted in my seat to give him a little more room, which drew a little flash of amusement.

Reminding myself I'd just divorced an Italian and had no intention of hooking up with another one, even if he was a charming doctor, I pulled out a pen and my list of potential victims from my tote bag to get down to business. "You mentioned a pattern yesterday. Along with Trudy Bergeson, two patients of Dr. Straitham's who died suddenly."

His gaze hardened. "We already talked about this."

"I know. I wanted to ask you about two other patients who died at the hospital—Rose Kozarek and Jesse Elwood."

Kyle frowned. "I don't recognize the names." He

reached for the spiral notebook in my hand. "May I?"

"They died over a year ago," he said after a quick scan of my victims list, then handed the notebook back to me. "I didn't start working here until last January, so I never saw them."

"There's an indication that they could have died under similar circumstances." I neglected to mention that the indication had come from Lucille.

"This might be an unusual request," and I was sure it was, "but could you find out who was on duty that night?"

He shrugged. "I can look it up."

"And while you're doing that, see what you could find out about how they died?"

"Anything else you'd like me to do?"

The laugh lines at the corners of his eyes deepened when I took too long to consider my options.

"Not officially," I said, all too aware of my burning cheeks.

I wrote my name and cell number on the back of one of Frankie's business cards and handed it to him. "I don't have any business cards yet." I also didn't know my phone number at the courthouse, but that was a pesky little detail he didn't need to hear.

He tucked the card into his breast pocket and started to push away from the chair.

"I do have a couple of questions about the other patients of Dr. Straitham that you mentioned."

Kyle's jaw tightened. "Okay," he said softly, his knuckles white as he settled back in his seat while his gaze played ping pong between a ringing telephone at the ER desk and a sandy blonde nurse zipping down the hallway.

Since this clearly wasn't a conversation he wanted to continue, I knew I needed to get to the point before my information source decided he'd rather play doctor than detective.

I pulled the four death certificates I'd printed from the inside pocket of my notebook. "Their death certificates don't appear to suggest anything unusual."

"I wouldn't expect them to."

Oh. "Then, maybe you can fill me in on what I'm missing."

I flipped the page and started reading. "Bernadette Neary, age seventy-six, died March 4th, three-ten a.m. Cause of death: Pneumonia."

He glanced in the direction of the unoccupied ER desk where a custodian was mopping the vinyl with a sudsy perfume of disinfectant. "Mrs. Neary's daughter brought her in to the ER because her mom had fallen and broken her arm. Mrs. Neary seemed disoriented and it turned out she also had pneumonia, so she was admitted and we pumped her with antibiotics and oxygen for three days."

I scribbled notes as he talked.

"I saw her each night on rounds. By day four, her lungs sounded clearer, her sats looked good enough for her to go home, then around three, she coded."

"Sats?"

"Oxygen saturation level. And hers had been improving, then she suddenly stopped breathing."

"She died?"

He nodded. "Pulmonary failure."

I sucked in a breath and flipped the pages in my hand to Rose Kozarek's death certificate. Cause of death: *Pulmonary failure.*

Just like Rose.

"And this is similar to what happened with Trudy Bergeson?"

Another nod. "Very."

"What about Howard Jeppesen?" I turned the page. "Age eighty-three. Died May 19th, two-seventeen a.m. Cause of death: Cardiac failure."

Kyle's dark eyes tracked the headlights of a car pulling out of the parking lot. "I'd seen him in the ER a couple of times—chronic bronchitis. Freaked out his wife and the paramedics would bring him in. Two months ago, he was back again, coughing up blood. The senior resident admitted him."

"And he started to get better?"

"Hell, no! He expired early the next morning."

"Well, where's the pattern in that?" Other than the fact that they were both patients of Dr. Straitham. And, of course, they were dead.

"It's how he died."

"Asphyxiation?" I asked, my voice mainly breath.

Kyle's lips pressed into a grim line as he watched the custodian push his bucket down the empty hall. I would have bet my first paycheck Kyle had just remembered something he didn't want to share.

His gaze hardened, his pupils constricted to the size of peppercorns. "Mr. Jeppesen's wife was sleeping in a chair by his bed. She woke up to the sound of her husband suffocating."

My hand flew to my mouth. "Oh God!" I didn't think I was going to spew, but the morning was young and anything was possible.

The pager on his hip buzzed. He read the display and then turned back to me. "God didn't have anything to do with this."

∽

Three hours and a pot of coffee later, I was buzzing with more than anticipation in Frankie's office while I waited for her to finish reading my notes from my early morning meeting with Kyle Cardinale.

Frankie's mouth tensed for a split second. "I can see where Dr. Cardinale would have some concerns."

Some concerns! If he was right, three people had been murdered. Including Rose, four.

"So what should we do next?" I asked. "Get a statement from Mrs. Jeppesen? Find out what else she might have seen?"

Frankie's lips thinned. "I understand that you flew solo with the Cardinale statement yesterday, but let's not get ahead of ourselves."

I felt an invisible leash tighten around my neck.

"We need to find out what Dr. Zuniga has to say before talking to anyone else," she added, meeting my gaze.

"Dr. Zuniga?"

"Henry Zuniga—a forensic pathologist who works out of Seattle. He'll be doing the autopsy tomorrow."

"At the hospital?"

She shook her head. "There's no morgue here, so we have a contract with Curtis Tolliver to use his facilities at the mortuary."

Three years ago, I'd seen Tolliver's Funeral Home up close and personal when I'd helped Gram make the arrangements for my grandfather's funeral. This included the sight of Curtis's cousin Eileen, the embalmer, emerging from a back room while I was on my cell phone with my mother and pacing the hallway. Behind Eileen I'd caught a glimpse of a metal operating table.

I shivered. No doubt that same room would be the site of Trudy's autopsy.

"Then, once we get the report of his findings," Frankie continued, "we'll know if we need to launch an official investigation. Until then, we'll just sit on this." She closed the manila file folder.

"And wait," I added without mentioning the four to six weeks. I didn't want her to know I'd received my information from Steve.

She flashed me a humorless smile. "You'll find we do a lot of that around here."

I was more of a stir, bake, and serve kind of girl, who had never been very good at sitting and waiting for six minutes, much less for six weeks.

This job was going to be tougher than I thought.

∽

I spent most of the following morning with Ben in Judge Witten's courtroom at the far corner of the third floor, where I'd been introduced as a Special Assistant to the Prosecution. The semi-lofty title meant that I could sit at a long wooden table with Ben and one of the assistant prosecutors, Lisa Arbuckle, during jury selection—my assignment for the next two days.

Earlier in his office Ben had made his expectations for these two days crystal clear: I was to sit quietly and observe the process, and if I had a strong opinion on any prospective juror I should pass Lisa a note. I got the message, the same one Duke had delivered on Monday. *Keep your yap shut.*

And that's exactly what I did. That was, when I wasn't yawning.

Two hours and a twenty-minute recess later, we broke for lunch early because the defense attorney had a meeting. Fine by me. With the mystery of Trudy's death not far from my thoughts, this gave me a little extra time to grab a quick tuna sandwich at Duke's, then head south on Main Street and walk the four and a half blocks to Tolliver's Funeral Home.

With every step something told me that I should do an about-face. The way I saw it, I could heed that advice, hightail it back to the courthouse and continue to play the waiting game, or I could roll the dice and maybe get lucky and catch Dr. Zuniga before he left town.

I spotted an unmarked white pickup with a rounded white canopy parked in the Tolliver's parking lot. Since the igloo on wheels didn't look like the typical vehicle belonging to the bereaved, I thought about going inside to see what I could find out, but the mere thought of asking, *"How's the autopsy going?"* made the tuna sandwich in my stomach do a belly flop. To avoid a sudden reappearance of my lunch on my slingbacks, I popped a peppermint and sat on a bench under a shade tree in the parking lot.

After about fifteen minutes, a woman in her early fifties

carrying a navy duffel bag exited the funeral home. A stout man hauling a matched pair of aluminum cases the size of carry-on bags followed the woman to the truck.

"Dr. Zuniga?" I called after him.

He turned. "Yes?"

With a thick head of salt and pepper hair and a face well worn with lines, Dr. Zuniga appeared to be around sixty. He smelled like antibacterial soap, reminding me that I didn't want to think about where his hands had just been.

"I'm Deputy Coroner Charmaine Digby." I showed him my badge.

He squinted at it, then his face crinkled into a smile. "I don't think I've ever seen one of those around here. You must be new, Charmaine Digby."

"Very. But I hope you won't hold it against me."

The creases around his warm brown eyes deepened.

"I've been working on Trudy Bergeson's case—"

"Have you." He sharpened his gaze. "I wasn't aware that this had already been made an official Coroner case."

I knew I'd just made a rookie mistake, so I thought I'd better fess up before I dug myself too deep a hole. "It's not exactly official."

The woman carrying the duffel opened the rear door of the truck canopy and glanced back at us over her shoulder. "Henry," she said softly. "If we want to make the one-fifty ferry, we need to go."

Dr. Zuniga winked at me. "My wife, the clock watcher."

I edged closer. "I'm sorry, but do you think this will become a Coroner case? Because there are some extenuating circumstances that—"

"Frankie will get my report tomorrow morning," he

said as he lifted the cases into the rear of the truck. "But I didn't see anything conclusive that would indicate a cause of death other than Mrs. Bergeson's rather advanced heart disease, which could certainly have led to cardiac arrest."

"There was nothing conclusive." Okay. "Was there anything that struck you as odd? Anything that didn't fit?" I said, using Kyle Cardinale's words.

Dr. Zuniga pursed his lips, hesitating. That would be a *yes*.

"Not typical," he said thoughtfully, "but I wouldn't call it terribly odd."

But something he found was niggling at him. I could see it as clearly as the roadmap of lines on his face.

"She had a secondary needle mark next to her intravenous needle site. Her chart didn't indicate any recent injections, but it happens sometimes. Usually a less experienced nurse. Probably nothing to be overly concerned about, but we'll run the usual labs. We'll know more in four to six weeks."

I may have only been on day three of my job, but I was already sick of that answer.

Chapter Seven

Saturday afternoon, I took a seat in the chapel of Tolliver's Funeral Home four rows back from a narrow table draped with an antique white, lace-edged runner. Two porcelain vases filled with red roses, carnations, and white calla lilies bookended the luminescent ceramic urn sitting center stage on the table, next to a framed photo of a smiling Trudy. Flanking the table, long ivory tapers atop brass candlesticks softly flickered while gentle strains of Mozart were pumped through the wood grain speakers mounted in the corners of the chapel. Since it was the hottest day of the year, pumping some air-conditioning into the room would have been a more effective mood enhancer.

"It feels like we were just here for Rose," Aunt Alice grumbled, easing down onto the padded folding chair to the left of my grandmother.

Gram answered with a pat of her younger sister's hand, but I knew that most of the senior crowd in attendance shared Alice's sentiments.

Marietta wiggled her hips into the aisle seat next to me.

"Mah, isn't this cozy," she said, fanning herself with Trudy's memorial brochure.

"Yeah, cozy." In a sweat-dripping-down-my-back kind of way that had me regretting my decision to squeeze into my black Nordstrom Rack pantsuit with the help of some control top panty hose to minimize the damage of the last ten pounds I'd packed on. Marietta wore a curve-hugging pomegranate knit dress with a V-neck that minimized nothing.

A couple of hours earlier, I'd made an effort with the hair dryer and beaten my hair into submission long enough to twist it into a chignon, plaster it with hairspray, and call it good enough. Not according to my mother, as she would attest if she'd stop with the sidelong glances at my hair and actually say what she was thinking.

I felt a tug on a strand that had escaped from my chignon, and turned around to fire on yet another hair critic.

Steve's face split into an evil grin as he took the seat behind me. He wore a charcoal business suit—probably the same one he wore when he had to testify in court. With his lean, athletic body, Steve could wear anything and look great, but with the cut of the suit, the pressed cornflower blue shirt, and his short, cropped, finger-combed dark brown hair, he looked finger-licking good.

He would have looked even better if Heather Beckett hadn't sat down next to him and given me the stink eye.

"Hey," I said to Steve. *Heather? Seriously?*

Heather had chewed him up and spit him out our junior year in high school. I thought he was too smart to fall for her act back then. He certainly hadn't gotten any dumber in the last seventeen years. At least I hadn't thought so before today.

"Steve, honay." Marietta turned and took his hand. "Oooh," she purred. "Now don't you clean up well."

"Have you met Heather?" Steve asked.

A smooth deflection move since it required Marietta and anyone within earshot to acknowledge Heather's existence.

I aimed a smile at my former nemesis. It may even have appeared to be sincere.

"I'm sure ah have," Marietta said in a tone of indifference that registered loud and clear on Heather's face.

My mother can be quite condescending at times, especially while channeling her inner Southern belle. This was one of those times and I didn't mind one bit.

Steve met my gaze. The tic in his cheek told me that he didn't share my opinion.

Marietta sighed as she turned to face forward. "Lovely man." She leaned into my shoulder. "You two never—"

"No." And not something I wanted to discuss, especially with him sitting right behind me.

"I didn't know Steve was seeing Heather again," Gram whispered in my other ear.

"That makes two of us." Again, not a subject for conversation today. "Oh, look." I pointed across the aisle at Sylvia Jeppesen. Steve wasn't the only one who could make a deflection move.

Gram waved at Sylvia, one of her exercise buddies from the senior center. "Who's that sitting next to her?"

"Who's sitting next to who?" Aunt Alice chimed in.

"Looks like Wally," I said.

Wally Deford was eighty if he was a day. He drank decaf, always had two eggs over easy for breakfast, and used to be a pie happy hour regular before his wife passed away back when I was at culinary school.

Two rows back from Sylvia and Wally sat Port Merritt's newest couple from the surviving spouse contingent, Jayne Elwood and Ernie Kozarek, with Gossip Central's Lucille and Kim in the seats directly behind them, no doubt to be within striking range should anything incriminating come up in conversation. Eddie, Rox, and Donna Littlefield, one of my best friends since junior high, sat in the rear, behind Nell and her new boyfriend.

There was no Dr. Cardinale in attendance, but the surviving family members of the names he'd provided me were well-represented. So was the hospital with a very stoic-looking Warren and Virginia Straitham sitting two rows back from Steve and Heather, along with Laurel and several members of the nursing staff.

"Really…Wally and Sylvia." Gram folded her arms under her ample breasts. "I've heard the rumors, but you know how people can be. Always leaping to conclusions." She arched an eyebrow at me.

At least I was being paid for coming to my conclusions.

"Aren't they cute together," Marietta said, fanning herself again. "When did they become an item?"

I'd venture a guess that it was sometime after Howard Jeppesen drew his last breath.

"All this is just wrong," Alice protested.

Duke patted her on the knee. "Give it a rest, honey, and let's just get through this."

She pulled out a handkerchief from her handbag and sounded like a Canadian honker as she blew her nose. If we were all very lucky, that would be all we heard out of my great-aunt for the next hour. Except there was absolutely nothing about today that felt lucky.

A minute later, Curtis Tolliver, the funeral director, led Norm Bergeson and his three daughters and their husbands to their seats in the front row. After the family was seated, Curtis turned, his beady eyes locked on my mother as he smoothed back his hair.

Uh-oh.

His fleshy face was flushed as he pressed his hand into hers and leaned close. "Very nice to see you again, Ms. Moreau."

"Marietta, please," my mother said, well aware that he was looking down her dress, especially since he had done the same exact thing at my grandfather's funeral.

His lips stretched into a wolfish grin as a bead of sweat trickled down his temple. "Miss Marietta."

She fanned herself with her other hand. "Curtis, honay, ah know you're terribly busy right now, but could ah trouble you for a teensy bit more air conditioning?"

"Of course," he said deferentially. "I'll see what I can do."

She leaned in, grazing his hand with her double Ds. "Ah'd be ever so grateful."

That was an empty promise if I'd ever heard one.

"Mary Jo," Gram whispered as soon as Curtis disappeared from view, "I didn't raise you to be such a...a..."

"Prick tease?" I said, filling in the blank.

Marietta rolled her eyes. "Chahmaine, that's not very nice. Ah was simply influencing him to make the right decision."

"Not exactly the technique we use at the department, but whatever works," Steve said in my ear.

Marietta's full lips curled with satisfaction. "Damned straight."

An hour and ten air-conditioned minutes later, Reverend Fleming's wife played *Ave Maria* on the organ to accompany Norm Bergeson and his family as they filed out of the front pew.

"That was a lovely service," Gram said after I helped her up from her seat.

"Lovely," Alice scoffed, sounding like she was rapidly reaching the end of her short fuse. "Is that what you call this?"

Gram gave her sister the *please keep your voice down* look while Duke stood and offered his hand to Alice. "Now, honey—"

Alice swatted his hand away. "Don't you dare 'now, honey' me." She narrowed her eyes at Steve. "This is all wrong and you know it."

Standing, Steve touched her shoulder. "I understand how you feel. You lost a good friend."

"You need to do something." Alice's voice broke as she choked back tears.

He met my gaze. "I would if I could."

But he was in wait mode for the autopsy results as I knew all too well.

"Time to go," Gram proclaimed like we were late for dinner. She elbowed me into the center of the aisle, where Heather was standing, waiting, with perfect, blonde-streaked hair, a dark blue, sleeveless sheath, and matching pumps.

I'd heard from Rox that after Heather's divorce last year from an advertising executive, she'd moved back home from Boston and was working at a Port Townsend boutique. If anyone ever had needed an employee discount to expand her designer wardrobe, it wasn't trim, tan, and more perfectly gorgeous than ever Heather. Why wouldn't Steve want to be with her?

The bastard.

"Nice dress," I said. I knew it sounded lame, but I had to say something to the conniving bitch I'd outed after she tried to steal Rox's boyfriend back in ninth grade.

Her gaze lingering on my chignon, Heather responded with a fake smile. "Thanks."

"Awkward," Marietta sang in my ear.

True, but the queen of awkward silences needed to cut me a little slack.

"See you later," Steve said to me as Heather sidled up next to him.

"Later." Which translated into another opportunity to make painfully polite conversation with Heather and Steve at the post-funeral nosh-fest at the Bergeson's that Gram and Alice had helped organize.

Goody.

Watching Steve and Heather make their way past Marietta, I noticed that they didn't hold hands, didn't touch. It didn't make me feel any better about seeing them together, but it didn't make me feel any worse, either.

"Keep moving," Gram said, waving me on like a traffic cop. "We need to get Alice out of here before she starts saying things she's going to regret tomorrow."

Easier said than done since Marietta was sauntering down the aisle as if she were working the red carpet at the Oscars.

She shook Dr. Straitham's hand and his gaze followed the swivel of her hips as she moved to the next row to schmooze Mr. Ferris, my high school biology teacher.

I wasn't the only one watching Warren Straitham's reaction to my mother. Virginia leveled a cold, hard glare at her husband.

Unfortunately, Mr. Ferris didn't have a wife by his side to put out the *no trespassing* sign.

Gram extended her hand. "Come along, Alice."

With her eyes fixed on Warren Straitham, Alice sidestepped my grandmother.

Gram sharply inhaled. "Oh dear."

"You have some nerve showing up here," Alice said, her voice cutting through the crowd like a butcher's knife through butter.

The tall, silver-haired gentleman in the cheap gray suit blinked. "Pardon me?"

Alice wagged her index finger at Dr. Straitham. "Don't think that I don't know what's going on."

He blanched to a doughy pallor, reminding me of the time I'd caught my ex-husband in the walk-in freezer with Brie, his sous chef. Unlike Chris who'd followed me out the door, all the while trying to spin his dalliance into a palatable confection, Dr. Straitham looked like a human popsicle frozen in place.

Duke reached for Alice's hand. "Honey, let's go."

She shook him off. "You're not going to get away with this," Alice said as she inched closer to Dr. Straitham. "I'm on to you!"

The doctor's silver-brown brows drooped, giving him the appearance of a blue-eyed bloodhound. "Alice," he said in a hushed tone, sounding like a sympathetic man who understood grief, but his thin lips stretched into something else—fear.

Standing ramrod straight by his side, Virginia flushed a bloody shade of crimson.

"That's enough," Duke growled, taking Alice by her thin shoulders and pointing her toward the exit. "We're leaving."

I grabbed my grandmother by the arm and squeezed out a smile at Virginia Straitham. "See you later." Maybe.

"Don't you think we should apologize?" Gram asked as we filed out of the chapel.

"No." Quite enough had been said. And learned.

Gram heaved a sigh. "What Virginia must be thinking of us!"

Based on the icy glare Virginia Straitham had directed at her husband, we were the least of her concerns.

"I hope you're satisfied," Gram said to her sister's back once we'd caught up to Duke and Alice in the foyer. "Ginny will probably never speak to me again."

"Or step a foot into the cafe," Duke grumbled.

Alice stopped in her tracks. "What's wrong with you? Didn't you see what just happened?" She locked onto my gaze. "Tell me you saw that look on his face."

"I saw it." I had a sick feeling that I had also just seen the face of a murderer.

～

A half hour after we left Tolliver's funeral home, my grandmother and I stood at opposite ends of a casserole and cake receiving line in the Bergeson's compact, U-shaped kitchen.

Having worked for friends in the catering business I knew from experience that people drink at weddings, but they eat at funerals. Around here, a funeral announcement signals the start of a bake-off that sends the senior set flocking to their recipe rolodexes and ends with lethal volumes of cheese, butter, and chocolate arriving at the doorstep of the bereaved.

Until Sylvia Jeppesen handed me a weighty glass serving dish with a distinctly fishy odor, Trudy's reception had been no exception.

"Chinese noodle and tuna casserole," Sylvia announced proudly.

"Yum." No cheese, no butter, no chocolate—a clear violation of the bereavement food code. At least it had arrived warm unlike the dozen casserole dishes awaiting their turn in the microwave.

I pushed aside a raspberry glazed bundt cake to add Sylvia's casserole to the smorgasbord laid out on the dining room table.

"Something in here has got to go," Lucille said, holding a steaming crock pot of Swedish meatballs.

My vote went to the tuna casserole.

"Move Ginny's bundt cake over here." Lucille angled the crock pot in the direction of an antique sideboard.

"Ginny?" Picking up the platter with the bundt cake, I scanned the crowd for Virginia Straitham, the last person I expected to see after what had happened at the funeral home. Okay, maybe Virginia ran a close second to her husband.

Lucille set the crock pot on the table. "Handed it to me just after I got out of my car. Looked like she'd been crying. I heard what happened between the doc and Alice," Lucille said at half her normal volume. "Do you think he did it?"

Maybe. I didn't want to fan any flames of suspicion, so I just shrugged.

"Did what?" Steve asked, stepping up to the table with a paper plate in hand instead of Heather.

Not that I would give a second thought to anyone he might be dating. The bastard.

"Murder Trudy," Lucille said to Steve in the same stage whisper.

The tic registered in his cheek. "No."

She narrowed her eyes at him. "Then how do you explain what happened?"

"I don't," he said with a casual indifference at odds with the tight cords of tension in his neck. Lifting the lid of Sylvia's casserole dish, he sniffed and wrinkled his nose at me.

I shook my head. "Sylvia's tuna."

He replaced the lid and continued clockwise around the table.

Lucille scowled. "I don't think you're taking this very seriously."

"And I think certain people around here have been jumping to some dangerous conclusions." Steve met my gaze. "There's been nothing to suggest that anyone's been murdered."

Lucille flushed. "Nothing? You didn't see Trudy the night before she died. I did. And now we're here again with another one of these damned tuna casseroles, and if you don't want to see it again in another few months," she said, pointing her finger at Steve's nose, "certain people will do something about it!"

"She makes a good point about the tuna casserole," he deadpanned after Lucille stalked back to the kitchen. "Someone should do an intervention before Sylvia buys another can of tuna."

"Be serious." I added some lukewarm lasagna to his plate. "It's not a big leap to think that Warren Straitham could be killing his patients."

He cocked his head. "Give me a break."

"Okay, it is, but you weren't there when Aunt Alice told him that she wasn't going to let him get away with it. He looked scared. Exposed."

"Hey, she once chased me out of her kitchen with a carving knife. Trust me, the women in your family can be plenty scary."

I ignored the cheap shot. "I'm just telling you what I saw."

"I'll take that under advisement," he said, sniffing another casserole dish.

"Sure you will. And that's Mrs. Lundgren's pesto

ravioli."

"What the hell is pesto?"

"Just try it and stop sniffing around."

His lips curled into a lopsided grin. "I will if you will."

"Am I interrupting something?" Suzy Harte asked, carrying a platter piled high with fresh veggies, her light blue eyes gleaming as they darted between Steve and me.

Suzy seemed to be the queen of part-time jobs—one as an ER nursing assistant, one as an aerobics instructor at the senior center, and one as a self-appointed dispenser of unsolicited advice. When it came to sticking a nose where it didn't belong, she even had Lucille beat.

I took the platter from her. "Not at all. Steve and I were just—"

"I don't see Heather anywhere," Suzy said. "Did she have to leave?"

All traces of Steve's smile vanished. "Something like that."

"What a shame." The tiny crow's feet at the corners of her eyes crinkled as Suzy beamed. Not at him, but at me.

Not the usual effect Steve had on women.

With short, straight, sandy blonde hair and a pert turned-up nose dusted with freckles, the slender aerobics instructor had the look of a middle-aged pixie.

The pixie leaned in, studying my face. "I hadn't noticed the resemblance before. You do take after your mother."

We had the same eye color. Other than that I took after *that French bastard*, but I didn't detect any deception in Suzy.

With eyes wide like a chocoholic in a candy store she gazed out the dining room window at Marietta, holding court with Mr. Ferris in the shade of a patio umbrella.

I'd seen the look on Suzy's face many times before. She was a fan, and I was somebody because I was a child of a *somebody*.

"Thanks for the veggies," I said, hoping she'd move on to the patio like a good little fan so that she could deliver her adulation in person.

"I thought there might be a few people who'd want a healthy alternative to all these heavy desserts," Suzy said as I set the platter next to the bundt cake on the sideboard.

No one I knew.

Steve grabbed a celery stick. "Bon appétit."

Ignoring him, I met Suzy's gaze. "Very thoughtful of you."

She smiled contentedly, watching as Steve headed into the living room where Donna and several others from our old high school gang had gathered. "You're cute together."

Huh? "We're just friends."

"Obviously good friends." Arching her eyebrows she waited.

"Just *old* friends."

She glanced behind me. "Like your mom and Barry Ferris?"

I turned and saw Marietta fanning herself, showing a lot of thigh as she sat cross-legged under that umbrella with Mr. Ferris. All she needed was a mint julep to make the Southern belle image complete.

Since the last time she had spent any time with him was when she'd showed up unannounced at my high school science fair, they didn't exactly meet the usual definition of old friends. But with the way she kept touching his hand, they seemed awfully chummy.

"I don't believe it," Aunt Alice muttered, rounding the corner.

My thoughts exactly, but I was pretty sure that she wasn't referring to my mother and Mr. Ferris.

Lucille lumbered up to the dining room table with a steaming casserole dish and stopped in her tracks when she spotted my great-aunt. "Uh-oh. What's wrong?"

"Carmen." Alice uttered the name of one of the Gray Ladies like she wanted to sic a gypsy curse on the woman.

What about her? I peeked into the living room and located Carmen sitting on the sofa with Norm Bergeson. She was patting his hand while Bonnie Haney, another widow, closed in on the empty sofa cushion opposite Carmen like a heat-seeking missile.

Lucille heaved a sigh. "Here we go again."

Chapter Eight

By the time Rox and Eddie left Trudy's funeral reception to head back to work, Bonnie, Sylvia, and Miriam Rybeck had each taken a spin through the revolving door of widows and divorcees vying for the seat on the sofa next to Norm. My mother even made a brief appearance on the comfort couch. Although she was clearly a benchwarmer in the Norm Bergeson sweepstakes, it didn't make the spectacle any easier for my great-aunt to watch. At least it gave Marietta's flirtation with Mr. Ferris a time-out.

Unfortunately, that was short-lived.

"What a delightful man," my mother said, back under the patio umbrella while Mr. Ferris trotted to the makeshift bar in the kitchen to refill our wineglasses.

My buddy, Donna, sat down next to me and whispered in my ear. "Please tell me she's not serious."

I shrugged. Considering Marietta's last husband had been eighteen years her junior and my former biology teacher was pushing fifty, I didn't think I needed to worry about Mr. Ferris asking me to call him *Dad* anytime soon.

Marietta leaned in with a bright smile. "So, what do you

want to do tonight?"

Go home, pull on my pajamas, and sleep for twelve hours straight in my own bed.

"Actually, we already have plans," Donna said before I could come up with a creative fib.

My mother's smile slipped. "We?"

"Char and me." Donna nodded at me as if to say *play along*. "Sort of a double date."

Sort of? If you're going to tell a whale of a lie, at least tell it with conviction.

"Really!" Marietta licked her ruby-red lips like a tigress anticipating fresh meat. "With anyone I know?" She cocked her head toward Steve.

"No, Mother," I said with all the disinterest I could muster.

She leaned back in her green striped, padded deck chair and blew out a sigh. Silent seconds ticked by while she scrutinized me from head to toe. "What time?"

I glanced at the Versace watch she had given me for my twenty-first birthday, back when her telephone still rang with the occasional movie offer. "We're meeting the guys at seven." A quick answer devoid of unnecessary details— key to telling a believable lie.

Marietta grabbed my left wrist and peered at my watch. "But that only gives you a little over an hour to get ready."

I'd made myself ready for real dates in less time. A fake one? "No problem."

She pushed to her feet. "We need to go."

"Really, you're making too much out of this." But since Barry Ferris was approaching the table with a glass of white wine in each hand, maybe this was the ideal time to say our goodbyes.

Disappointment etched into the furrows of his graying brows. "Leaving so soon?"

"Oh, Barry," Marietta cooed. "Ah'm so sorry, but we have a little family emergency."

"It's nothing really," I assured him.

She grimaced at my hair. "Trust me. It's not nothing." She took a glass out of Mr. Ferris's hand, took a sip, then pressed her palm in his. "It's been a pleasure."

His eyes darkened as he kissed her hand. "The pleasure has been all mine."

Gag.

I turned to Donna. "See you at Eddie's at seven."

She grinned. "I can't wait."

That made one of us.

Marietta's eyes were still locked with Mr. Ferris's.

Way to let him down easy, Mom.

I angled between them and pushed my mother's clutch bag into her ribs. "So, are we going or what?"

She gave my chignon a sideways glance. "I'm afraid we must."

Waving her clutch at my grandmother sitting in the sunshine with Alice and Sylvia, Marietta shuffled toward the French doors in her stilettos. "Mom, we're leaving."

Gram aimed a frown at her. "What's the rush?"

"Char has a date."

"A date!" Gram held out her hand for Steve to help her get to her feet. "For pity's sake. Why didn't someone say something about this earlier?"

"Have fun," he said, standing by the French doors as I followed Marietta into the house.

Like that could happen. "Tell me you're wearing your gun."

"Don't usually wear it to funerals."

"Too bad. I need somebody to shoot me."

∽

Eddie was filling a pitcher from the tap when I entered the bar a few minutes after seven. He did a double take when he saw me. "What the hell happened to you?" he yelled over the ZZ Top guitar riff blasting through the speakers.

I batted the eyelash extensions Marietta had spent most of the last hour applying. A few more coats of mascara and I could probably achieve lift off. "My mother happened to me."

Eddie's heavy brows knitted together. "You look…"

Ridiculous. He didn't have to say it. I already knew.

"…a little like your mom."

"Yeah, on steroids."

"White wine?" Eddie asked as Rox zipped past me with a steaming hot pizza in one hand and a short stack of plates in the other.

"Make it a double."

I didn't have to search the room for Donna. I knew I'd find her at her usual barstool.

"You look hot!" she said as I slid onto the seat next to her.

Since the a/c was out in the Jag and my bangs had pasted themselves to my forehead, I felt hot and not in a good way. "That's because I am."

Donna, a cosmetologist and owner of Donatello's, the local cut and curl, finger-fluffed my bangs. "Will you please just accept a compliment? You look great."

The suck-it-all-in pantyhose I had on under my black jeans added a roll below my rib cage that threatened to send the bottom button of my green silk blouse into orbit. Short of some emergency liposuction, looking great was a physical impossibility, especially since I was working up a sweat sitting still.

Donna was the one who looked smoking hot. Sultry charcoal lined her sapphire almond eyes. A touch of bronzer lent a shimmery glow to her perfect peaches and cream complexion. Her favorite low rise blue jeans showcased her pierced navel, and the white eyelet lace cotton top hugging her breasts had a deep scoop neckline and spaghetti straps that revealed sun-kissed, freckled shoulders.

"Whoa, look at you!" Rox said, beaming at me on her way back to the kitchen. Then, she stopped dead in her tracks. "Holy crap! You look like your—"

I made a stop sign with my hand. "I know."

"I love what you did with your hair," Donna said.

I hadn't done anything. "Marietta flat-ironed it."

Donna's gaze zeroed in on my eyelashes and she leaned closer, ignoring Eddie, who was delivering my drink and ogling the cleavage enhanced by her push-up bra.

Rox slapped Eddie on the back of the head. "Don't be a dirty old man."

"You know I only have eyes for you, sweetheart," he said to her backside as she swung open the kitchen door.

Eddie winked at me, keeping the moment light, but the

way his gaze had followed his wife gave me a little pang of envy.

I reached for my drink but froze in my seat when Donna scooted her chair next to mine. "Trust me, I look better from a distance."

"Shut up," she said, staring at my left eye. A tiny frown line cracked the creamy skin between her perfectly arched brows. "What'd you use? Extensions?"

"Marietta's." I took a sip of wine. "Part of her new makeup line."

More like a cosmetic line my mother was being paid to rep in infomercials—a career move birthed from the harsh reality that she hadn't worked in anything but an indie film in the last five years but wanted to keep her house in Malibu.

"Well, you look awesome. Justin's going to be so impressed."

"Justin?" I smelled a set up.

"He's a new client of mine. A landscaper." Chewing on her lower lip, Donna tilted her head and her long, blonde hair spilled over her shoulder. "Or was he the scuba instructor? Anyway, he's outdoorsy and very nice. You'll like him."

I cringed. "What have you done?"

"Nothing! I just happened to mention that a few of my friends might be hanging out here Saturday night and since he was new in town that he might like to join us."

"Uh-huh." That sounded too much like how the former Donna Grazynski met her second ex-husband.

I wasn't in the market for a second anything, but since the alternative was heading home and telling Marietta and

Gram all about the *date* I didn't have, I sucked down some more wine and scanned the room for an outdoorsy type. That could describe half the guys in the bar, including Eddie and Little Dog. "Is he here?"

"I haven't seen him yet," she said, frowning at my right eye.

"What?"

"I think you're losing an eyelash."

"Great." Marietta had warned me to stay out of the heat until the glue set. I hadn't realized that also included my car. "Just pull it off."

Donna plucked away the offending eyelash with her thumb and index finger. Then she squinted and plucked at another one. "Uh-oh."

"Now what's wrong?"

"You have a little problem."

I'd thought I'd left her at home with my grandmother.

Donna cupped three eyelash extensions in her palm. "If you brought the glue, I can fix this."

"Do I look like someone who'd have eyelash glue in my tote bag?"

"At the moment, you look freakishly like your mom, so yes, you do."

Lovely.

I drained my glass and made tracks to the ladies room to assess the damage. Five minutes and sans a couple dozen lash extensions later, I stared at my reflection in the bathroom mirror. Tonight, I had my mother's green eyes. Maybe not all her lashes, but with her makeup and the right lighting, maybe I did look a little like her in a puffy Pillsbury Doughboy-as-my-father kind of way.

"Well, Justin, I hope you like brunettes."

I unbuttoned the top button of my blouse to give him a glimpse of the girls, then painted on a fresh layer of raspberry lip gloss and smiled at the mirror. "It's show time."

When I returned to the bar, Steve was sitting where I had left Donna.

"What'd you do with Donna?" I asked as I slid onto the barstool.

"She hooked up with Justin somebody. Assuming you're interested, they're sitting by the window."

So much for Justin meeting the girls.

I was considering buttoning up and calling it a night when I noticed Steve staring at me. "Why are you looking at me that way?"

"What'd you do to yourself?"

"I'll have you know that I'm on a date, and I think I look pretty good." At least from the boobs up.

"I never said you didn't."

"You insinuated."

His gaze dropped to the swell of my breasts straining against the tiny buttons of my silk blouse.

I leaned closer to give him a better look.

The frown line between his brows deepened. "What the hell are you doing?"

"I could ask you the same question."

His lips curled into the hint of a smile. "I was just noticing that you might have missed a button."

Sure. "Yeah, that's what I figured."

"So, who's the date?"

"No one you know." I reached for my refilled wineglass.

"In fact, you shouldn't be sitting here."

"And why not?"

"My date might get the wrong idea."

"Don't see why. Just two friends having a drink. Besides, I'd like to meet him."

So would I. "He might be running late."

"Then I'll keep you company until he arrives."

I looked over my shoulder at Donna and Justin. It didn't look like that would happen anytime soon. "Okay, but on one condition."

Steve gave me a sideways glance.

"You have to talk to me."

"I don't suppose I need to ask what we're going to talk about."

"Nope."

He blew out a breath. "Go ahead."

"Don't you think it's strange that Nell Neary, Jayne Elwood, Ernie Kozarek, and Sylvia Jeppesen are all in new relationships?"

"You aren't going to let go of this, are you?"

No. "It's too coincidental."

I watched for a reaction as Steve stared at his sweaty beer bottle. As usual, nothing.

"Think about it. They were all caregivers," I said, edging closer. "For years Nell took care of her mom. Jayne and Sylvia each had a decade of tending to a sick husband. In Ernie's case, a bed-ridden wife. Then suddenly, Bernadette Neary, Mr. Elwood, Rose Kozarek, and Howard Jeppesen—all patients of Dr. Straitham—die. Months later, Nell has a boyfriend and Ernie shows up at Clark's Pharmacy with a prescription for Viagra."

Steve hung his head. "Can't anyone in this town keep their mouth shut?"

He knew the answer to that question as well as I did. It explained why he and Eddie used to go to Port Townsend to buy condoms. Steve still did for all I knew. And I really didn't want to know.

"And Ernie's not the only one." At least according to Lucille.

Steve swallowed the last of his beer. "Are you telling me there's a Viagra connection between these deaths?"

Maybe, but that sounded so ridiculous I wasn't about to admit it aloud. "Actually, I think it's more like a matchmaking connection."

I heard him string together a few choice expletives.

Okay, I'd be the first to admit that matchmaking didn't sound much better. "Just hear me out."

"I can hardly wait," he said, wearing a smirk that I didn't much care for.

I leaned closer so that I didn't have to shout over Billy Squier belting out *Everybody Wants You*. "All four of these deaths have resulted in *matches* – you know...couples."

The corners of his lips tightened. "I know what a match means."

There was no evidence of that fact from the assortment of women he'd dated over the years, but I had no desire to debate the merits of his sex life.

"Nell hooks up with a guy and has a relationship for probably the first time in her life. Jayne and Ernie become suddenly single within eight months of one another, and now they're inseparable. And lately, Sylvia Jeppesen and Wally Deford seem to have become an item. It's like Lucille said—"

"Figures that she'd be mixed up in this somewhere," Steve muttered, shaking his head.

"—this just seems too convenient."

"The only thing convenient about this is Lucille jumping to some very big conclusions."

"There's something going on, and you know it."

Steve's eyes tracked Rox delivering another pizza. I had a feeling it was to avoid my gaze.

"What I know," he said, "is that we need to wait for the lab results to come back."

"Right. What about how Dr. Straitham reacted when Alice told him that she was on to him?"

Steve leaned so close I could smell the beer on his breath. "You can't really think the doc is killing his patients to play matchmaker."

I knew Kyle Cardinale suspected something, and I knew what I'd seen at Trudy's memorial service, so I was convinced to a level of a definite maybe. "It's a possibility, isn't it?"

"Only if you can give me a good reason why."

I couldn't even think of a bad reason.

"That's what I thought." Steve uncurled his legs from under the bar and tossed several dollar bills on the counter. "But I'll make a note of your theory in the file."

I didn't believe that for a minute. "And what file is that?"

He grinned. "It's where I keep all of Lucille's Elvis sightings."

Bastard.

Chapter Nine

I was sound asleep Monday morning when my cell phone rang. I squinted at my alarm clock as I grabbed my phone. Six-twenty-seven. "No one I know would call this early," I croaked.

"Sorry. I'd assumed you were an early morning person."

I recognized Kyle Cardinale's voice and cringed. *Stupid. Stupid. Stupid.* I needed this guy and couldn't afford to give him an excuse never to call me again.

"Did I wake you?" he asked.

"No, I...just haven't had my coffee."

"If you make that two coffees, I might have that information you asked me to look up for you."

I sat up straight, the Crippler poking me in the butt with a bed spring. "When can we meet?"

"How soon can you get to the hospital?"

"I'm in the middle of something." He didn't need to know it was my grandmother's hide-a-bed. "Maybe in about an hour."

After I set a land speed record in the bathroom, I threw

on a denim shirtdress, strapped on a pair of navy wedge heel sandals, then hightailed it to Duke's for two coffees to go.

Ten minutes later, I stood in front of a coffee machine, sputtering to finish its brew cycle. "Come on," I said, urging it to completion as I stifled a yawn.

Lucille squeaked behind me. "Late night or hung over?"

That got me a parental glare from Duke, tending the grill.

"I'm not hung over," I assured him as I filled two tall paper cups. And I didn't want any lectures about getting to bed earlier. I would if I could. Unfortunately, my mother had staked a claim on my bedroom. "I'm meeting someone for coffee."

Duke pointed his spatula at me. "Why the hell can't you meet him here? Then one of you might actually pay for the coffee."

I shrugged. "He's shy. Not ready to meet the family yet."

Duke cursed under his breath while Lucille followed me to the bakery shelf behind the cash register. "Is he your date from Saturday?" she asked, handing me a white bakery bag.

"He's somebody else." Okay, that didn't do much to unravel the tangled web Donna had helped me weave in the fake date department, but at least it wasn't a total lie. I dropped two lemon poppy seed muffins, some creamers, and a couple of napkins into the bag, and hoped Lucille got the hint that I had nothing else I wanted to say on this subject.

Lucille nodded her approval. "Good for you. There's

no reason to put all your eggs in one basket."

"That's my motto," Stanley added from his usual perch at the counter.

My motto this morning was get in and get out, especially since I didn't want to be late for my non-date with a hot doctor who had some information for me. I said my goodbyes and sprinted for the door with the coffees in a paper takeout carrier in one hand and the bakery bag in the other.

The door opened just as I was about to reach for the knob.

Standing in the doorway, Steve glanced down at the white bag.

So much for making a clean getaway.

He cracked a smile. "Don't suppose you were bringing that over to the station for me."

"Sorry, no bribes today."

"Too bad. And they were usually so effective, too."

"Can't blame a girl for trying."

"She has a breakfast date," Lucille chimed in.

Not helpful.

The get in and get out motto didn't include providing too much information to any of my friends, especially this one.

Steve and I locked gazes.

"Another date?" he asked, holding the door open for me.

"Sort of." I knew he'd see it as a lie, but at least I had the two cups to back me up.

"You're a busy girl."

You don't know the half of it.

"And I'm late," I said, making a dash for the car to avoid any more unsolicited opinions about my nonexistent love life.

Ten minutes later, after applying a fresh coat of lip gloss and a blast of breath freshener, I followed Kyle Cardinale into the doctor's lounge and sank my butt into the same aqua blue vinyl seat that I'd sat in a week ago. I handed him a to-go cup. "Here you are, as promised."

He popped the top. "Thank God. The coffee here is like diesel oil."

He'd soon find out that Duke's coffee wasn't much of an improvement—just fresher crude. I opened the bakery bag and passed him a couple of creamers. He was going to need them. I also offered him a muffin.

He reached in the bag, lifted one to his nose and inhaled. "Lemon?"

I nodded.

"Did you bake this?"

If I had, unlike the baker who worked the Saturday through Monday morning shift, I would have used fresh lemon juice, and they would have been golden brown, not eggy-yellow. "No, but they're compliments of Duke's."

"Ah." He smiled. "I only asked because Laurel told me that you bake."

Kyle Cardinale had talked to Laurel about me? Not that it was of any consequence, but my heart skipped a hopeful beat anyway.

He pulled off a chunk of muffin and popped it into his mouth. "Mmmmm…." He washed it down with a gulp of coffee. A dribble escaped down his chin and he swiped at it with the back of his hand.

I passed him one of the napkins from the bakery bag.

His lips curled into a sheepish smile. "You must think I was raised by wolves."

I thought he was dangerously charming, much like the Italian I'd been married to for seven years. "You're a guy. I'm sure it's in the guy manual that the hand can be substituted for a napkin."

"Knew I picked that up somewhere," he said, his whiskey gaze fixed on me, lingering on my mouth.

To save time this morning, I'd pulled my hair back in my tortoiseshell clip. The longing I felt stirring in the pit of my stomach echoed my regret that I hadn't hit the flat iron before I'd run out the door.

Since I'd left the other muffin in the bag, at least I knew I didn't have any poppy seeds hanging from my lips.

What? I mentally slammed on the brakes. I shouldn't care how I looked to this guy.

Dammit! What was it with me and Italian men?

I took a sip of coffee to kill the longing with an acid bath. "So…" I smiled deferentially. All business, no pleasure, no how. "You have some information for me."

Kyle's jaw tightened. He wasn't happy about the change of subject.

Join the club, pal.

He reached into a pocket of his white coat and handed me two folded sheets of paper.

Rose Kozarek and Jesse Elwood's names were listed at the top of each page.

"It's a hard copy of the last entries in their charts," Kyle said. "The vitals, drugs administered—it's all there."

I scanned the pages. What was also there was the same

doctor's name on both sheets of paper—R. Forsythe. I didn't recognize the name, but I intended to make this doctor's acquaintance.

One set of initials accompanied most of the drug entries in the early morning hours. "C.T."

"Cindy Tobias," Kyle said. "Worked graveyard for a couple more months after I started, then she switched to days."

I wasn't overly concerned about Cindy, but I knew I'd better chat with her to see if she shared any of Kyle's suspicions.

The recurring initials of *T.N.* indicated that another nurse had been working similar hours to Cindy's. "T.N. is..."

"Tina Norton. Still works that shift. Mostly weekdays, I think."

I handed Kyle the computer printouts. "Do you see anything unusual here? Anything that doesn't look right?"

His gaze traveled the length of both pages. "They both came in with pneumonia. Everything looks like I'd expect other than the fact that her sats were improving."

"So, Rose was getting better."

He nodded.

"Then what? She just dies?"

Another nod.

"Asphyxiated?"

"Looks that way."

I turned to the other page. "What about Mr. Elwood?"

Kyle shook his head. "He had a pulmonary embolism shortly after admission. No matter what anybody did, he wasn't going home." He folded the paper and handed it back to me. "At least he didn't suffer long."

"What do you mean by that?"

"Nothing. It was just quick."

"Unusually quick?"

His gaze tightened. "Are you asking if I think that someone hurried the process along?"

He was the one who'd called Frankie with his suspicions about Trudy's death. So, yes. That was exactly what I was asking.

I nodded.

"There isn't anything there," he said, pointing at the paper in my hands, "to suggest anything that I'd call unusual."

That didn't answer the question. "If you were going to kill one of your patients, wouldn't you make sure that nothing unusual was recorded in his chart?"

"I'd be stupid not to."

Warren Straitham's name was conspicuously absent from these pages. If nothing else, it confirmed what I already knew. He was guilty of something, but it wasn't stupidity.

"Thanks for this," I said, tucking the printouts he'd given me into my tote bag.

"What are you going to do with the information?"

Other than talk to Cindy and Tina, I didn't have a clue.

ⴰ

It was a few minutes after eight when I huffed and puffed my way up the steps of the courthouse. Patsy arched an eyebrow at me as I passed her desk, my to-go cup in hand.

"Late night?" she asked.

I ignored the Chimacam County Courthouse Hall Monitor's insinuation. "Early morning."

She glanced at the glass-domed gold anniversary clock ticking next to her computer monitor and her mouth formed a lemon-worthy pucker. "Uh-huh."

For being on the receiving end of this much disapproval I should have been having a lot more fun.

I noticed that the overhead light in Frankie's office was off. "Is she in?"

"She's in a meeting with Ben. She told me to give you this."

Patsy handed me a white envelope addressed to a Dr. Roland. From the Seattle street address, I ventured a guess that Dr. Roland's office was in one of the Pill Hill area medical buildings near Swedish Hospital. "What is it?"

"A subpoena, and it needs to be delivered today. He's going to be called as a witness next week."

If I had been told about this yesterday, I would have cut my visit short at the hospital and driven straight to the ferry terminal to catch the eight o'clock sailing. Given the lines during the busy summer tourist season, I'd be lucky to get out of Seattle before one.

Patsy's telephone rang. "Everything you need to know is in the envelope," she said, reaching for her telephone receiver.

En route to the break room to refill my cup, I opened the unsealed envelope and pulled out a list of instructions. Identify myself, confirm the recipient's identity, serve the subpoena. Sounded easy enough. As a process server, I'd delivered dozens of notices to appear; I could certainly serve one measly subpoena. At least it would give me a reprieve from making coffee for the next few hours.

Eighteen minutes later at the ferry terminal, I forked over the last twenty in my wallet for a round trip ticket and pulled behind a black Suburban idling in the second row of a long line of cars waiting for the 9:10 sailing to Seattle. Since I had a fifteen-minute wait until the ferry arrived and had just drained my to-go cup, I figured I'd better make a fast pit stop at the picnic area restroom before boarding.

Killing the engine, I climbed out of the Jag and was promptly greeted by gusts of briny wind blowing in from Puget Sound. With the hem of my shirtdress whipping around my knees as I approached the pier, I noticed a mother with a pair of towheaded toddlers feeding the ducks on a patch of grass across from the restroom, much to the chagrin of the squawking gulls circling overhead.

It seemed like a typical summer scene at the ferry dock until I spotted Heather Beckett sitting alone at one of the picnic tables as she stared out at the waves glistening like sugar crystals under the morning sun.

The last thing I needed this morning was some stink eye from Heather so I did an about face and scurried back to my car. "No problem," I said to myself as I unlocked the car door. Nature might be calling soon, but there were restroom facilities on the ferry. This time I had no problem with waiting.

By nine-thirty I had a little problem. Not only was Heather on the ferry, her blue Prius was parked next to the stairway leading up to the passenger deck where most all the other ferry riders were enjoying the view, and more importantly, had access to a bathroom. Most everyone but Heather and me.

Now, I'm all for avoiding confrontation with certain females from my past whenever possible, but I needed to pee and that trumped any amount of stink eye Heather could hurl my way.

Just as I reached for my door handle, I saw Heather climb out of her car. From the swipe she'd just made at her cheek, it looked like she had been crying. Because of Steve? I didn't want to know.

Okay, I was dying to know, but after twenty years of being snubbed by Heather Beckett, I knew I was the last person on Earth that she'd pour her heart out to.

I watched her head up the stairs, no doubt to repair her perennially flawless face in the ladies room, exactly where I should have gone the second I drove onto the ferry and switched off my car's ignition. I certainly couldn't go now, not with Heather in there. *Damn.*

Ten minutes later, she returned to her car grasping her cell phone. Whoever she was speaking to was getting an earful.

I rolled down my driver's side window. Not that I make a habit of eavesdropping on private conversations, but since it was Heather, good manners seemed optional.

"I don't care!" she yelled, gripping the phone as if it were a hand grenade she wanted to launch at someone. "You *have* to do this."

Do what?

I held my breath waiting for an answer, but the only response I heard was the slam of her car door.

I'd wager that Heather had just been told *no*. Obviously wasn't happy about it, either, which didn't break my heart one little bit, especially if that *no* had come from Steve. Really, did she expect him to drop everything—including the murder investigation that he should be working on— and join her in Seattle for some sort of rendezvous?

Even Heather's allure couldn't be that irresistible. Could it?

I was asking myself the same thing five minutes later, while I watched Heather drive down the ferry ramp. Not that I cared what she and Steve did.

Once she was out of my sight, I turned the key and the Jag rumbled to life. "I don't care." Because it didn't affect me in the slightest.

Liar.

"It doesn't matter," I said, easing down the ramp. No more than it had mattered seventeen years ago.

The SUV in front of me slowed to a stop behind a string of cars at a red light to turn left onto 1st Avenue South. I merged into the right lane after I made the turn and saw a blue Prius five cars ahead of me.

According to the driving directions to Dr. Roland's office that I'd printed, I was supposed to turn right on South Jackson. The Prius went straight through that intersection toward the heart of the city, where my grandmother used to take me shopping each August before school started. And beyond Nordstrom and the upscale shops of Westlake Park stood countless hotels that rented by the hour.

My grip tightened on the steering wheel. Should I turn or go straight?

Turn and act like a mature adult who had a job to do or

run the light that had just turned yellow and find out what Heather was doing in Seattle?

The job could wait a few minutes.

I hit the gas. "Please be going shopping."

Heather turned right on Yesler, veering east from the downtown shopping district and my heart sank.

I let a yellow taxi cut in front of me to add some distance between me and the Prius, then made the right turn onto Yesler.

As I followed Heather onto Broadway she wove her way past Swedish Hospital, finally turning onto East Madison—not an area of town I was familiar with.

Wherever Heather was heading, my bladder needed her to get there. Quickly.

After a couple of blocks she turned onto a tree-lined side street near Seattle University, then pulled into a parking lot behind a bank.

I breathed a sigh of relief. Not a no-tell hotel in sight. So what was this? A doctor's appointment?

I parked in the lot of the convenience store on the opposite corner and watched her disappear inside a two-story office building.

A few seconds later, I eased out of the lot and read the carved wooden sign next to the building entrance. *Elliott Bay Psychological Services.*

Holy cannoli. It was a doctor's appointment all right. For therapy. And by coming here, Heather was going well out of her way to get it. Understandable since news about her seeing a shrink would spread like a white hot wild fire in Port Merritt.

Besides me and maybe her mother, the only other

person who knew that Heather had this appointment might have been at the other end of that phone call.

You have to do this.

I sucked in a breath as icy fingers of realization crawled up my spine. This wasn't just therapy, this was *couples* therapy. And Steve could be here any minute. "Shit!"

A car horn blasted behind me. With my pulse racing like I'd just mainlined a gallon of Duke's coffee, I peered into my rear view mirror and released the breath I'd been holding when I saw an elderly woman gesturing at me to move. Since I needed to make myself scarce before Steve arrived, she'd get no argument from me.

After a quick bathroom break at a fast food restaurant on East Madison, I drove straight to Seattle's Pill Hill to lay a subpoena on Dr. Roland. Exactly what this deputy coroner should have done in the first place—focus on her job instead of taking a side trip into too much information land.

Because Dr. Roland's pissy receptionist made me wait until the doctor had finished with his last morning appointment before I could slap the subpoena into his hand, it was almost two o'clock by the time the ferry docked back in Port Merritt. My brain spent the entire crossing chewing on everything I'd learned this morning, worrying about what secrets the medical records in my tote bag held and how angry Steve would be if he knew those records were in my possession. Worse, if he ever discovered that I'd followed Heather to their appointment.

All my mental mastication made my head feel like it was being squeezed through a pastry bag, so I headed for Duke's for some edible relief—preferably in the form of a grilled turkey club on the house.

While on the hunt for a parking space near Duke's, I noticed a tall woman with perfectly straight hair glinting red in the afternoon sun—Nell Neary. As she walked down the sidewalk, her bright pink sundress swayed with every step. Unlike Heather and me, Nell had the relaxed appearance of a woman who didn't have a worry in the world.

Given everything I'd learned today, I had enough worries for the three of us.

The turkey club could wait a few minutes.

I parked the Jag in front of Clark's Pharmacy and followed Nell inside. Grabbing a plastic shopping basket from a stack by the entrance, I ventured down the candy aisle and tossed in a Snickers bar while keeping a watchful eye on Nell. When she stopped to peruse the hair color Clark's had on sale, I meandered over and picked up a box with a redhead on the cover.

"Have you tried this brand?" I casually asked.

Her face brightened. "Charmaine?"

"Nell? Wow, look at you. I hardly recognized you." Which would have been true if I'd said it a week ago.

She beamed. "I know. Donna talked me into going red a few months back. And of course the contacts help. You look…" her smile slipped for a fraction of a second, "… great."

Since the dark circles under my bloodshot eyes were giving me a Queen of the Undead look, it didn't take any skill to see she was just being kind. "Thanks."

"I heard you were back home," she said, glancing down at the aging linoleum. "In fact, I saw you at Trudy's funeral."

I couldn't admit that I'd also seen her so I had to go with a safer response. "You should have said hello."

"I meant to, but I was with my boyfriend and since he had to go back to work, we didn't stay long."

"What kind of work does he do?"

"He's a ranger for the Forest Service." Her cheeks flushed with pride. "You know, one of those outdoorsy types."

I wondered if he knew Justin. "How did you meet?"

Since Nell was a tax accountant with a home office and had spent most of her adult life taking care of her mother, I was more than a little curious, especially if it had anything in common with how Jayne Elwood or Sylvia Jeppesen had hooked up with the new men in their lives.

Nell shrugged. "You're going to think it's silly."

Doubtful. "Try me."

"We met last month at a dance. Thomas was there with his mother—"

"His mother?" Was this outdoorsy guy one of those forty-year-olds who still lived with his mother?

"Oh, yes. She's a very good dancer."

Okay. Maybe this was the silly part.

"So..." Nell looked up as if she were replaying the events in her head. "...it was Tango Tuesday and I had punchbowl duty."

"Tango Tuesday?" She was losing me.

"At the senior center, like it is every Tuesday night."

Oh. I hadn't received the memo.

"So, there he was, hanging around the punchbowl, and we struck up a conversation," she said with a sweet smile.

"No one introduced you?"

"Oh, no, nothing like that. Then, one thing led to another." Nell shrugged. "And here we are."

And here I was, getting nowhere fast. "Sounds like it's getting serious."

Nell nodded. "We're going into Seattle next weekend to look at engagement rings."

"That's great." Except everything she'd told me made Swiss cheese out of my matchmaking theory. Maybe Steve was right and Bernadette Neary's death was just coincidentally similar to several other deaths in the past couple of years.

Nell touched my wrist. "I'm sorry, I got completely caught up. I don't think I answered your question."

"My question?" It seemed like she had answered everything I'd asked and then some.

She pointed at the box of hair color in my hands. "About trying that brand."

"That's okay." I placed the box back on the shelf. "I don't know that I'm ready to make a big change. I think I'm just in a little rut."

Nell nodded, no doubt familiar with the concept after spending over a decade as a caretaker to her mom.

"Maybe I'm just tired." It wasn't a stretch.

"You do look a little peaked."

"I haven't been sleeping that well. Actually, for a while now." For exactly a week, since my mother had breezed into town, but who was counting? "Maybe I should make an appointment with Dr. Straitham," I said to see if Nell would react to the mention of his name.

I waited, watching, but there was nothing except some possible concern on my behalf. Nice, but not helpful.

"You probably should. I'm sure he could prescribe you something or maybe Clark's has some over the counter medication that could help."

Again, that didn't get me any closer to fitting together the puzzle pieces that connected the deaths of Dr. Straitham's patients.

Although making an appointment with the doctor wasn't a bad idea, and I happened to know just the former patient who needed to see him.

Chapter Ten

It was almost two forty-five by the time I got back to the office with a turkey club and a can of Diet Coke.

Sitting at my desk, I slammed back a couple of aspirin with the Diet Coke to do battle with my headache and waited for the carbs in the turkey club to send me to my happy place. Stopping for a mocha latte on the way back would have sent me there faster, but I'd already blown my diet with the Snickers bar and the poppy seed muffin, so I was in damage control mode. Tomorrow, no muffin and no candy. Well, maybe just no candy. I didn't want to shock my system.

After I dropped off my expense report with Patsy, I poked my head in Frankie's office. "Would you mind if I left early one day this week? I need to make a doctor's appointment."

Frankie looked at me over her bifocals. "This wouldn't have something to do with Warren Straitham, would it? Because if it does, we need to talk."

Busted. I needed some deflection, pronto. "Actually, it's for my mother."

Frankie arched an eyebrow. There was nothing like the

promise of salacious celebrity gossip to draw someone's attention. All the better when it drew that attention away from me.

"Nothing serious." Which was true. "Just something that requires a driver." Not so true, but I was counting on Frankie respecting Marietta's privacy and not asking any questions. "So if you could spare me for a couple of hours…"

"Do what you need to do," she said, reaching for her ringing telephone.

I wasn't sure she believed me, but it was a *yes*. That was all I needed to hear to head back to my desk and punch in the number for Warren Straitham's office to schedule some face time with the doctor.

A monotone female voice answered the phone, and I told her that I wanted to make an appointment for my mother.

"Is your mother a patient of Dr. Straitham's?"

"A former patient. It would be under the name Mary Jo Digby."

There was a long pause. "Mary Jo Digby…the actress?"

I wasn't surprised the receptionist had made the connection. Most of the old-timers in town called my mother by her real name. "Yes."

"Cool," the receptionist said with a breathy giggle. "And what seems to be her problem?"

If she wanted an unbiased opinion, this chick was asking the wrong person.

"I think she might need something to help her sleep." At least one of us did.

"The doctor will want to do a brief physical first…"

Based on how he had ogled Marietta at Trudy's funeral, I had no doubt of that.

"…but I'm sure he can prescribe a little something to help her get some sleep."

I and all the sheep I'd been counting for the past week were depending on it.

By the time I hung up the phone, Marietta had a Tuesday appointment at two-thirty. Now, all I had to do was break the news over dinner.

I called Gram to make sure there was plenty of wine in the house.

Sitting in my grandmother's dining room almost four hours later, Marietta's fingertips traced the hollow of her throat as she stared across the table at me. "You want me to do what?"

I picked up the bottle of merlot and refilled her glass. "I want you to see Dr. Straitham tomorrow. You have a two-thirty appointment."

Her extended eyelashes fluttered. "Whatever for?"

"I need to talk to him, but given how things went at Trudy's funeral, I think he'd be more willing to see you than me."

Gram scowled. "Rather underhanded, don't you think?"

Maybe. I topped off her glass for good measure. "You know it's true."

"What I know is that you're poking your nose where it doesn't belong," Gram said.

"I'm just going to go along and ask a few questions."

Marietta's eyelids tightened as she met my gaze. "While you're there at my appointment?"

I had no intention of being in the examination room with her. "More like before and after your appointment."

"I see," she said thoughtfully. "So, what you're really sayin' is that you need my help to get to the bottom of the mystery of poor Trudy's death."

I wouldn't have used those exact words, but.... "Yes."

Her collagen-enhanced lips curled into a satisfied smile as she reached for her wine glass. "Well, if you put it that way. I'll let Barry know that I'll have to cut our lunch date a little short."

She couldn't be serious. "You have a lunch date tomorrow with Barry Ferris?"

"He's so sweet. Persistent, too. Ah do like that in a man."

I didn't, especially when he was my former biology teacher. "Isn't he a little old for you?"

"Chah-maine, don't be silly."

"He's practically *your* age."

Marietta's eyes darkened. "Which gives us a lot in common," she said without a trace of the Georgia peach accent.

Gram and I exchanged worried glances as Marietta sipped her wine.

My mother pointed a manicured index finger at me. "I saw that look."

Gram pursed her mouth, accentuating the puckers gathered around her lips. "He's a nice man, Mary Jo."

"Don't you think I know that? I wouldn't be having a lunch date with him if he weren't. Ah swear, you two are making mountains out of molehills. It's not like I'm gonna marry the man. I'm just having some fun."

That's what I was worried about.

∽

The next morning I woke up to a metal bracket in the Crippler poking me in the butt like a cattle prod. I lifted an eyelid to peek at the clock. Five twenty-seven.

I'd wanted to get over to Chimacam Memorial to talk to Cindy Tobias before I had to be in court, but even my ex-husband had the good sense not to poke me this early with any appendage he wanted to keep.

After a long, hot shower, I took a little extra time doing the hair and makeup thing. If I was going to make an appearance at the hospital, I might as well look halfway decent doing it, especially if I was going to run into Dr. Forsythe. Or any other doctor for that matter.

An hour later at Duke's, I ladled some oatmeal into a white ceramic bowl, grabbed a small dish of strawberries, and took them over to the counter and sat next to Stanley.

The ninety-year-old stared through his thick glasses at my bowl.

"What?" I asked, dumping the sliced strawberries into the oatmeal.

He gave me a curt nod. "Very sensible."

"It happens every once in a while."

"Must be a full moon," Steve said as he parked himself on the barstool to my right.

I shot him my best glare.

He stood deferentially. "Where are my manners? I should have asked. Is this seat taken?"

Between Stanley and a burly trucker slurping his coffee at the other end of the counter were seven empty seats, including Steve's usual spot in front of Duke's grill.

I shrugged. "Sit wherever you want."

Settling back into his seat, Steve motioned Lucille over with the coffee carafe. "I thought I'd better ask in case you were waiting for a *date*."

I was tempted to ask whether he'd had a date in Seattle yesterday but kept my mouth shut.

Lucille's gaze shifted to me as she poured his coffee.

"Nope, I'm flying solo this morning," I said.

Stanley elbowed me as Lucille topped off his coffee cup. "What am I, chopped liver?"

"Sorry, Stanley." I turned to Steve. "You and everyone else will have to get in line."

"Now you're talkin'," Stanley said with a rheumy chuckle. "I do like my women to have spunk."

Steve stirred creamer into his cup. "You're living on the edge with this one, Stan."

Stanley reached past me for the sugar. "What can I tell ya. I'm a livin' on the edge kind of guy."

What a happy bunch of liars we were this morning.

"The usual?" Lucille asked Steve.

He glanced at my bowl. "I'll have what she's having."

One corner of Lucille's mouth twitched into a hint of a smirk as she refilled my coffee cup. "It must be a full moon."

After taking a sip of the steaming, dark-as-molasses brew, Steve dumped in another mini-cup of creamer. "So, what's going on today?"

I figured I'd better steer clear of any topic of conversation that involved Heather, Warren Straitham, Kyle Cardinale, or Trudy, so that left just one thing to talk about.

"Marietta has a lunch date with Mr. Ferris."

Steve grinned. "No shit."

"It's not funny."

"I think it's kind of funny," Stanley chimed in.

Swell. "I don't."

Steve stirred his coffee. "I'm sure it's harmless. He's too old for her."

I scraped the bottom of my bowl for the last spoonful of oatmeal. "That's what I told her."

"And?"

"She didn't take it very well," I said as Lucille delivered Steve's breakfast.

"How much longer is your mother going to be in town?" he asked.

"Good question." One that I had been asking since the day she arrived.

Aunt Alice inched around the corner with a tray of doughnuts. What had me concerned more than her slow progress to the bakery display case was the sight of her walking with a slight limp.

Lucille reached out to take the aluminum tray. "Let me help you with those, hon."

"I can manage," Alice barked.

Steve turned to me. "Why is she limping?"

"I don't know." I twisted out of my seat. "But I'm going to find out."

I grabbed a cup from the rack under the counter and filled it from a freshly brewed pot of coffee. "Good morning," I said to Duke as I entered the kitchen.

Grimacing, he flipped a pancake on the grill. "Don't be so sure about that."

I edged closer. "What's wrong?"

He fixed his gaze on his wife. "Something's hurting her. She won't tell me what."

I didn't think she'd tell me, either, but I needed to give it a try.

I followed Alice back to the table in the center of the kitchen and set the coffee cup down in front of her. "How's it going?"

"Peachy," Alice grumbled, wincing as she eased herself down on the wooden barstool.

I didn't have to read the strain in her eyes to see that something was very wrong. "Do you feel okay?"

"I'm fine! I wish everyone would stop asking me that." She picked up her rolling pin and a ball of piecrust dough. "I'm right as rain."

Yeah, and I'd been sleeping like a baby.

"Why are you limping?"

"I stubbed my toe," she said, rolling out the dough like I'd seen her do a thousand times.

"Liar."

She glared at me. "Don't you need to get to work?"

"Soon."

I took the next few minutes of silence as my cue to get out of her kitchen.

"I'll be back for lunch," I told Duke as I walked past the grill.

"Why am I not surprised?" Duke deadpanned. "I'm going to have to start calling you *Free Lunch*."

"If she's any worse," I said, ignoring the old coot, "I'll take her to the doctor. I have an appointment later this afternoon."

Duke raised a silvery eyebrow.

"I'm fine. It's nothing. In fact, it's Marietta's appointment." Deflect, deflect, deflect.

"What the hell's wrong with her?"

"You're kidding, right?"

Duke cracked two eggs on the grill. "Sorry I asked."

Stepping behind the counter, I grabbed the coffee carafe and refilled Steve's cup. "I didn't find out much. She's not talking but she's obviously in some pain. Denies it of course."

"Of course." Steve stood, pressing his palm to my shoulder. "I have to get to work, but I'll stop by later to see how she's doing."

The warmth of his touch lingered for a moment, heating my core like a steaming mug of cocoa on a blustery winter morning.

Good thing I was a mocha latte girl.

"Oh, Free Lunch," Duke sang out as I watched the door shut behind Steve.

I wheeled around. "You're not really going to call me that, are you?"

"If the sandwich fits." He pointed his spatula at Arlene Koker, who was sitting alone in a booth by the window. "Earn your keep and get Arlene's breakfast order."

Arlene was a perky sixty-something with soft champagne blonde bangs sweeping her forehead and had been the activity director of the senior center for most of the last decade. You could count on her always wearing a smile and never varying her breakfast order—two poached eggs and a side of whole wheat toast, unbuttered.

I took the coffee carafe to her table and filled her cup. "Good morning. The usual?"

Arlene nodded, her smile dimming as she looked up at me. "Charmaine, I thought you had started a new job at the courthouse."

"I did. I'm just working off my breakfast." Taking it out in trade was probably more like it.

"You should come on over to the center. We have all sorts of good ways to work off calories." Her gaze shifted to my thighs. "Aerobics, too. In fact, a class is going on right now. Your granny's a member, so that gives you a family discount."

"Thanks, Arlene. I'll be sure to keep that in mind," I said, hoping she'd get the hint that I had no intention of becoming an honorary Gray Lady.

She tore open a blue packet of sugar substitute and stirred it into her coffee. "And of course you know about Tango Tuesday."

"I've heard of it." Specifically from Nell.

Arlene pointed her spoon at me. "You should come. Bring Steve."

Right. Like I could drag him onto a dance floor with a bunch of seniors. "That might not be Steve's cup of tea."

"Really? He seemed to have fun last time."

Last time?

She reached for her cup. "He was a big hit with the ladies."

"He always is."

⟳

I arrived at the hospital around seven-forty. At the second floor nurse's station I'd been told that Cindy Tobias was working in the ICU, so I took a right turn down a long hallway, pushed open the door marked *Intensive Care*, and found her standing at a monitor next to an elderly patient's bed.

She didn't look pleased to see me.

"I figured I'd be seeing you sooner or later," she said softly, exiting the patient's room.

I followed her to a dimly lit desk at the opposite side of the hallway. "Why do you say that?"

She sat at the computer station and made a few mouse clicks. "You want to talk to me about Trudy Bergeson, don't you?"

And Rose and Mr. Elwood. "Do you have a few minutes?"

She blew out a breath, then pointed to a nutmeg brown upholstered chair next to her workstation that looked like it was held together with duct tape. "Have a seat."

Ignoring the lumpy seat cushion, I scooted the chair a little closer to get a better view of Cindy's face. "I'm just trying to get a sense of what happened."

"Because of Dr. Cardinale calling Frankie Rickard."

She knew. It made me wonder what else she knew. "Because it seems like Trudy died rather suddenly."

The flicker at the corners of Cindy's lips told me

I'd struck paydirt. She opened her mouth, then pressed it closed. Whatever she'd thought about saying, she had censored herself.

"You were surprised when it happened," I said for her.

She stared at her keyboard for several seconds. "We all thought she was going home the next day."

"She was being dismissed from the hospital?"

Cindy nodded, her blunt-cut honey brown hair bobbing at her shoulders. "There was a notation in her chart about it."

"From?"

"Dr. Straitham."

No big surprise since he was Trudy's doctor, but I wrote it down in my notebook. "I understand that Trudy Bergeson coded around three forty-five."

"That's when I did a bed check and discovered she wasn't breathing."

"There wasn't an alarm that went off?"

Cindy shook her head. "She'd been moved out of the ICU and wasn't on a heart monitor."

Which would make it a little more convenient if someone wanted to kill her.

"Then what happened?"

"I called for help and started CPR. Dr. Cardinale arrived a minute later, but there wasn't much he could do."

"What about Tina Norton?"

Cindy's mouth quirked. Maybe she'd been asking herself the same question.

"Was Tina working that night?" I asked.

"No."

That didn't explain the reaction I'd just seen. "Did you

see her that night?"

"No." She folded her arms across her chest, which I took as a cue that she wanted this to be the final word on the subject of Tina.

I decided to try a different approach. "Prior to discovering Trudy wasn't breathing, did you notice anything unusual that night? Anything or anyone out of the ordinary?"

Cindy gave me another little headshake. "Until I went into Trudy's room, it had been a pretty slow night."

"Had you seen Dr. Forsythe prior to that?"

"No, he doesn't work weekends."

"What about Dr. Straitham?"

She shrugged, her lips pressed together. "He doesn't usually keep those hours."

There was something about the way she said *usually*.

"You'd seen him here other nights?"

"Not really. I'd just seen Dr. Straitham's car a couple of times when I went out for a smoke."

"But not him."

She hung her head. "No."

What the hell? His car was here but she never saw him?

"Did you see his car the night Trudy died?"

"Only after Dr. Cardinale called him. I didn't notice it before that."

That meant that she couldn't help me with the timeline for Warren Straitham's whereabouts at the time of Trudy's death.

"Cindy, what about the early morning that Rose Kozarek died? You were working that shift, right?"

She nodded.

"Do you remember if you saw Dr. Straitham anytime during your shift?"

"You're the second person to ask me that this week."

That was the last thing I'd expected her to say. "Who was the first?"

"Steve Sixkiller."

Chapter Eleven

After a torturously long morning hunched over a row of filing cabinets, I made a break for Duke's. My growling stomach hankered for one of his patty melts, but more importantly, I wanted to see how Alice was doing.

Typical for the noon hour, the savory aroma of burgers and bacon sizzling on the grill hung on the air and most every table was occupied. Not so typical, there was no sign of Alice in the cafe.

I went to the juice dispenser, poured two glasses of orange juice and set one on the counter in front of the grill.

Duke glared at the juice glass like I'd spiked it with arsenic. "What's that for?"

"It's good for you." And if I knew him, he hadn't had much to eat or drink all day.

"You paying for it?"

"Hadn't planned to."

"So what else is new?"

Ignoring the wisecrack, I watched him suck down the juice in three big gulps. "How's Alice doing?" I asked.

He wiped his mouth with the back of his hand. "She

keeps saying she's fine, but she went home early. That should tell you how fine she is."

It did, and now I was even more worried. "Do you think there's any way I could talk her into seeing Dr. Straitham?"

"See the doc after what happened last Saturday?" Duke flipped a burger. "Pigs would have to fly out of my butt first. I'll take her to the ER if it gets any worse."

The ER, where Trudy and Rose had arrived a couple of days before they took their final breaths? "That might not go over real well, either."

"I'm bigger than she is. I'll *insist*."

I'd been down that road before with Alice. Insisting that my great-aunt do anything she didn't want to do met the same reception as a cat facing a sink full of sudsy water.

Lucille squeaked up behind me while I asked Duke to make me a patty melt. "So, what did you find out at the hospital?" she asked.

"What did you do—put a tail on me?"

"I have my sources."

And if they worked at the hospital I wanted to know what else she had found out.

"Did your sources tell you where Dr. Straitham was the morning of Trudy's death?"

"Jay-sus!" Duke rolled his eyes. "Don't encourage her."

Lucille glared at Duke. "All I know is that he managed to get to the hospital pretty damned quick to break the news to Norm."

That confirmed Kyle Cardinale's statement but didn't shed even a glimmer of light on where Dr. Straitham had been when he received the call from the hospital.

"Order up!" Duke barked. "Some nice people would

like to eat sometime today."

"If you hadn't noticed, some nice people are being killed off around here." Lucille cocked her head. "Which do you think is more important?"

Glowering, Duke pointed his spatula at me. "See what you started?"

"Who me? I'm just here for my free lunch."

I caught a fleeting smile as he plated the patty melt. "Yeah, right."

I kissed his grizzled cheek, grabbed the plate, then surveyed the small crowd and spotted Jayne Elwood sitting alone near the door.

It seemed like a good opportunity to have some casual chitchat with Jayne so I slid onto the seat at the next table, facing her.

"Waiting for Ernie?" I asked.

She glanced out the window with a wistful smile on her lips. "He must be running a little late."

I took a bite of my patty melt and watched her cross her legs, smoothing her pale yellow skirt over her knees. A tan leather flat dangled from her left foot. It looked new.

I wanted to keep the conversation going to hear how she'd hooked up with Ernie. Since it wouldn't help me to appear too eager, I used what she was giving me. "Those look like comfortable shoes."

"Oh, they are. I could wear them all day, and they're marvelous for dancing."

"Dancing?" Had everyone in town taken a sudden interest in dancing?

Jayne smiled, leaning my direction. "Honey, it's Tango Tuesday. You should put on your dancing shoes and join us," she added as Lucille topped off her coffee.

"Dancin' shoes!" Lucille scoffed. "Char?"

"Sounds like fun," I said. Even more, it sounded like something I shouldn't miss, especially if Steve was going to make an appearance.

Lucille gaped at me. "It does? Don't you have someplace else you'd rather be than the senior center?"

"Not on Tango Tuesday."

∽

At two twenty-five I parked the Jag in a shaded spot near the front door of the medical building on 2ⁿᵈ Street that Warren Straitham shared with my former orthodontist.

"Ah don't know that this is such a good idea," Marietta said, using the passenger vanity mirror to fluff her cropped hair.

"It'll be fine. I'm just going to ask the girls in the office a few questions while you're in with the doctor."

She smiled at the mirror, checking her teeth. "What's my problem again?"

Sometimes my mother made it way too easy to take a cheap shot.

Since I needed an ally willing to play her part, not a pissed off actress, I took the high road. "You're having trouble sleeping," I said, stifling a yawn.

"Ah'm sleeping just fine as opposed to some people around here."

"You're a skilled actress. You can fake it."

I was sure it wouldn't have been the first time.

Marietta's lips curled in satisfaction at the sugar-coated

praise.

"Think of it as improvisation," I added as we got out of the car. "And don't let him leave the room before he writes you a prescription."

She sighed. "Ah really don't need a prescription."

I did.

Warren Straitham's waiting room hadn't changed much in the twelve years since I'd been here last. Maybe an upgrade in the wall-to-wall carpeting and a few new prints by local artists. What I found most remarkable about Dr. Straitham's office was that every chair in his cramped waiting room was occupied by a middle-aged woman with her gaze fixed on my mother.

A half dozen cell phones and cameras took aim at us, clicking and whirring.

Fans.

My mother beamed with delight as she touched the base of her throat in mock-surprise. "Oh, mah, the doctor must be very busy today."

Yeah. Like hormone therapy was the special of the day.

"Ms. Moreau." Claudia, the receptionist, who had been two years behind me in high school, handed Marietta a clipboard and smiled reverently. "We just need to update your history."

"Mah history?" Marietta leaned against the reception desk. "Ah am sorry, but there's been a little misunderstandin'. This appointment is actually for Chahmaine."

My jaw clenched so tight I could have broken a molar. "What?"

Her gaze soft as silk, Marietta touched my cheek. The last time I'd been bathed in so much motherly affection, she'd powdered my other cheeks. "It's the only way ah could get her to come in and see the doctor about her sleepin' disorder."

Claudia's eyes widened.

I shook my head. "I don't have a disorder."

Marietta pushed the clipboard at me. "As you can see, she's in a bit of denial."

I pushed it back. "What are you doing?"

"Do you know how much one of the scandal rags would pay for those pictures?" she whispered in my ear. "I don't need that kind of press."

Like some dweeb at a tabloid would care about one of Hollywood's many beauty queens whose reign had been reduced to hawking her wares on cable TV infomercials.

Claudia handed me a ballpoint pen. "If you'll just fill out the form, the doctor will see you in a few minutes."

Marietta sighed contentedly. "Thank you ever so much." She leaned in, resting her elbows on the half wall. "There's just one more teensy little thing."

Claudia smiled. "What can we do for you?"

"If it isn't too much to ask, is there somewhere back there that ah could wait for mah daughter? It's a little crowded out here, if you know what ah mean."

"Of course there is," Claudia said, bounding from her seat.

Marietta winked at me. "Isn't this fun?" she whispered.

"Yeah." At least one of us was having a good time.

"It's like that episode when ah had to wear a bikini to distract the bad guys while Josie rifled through the accountant's safe for evidence that he was the one embezzling the funds." Marietta shrugged. "Except for the bikini part, of course."

And the accountant.

And the embezzling.

The waiting room door closed behind my mother and ten menopausal women stared at me like I was personally responsible for sucking all the fun out of the room.

I wasn't too crazy about the situation, either, especially when one of them snapped my picture.

At least I didn't need to worry about landing on the cover of a scandal rag. And given the doctor I'd soon be seeing, what the mad snapper planned to do with that photo was the least of my concerns.

Three minutes later, a forty-ish nurse I didn't recognize opened the door. "Charmaine?"

"I'm Shannon," she said with a smile as she took the clipboard.

As I followed her down the hall, I heard several women laughing, one of them my mother.

Shannon glanced back over her shoulder. "Your mom's a hoot."

Not exactly the first word that came to mind when describing Marietta, but as long as she was a hoot who could be discrete for the next fifteen minutes, I could live with it.

Shannon stopped at a scale. "Let's get you weighed in."

I'd sooner let my mother give me a facial. Every day for a month.

I slipped off my shoes. "Every little bit helps, right?" If I could have stripped naked and kept a shred of my dignity, I would have.

"Of course." Shannon set the bottom scale weight to

one hundred fifty, and kept sliding the top weight until the scale leveled off at one sixty-four.

Holy crap!

"Okey dokey," Shannon chirped after a little lip press. Incongruity. Words and action mismatch. Pretty typical in friends' white lies, customer service representatives working on commission, and weigh-ins by skinny nurses at the doctor's office.

Shannon led me to an examination room at the end of a short hallway, and I took a seat on a paper-covered padded table. She took my vitals and a few minutes later, I heard a knock on the door.

"Hello, Charmaine," Dr. Straitham said in a businesslike manner with Shannon hot on his heels. No smile, no attempt to put me at ease.

No big surprise. Given what had happened at Trudy's funeral it would have been a wasted effort because there was absolutely nothing he could do short of giving me an injection to help me relax. And given why I was here, especially not that.

He sat on a short black stool with caster wheels and looked up at me after he scanned my chart. "So, you've been having some trouble sleeping."

I nodded.

"How long has this been going on?"

"Over a week."

He made a note in the chart, then flashed a penlight in my eyes. He crossed his legs and jotted some more notes. "Getting enough exercise?"

"Uh…probably not." Although I was getting a lot more now that I was chasing down anyone who might know where he had been in the early hours of last Monday morning.

"What about your diet? Sometimes the foods we eat can keep us up at night."

"I don't think food's the problem."

Dr. Straitham's gaze transferred to my hips, then back to my eyes. "Looks like you've gained a few pounds in the last several years." He flipped a couple of pages in my chart. "Thirty-two since you were in last."

That meant I'd gained an average of less than three pounds a year. If I hadn't just tipped the scales at a hundred and sixty-four pounds, I might have thought that was pretty darn good.

He pursed his mouth. "What'd you have for breakfast this morning?"

"Oatmeal." I neglected to mention the half-cup of creamer I'd dumped in my coffee.

"Lunch?"

"A patty melt."

He set the chart down on the desk and met my gaze. "Charmaine, I know you're a smart girl. What are you trying to do?"

Excuse me? "I'm just trying to get a little more sleep." *And find out what the hell you've been up to.*

"Hmmmm." He twisted off the stool, tapped my back, then listened to my heart. "You having headaches?"

"Sometimes."

"You have a new job, right?"

"Yes."

"Could be stress-related."

"Things have been a little stressful lately," I said,

watching for his reaction.

He offered up a humorless smile.

"Lot's going on. You know, with Trudy Bergeson's death and all."

Eyes downcast, he slowly nodded. "Very sad."

And he clearly felt sadness, which proved absolutely nothing. After Chris asked me for a divorce, he had the same exact expression. Didn't stop the jerk from telling me he wanted out, didn't make me feel better, and didn't alter the outcome of the situation one iota.

"Thanks, Shannon," he said as she clicked the door shut behind her.

Uh-oh.

Dr. Straitham sat back down on the stool, leaned back against the wall, and stared at me for several ticks of the wall clock near the door.

The corners of his eyes tightened, his brows drew together.

Mistake, my brain screamed at me. I was now alone with a possible killer. If he reached for a syringe, what was I going to do? Fend him off with the paper lining from the examination table?

"Charmaine, I'm going to write you a prescription for a mild sedative that should help you sleep."

Great. I could use a little something right now to get my heart back to a normal rhythm.

"I'd also like you to think about your lifestyle."

"Okay." I wasn't sure where he was going with the bit about my lifestyle, but if it meant I'd live to suck down a mocha latte another day, I could think about pretty much anything.

"You only have this one body," he said as he pulled a sheet of paper from the desk drawer. "You need to take better care of it."

So was that the problem? Trudy and the others weren't taking care of their bodies? Weren't following doctor's orders? Seemed crazy harsh for a doctor to sit in judgment of his patients this way, but everyone had their breaking points.

"Okay."

I looked down at the paper he'd just handed me and tried to keep my hand from shaking long enough to focus on the words, *heart-healthy* and *food groups*.

"I think you'll find that this plan is easy to follow, and as a bonus you'll probably start sleeping better."

Swell. My prime suspect had just put me on a diet.

Chapter Twelve

As soon as she got into the car, Marietta pulled off her broad-rimmed dark glasses and beamed, hitting me with the full force of her chemically whitened teeth. "I have big news!"

Cursing under my breath, I started the engine. I felt stupid to be leaving Dr. Straitham's office with nothing more than a prescription for the problem in the bucket seat next to me. Oh, and a diet, so make that stupid and fat and in no mood to hear Marietta's breaking news.

"Don't you wanna know what I found out?" she asked.

I shifted into reverse and eased out of the parking space. "I'm listening."

She flicked her wrist, the three silver bangles adorning it colliding inches away from my ear. "You might want to pull right back in this spot and give me your full attention."

What I wanted was to drop Marietta off at my grandmother's house and hightail it to my favorite espresso stand for a mocha latte. "What've you got?"

"Dr. Straitham is having an affair!"

I slammed on the brake. "What?"

Bracing herself against the dashboard, my mother bit

back a frown. "Did I not tell you to park it?"

I'd noticed she'd been toning down her southern-fried accent when she wasn't around her adoring public. Now there wasn't a trace. Plus, she sounded like a pissed off mother which wasn't helping my mood.

I pulled off on a side street and parked in the shade of a thicket of Douglas firs that bordered a realtor's office. "Who told you Doc Straitham is having an affair?"

"His nurse, Shannon."

"But she was in the office with me most of the time."

"And then she joined in on the conversation when I mentioned how guilty Warren looked at Trudy's funeral." Marietta's lips curled into a wicked smile. "Turns out he has good reason for that guilty look."

Assuming that's all he was guilty of.

"An affair." The doctor certainly had a roving eye. I'd observed that myself, as well as Virginia Straitham's reaction to it. "Did Shannon give you the name of the woman?"

"No name. But she's pretty sure that it's someone at the hospital."

That would explain what Cindy said about the doctor's car in the hospital parking lot at odd hours.

"Does Virginia know?"

"Trust me, hon, she knows." Marietta gazed out the passenger side window. "We always know."

Marietta didn't have the greatest track record picking husbands. Then again, neither did I. Short of holding hands and turning this into a mother/daughter therapy session, I passed on sharing and made a mental note to pay Cindy another visit.

"So, this afternoon might not have gone exactly as

you'd planned, but did I do good or what?" Marietta asked with a gleam in her green eyes.

I had to give credit where credit was due. "You done good."

"That's what I thought." She patted me on the thigh. "We make a good team, you and I."

Team? This was a one-time performance of the Digby and Digby show. "I really don't—"

"So what's next? Do we try to find out where Warren's been dippin' his wick?"

There was that *we* thing again. "Leave any matters having to do with wick dipping to me."

"Well, if you insist, but I do believe I might have a little more experience in this area than you."

"I have plenty of experience."

That earned me another pat. "You are such a bad liar."

"Takes one to know one."

She reached into her purse for a lipstick. "Honey, I've been at the lying game a long time. Do it well and it's called acting."

"Says you," I muttered under my breath, easing away from the curb and turning right at the corner to take Marietta back to Gram's.

"So, what do you say we celebrate how things went today with a little piece of pie." A hopeful smile played at the corners of her cherry red lips. "It does happen to be pie happy hour."

I wouldn't say the news about Dr. Straitham was a cause for celebration. It helped a puzzle piece click into place, but it failed to get me closer to any answers about how Trudy died.

"You want pie?" Seriously?

"Lunch with Barry was a bit of a rush so I have to admit I'm a little hungry."

The mention of my biology teacher's name set off my radar. She might be hungry, but I was willing to bet the four dollars in my wallet that I'd been saving for a mocha latte that it wasn't for pie.

Since I could keep my four dollars by letting Duke supply my caffeine fix, I gave her the benefit of the doubt and took the right at the corner and the next left onto Main.

Two minutes later, the silver bell above the cafe door signaled our arrival.

Duke sat sipping a cup of coffee at the far end of the counter next to Stanley. Pie happy hour was his chew the fat time with the regulars before turning the grill over to the night shift and heading home to spend the rest of his evening parked in front of the tube.

His brows furrowed the second he met my gaze. "Do you ever actually work at this new job of yours?"

"I got time off for good behavior," I said, heading for the coffee carafe while my mother slid onto the bench seat of a booth by the front window.

He scoffed. "Bullshit."

"Such language!" Marietta said, her bangles clattering.

Duke growled like a junkyard dog warning her to keep her distance. "What's she doing here? Was the Ritz Carlton closed?"

I smiled with enough sugar to induce a diabetic coma. "She wanted pie."

He eyeballed her as I topped off his coffee cup. "Bullshit to that, too."

Stanley nodded his agreement as he pushed his cup at me. That made it unanimous.

"How's Alice doing?" I asked.

Duke shook his head. "She's home. Beyond that, she's not sayin' much. Keeps telling me she's fine."

No shock there. My great-aunt wasn't a complainer. But I didn't need to be able to read her body language to see that she was far from fine.

I grabbed a couple of white porcelain coffee mugs. "And I call bullshit to that."

I approached the table, where Marietta was leaning against the window and looking down the length of the street.

"What are you looking at?" I asked, following her gaze.

"Nothing."

Sure.

As I filled our coffee mugs, her eyes shifted to a man with a shopping bag walking by the window. A little sigh echoed the fact that this wasn't the man she was hoping to see.

"I just thought I recognized someone." She flashed me a fake smile, utterly lackluster by Marietta standards. "My mistake."

The sunshine streaming in through the window illuminated the fine lines around her eyes and mouth. Not exactly the soft lighting Marietta Moreau had grown accustomed to in her infomercials, but at fifty-six she was still striking, still an irritatingly fascinating beauty.

A minute after Kim took our pie order, two apple pie ala modes arrived at our table along with a spicy cologne chaser.

"Hello, ladies," Barry Ferris said, his gaze fixed on my mother, whose fork clattered to her plate.

"Barry, what a nice surprise." She scooted over on the bench seat to make room for him.

Surprise my ass. Barry Ferris didn't just happen to show up for pie happy hour freshly shaven, wearing a pressed white shirt and new Levis. Even without the spicy cologne he'd splashed on, this reeked of a set up.

He glanced across the table at me. "I hope I'm not intruding."

"Of course not." I had just become the intruder.

He leaned back and pointed at my plate. "That pie sure looks good."

"Would you like some?" Marietta pushed her plate toward him. "Truly, there's no way I can eat this all by myself."

Big fat lie. She could pack it away as easily as I could.

"Honey," she said to me, "be a dear and fetch Barry another fork."

I stepped away from the table and grabbed a fork from the bin under the counter along with a clean cup. As I stopped at the coffee pot, Duke crooked a finger at me.

He was a caffeine addict after my own heart, so I brought the carafe with me.

Duke's face screwed up like he'd been force fed Sylvia's tuna casserole. "Why the hell is Barry Ferris sniffin' around her porch?"

"If you have to ask, you need glasses more than I do," Stanley quipped, shoving his black horn rims up the bridge of his bulbous nose.

I topped off Duke's cup. "What he said."

Duke directed a steely-eyed glare at my mother. "I don't like it. Barry Ferris is a nice guy. She needs to go home and leave well enough alone."

"Amen to that," I muttered, heading back to the table.

I handed Barry the fork, poured him a cup of coffee, and reached for my plate while racking my brain for a believable lie because there was no way I was going to sit across from my mother and watch her make goo-goo eyes at my old teacher.

Fortunately, what I came up with wasn't much of a stretch. "Duke's a little down. I'm going to keep him company at the counter."

The corners of my mother's lips telegraphed her approval. And I knew it wasn't because I was being such a wonderfully kind-hearted great-niece.

"Okay, honey," she said. "We understand." She turned to Mr. Ferris, who was staring into her eyes like he was the luckiest man in the world.

The poor sap.

I didn't know what she thought she was doing with a high school biology teacher and considering the subject he taught, I didn't want to know. And I didn't want to think about him getting lucky with my mother. I just wanted to slap some sense into the man.

He didn't know her. He might have seen some glimpses of the small town Mary Jo that made Marietta Moreau seem like a real woman. But the fairytale ride in this coach was going to come to a screeching halt when it turned back into a pumpkin. It was just a matter of time—an internal clock ticking inside my mother. Something kept her on the move, navigating the waters like a shark, always hunting, always on the lookout for the next big thing to keep her face in front of the camera. Lately, that meant making personal appearances in metropolitan areas—part of her contractual obligation as the cosmetic line's spokesperson.

Port Merritt was no metropolitan area, and I was quite sure that her clock was going to strike midnight really soon. It always did.

After all the parent/teacher conferences she'd cancelled, all the empty promises I'd heard about how she'd make it up to me next year, I only hoped that Barry Ferris was smart enough to realize that pumpkin time was around the corner.

I carried my plate over to the counter and sat next to Stanley as the bell over the door announced the arrival of another happy hour customer.

Duke leaned my direction. "What? Was three a crowd?"

"I have a more important question," Steve asked, tucking his legs under the counter and taking my fork from my hand. "Aren't you supposed to be at work?"

"Sheesh, you're so suspicious. You'd make a good cop."

The lines at the corners of his eyes creased as he worked on a mouthful of pie. "So, what are you doing here?"

"I had an appointment this afternoon."

"What with—a piece of pie?"

That got a snicker out of Stanley. Although I didn't appreciate it nearly as much as he did.

"Very funny. I had to take Marietta to the doctor and after—"

"You didn't."

"Uh...her local fan club was having a meeting." Almost the truth.

Steve pushed the pie plate away. "Now you're getting your mother involved in this? What the hell are you doing?"

"If it makes you feel any better, she didn't see the doctor. I did."

"Dammit, Char! Leave the man alone."

"I'll have you know that I found out something big while we were there," I whispered, leaning close. "Something huge."

Steve's dark eyes hardened. "You are way out of line."

"But this is really big news!"

Shaking his head, he twisted out of his seat and stalked toward the door.

"Wait a minute!" The silver bell jingled behind me as I ran after him. "Don't you want to hear what I found out?"

He turned around and took an open stance like he was ready to throw me against the side of the building and slap a pair of handcuffs on me if I made one wrong move.

I had no doubt that he thought I'd already made it, but he might feel differently once he stopped acting like a ticked off cop and actually heard what I had to say.

I looked behind me to make sure we were alone. "Warren Straitham is having an affair."

"Which is no business of yours," Steve said, walking away from me.

"You knew?" I yelled at his backside as he rounded the corner. "Son of a bitch!"

Marietta filled the three wine glasses on Gram's dining room table with the Chablis we bought on the way home— her contribution to dinner. Then she sat back and aimed a frown at me as I walked in with flatware and napkins.

"He already knew?" she asked.

"Yep."

"You're absolutely sure. That lie-dar of yours isn't just having an off day?"

"No, Mother." There wasn't the slightest glimmer of surprise. Steve definitely knew and he wasn't the least bit pleased that I now knew.

She sniffed her wine glass. "Well, that Shannon can't keep her mouth shut."

I doubted that Steve's sources had been the same as my mother's, but I had no intention of debating the point with her.

All I wanted to know was why he kept trying to call off the dogs every time I mentioned Dr. Straitham.

Not that I'd refer to myself as a dog here, but I intended to keep sniffing around Warren Straitham like a bloodhound until Steve gave me a good reason not to.

I pointed at her with a butter knife. "But we will keep our mouths shut. No sharing this with Gram or Aunt Alice, Barry Ferris, or anyone."

"Charmaine, you want me to keep secrets from my own mother?"

"I don't like the sound of that," Gram said, standing in the dining room doorway. "What's going on?"

Marietta shrugged. "I guess I'm sworn to secrecy."

Gram planted her hands on her hips. "You know I'll find out sooner or later. You might as well tell me."

Not a chance. "When's dinner?" I asked, changing the subject.

"Not for a few minutes." Her mouth puckered. "So

that's it. You're really not going to tell me?"

"Sorry, Gram. It's official deputy coroner business." Sort of.

My grandmother heaved a sigh, sounding as deflated as my first chocolate soufflé. "You're no fun."

"Sure I am. In fact, I'm so much fun I'm taking you out tonight."

She blinked. "Huh? Where?"

"Gram, it's Tango Tuesday. Need I say more? Now, I need to change." I kissed her on the cheek and made a break for the stairs while the getting was good.

"Change into what?" she called after me.

A dog who was going to have her day.

Chapter Thirteen

Twenty minutes after Marietta drove off on a date with Barry Ferris, I handed my grandmother a battle-scarred tube of lipstick that I probably played dress-up with back in the second grade.

She wrinkled her nose. "Too pink." She handed it back to me. "What do you think of Barry?"

"I don't." And if I ever wanted to sleep for more than three hours straight, the less I thought of him showing up on our doorstep like my mother's prom date, the better.

I searched the contents of Gram's bathroom drawer for a shade a bit more sophisticated than bubble gum pink.

"He's a very nice man," Gram said.

"Too nice."

She sighed. "I hope your mother knows what she's doing."

So did I.

I found a silver tube labeled Cherry Bliss. "Try this one."

"Oooh, no. Too red. Your grandfather said it made me look like I should be standing on a street corner in fishnet stockings and platform shoes."

Cherry Bliss sounded like she'd know how to strut her stuff, but my eighty-year-old grandmother was more of the support hose type.

She pushed back a curl of peachy spun sugar from her forehead and hit it with a shot of Aqua Net. "What do I have to get all dolled up for anyway? It's Tango Tuesday, not ballroom dancing at the Waldorf."

"You never know who might ask you to dance."

Especially since this dance class seemed to be where several of the senior set had been making their love connections.

She stared at my reflection in the mirror. "The women will outnumber the men at least five to one. If I dance with anyone, it will be with you."

"I don't know how to tango."

"Then you're damned well going to learn. I'm not being dragged to this wingding for nothing."

"Fine." As a bonus I'd burn a few calories.

I dug through the sample case my mother had left in the bathroom and inspected two likely lipstick prospects. "Bronze Goddess or Tempestuous Tan?"

I got another nose wrinkle. "Tempestuous Tan? Is your mother coming up with these names?"

I doubted that the brain trust at Glorious Organics wanted to hear anything from Marietta unless she was hawking their cosmetic line in front of a camera. "That job probably belongs to some twenty-year-old in the marketing department." I held the two tubes of lipstick in front of my grandmother. "So, what'll it be because I want my date to have some hot looking lips."

"Bronze Goddess," she said with a sigh of resignation.

A minute later, Gram turned to me and smacked her bronze glossy lips. "So, am I hot enough for you?"

"Yep. Let's roll."

If the senior center parking lot was any indication, Tango Tuesday was a more popular draw than Friday night bingo. Since there wasn't a parking spot larger than a postage stamp, I dropped off Gram at the door, then parked her Honda Pilot half a block away.

The breeze wafting in from Merritt Bay took the edge off the heat radiating from the asphalt under my feet. Wind gusts played havoc with my calf-length, blue gauze skirt, blowing it skyward a la Marilyn Monroe cooling her jets in *The Seven Year Itch*. Only I was no Marilyn and the male ogling me was a twelve-year-old on a ten-speed who probably thought he was going to get to see something from Victoria's Secret.

"Think again, kid," I muttered, gathering a fistful of the sheer material. My tighty whities were from the local Walmart.

I scanned the side street behind the senior center parking lot and spotted Steve's sterling gray F150 parked in the shade of a sprawling hemlock. He either hadn't arrived early enough to claim a good parking space, or he'd wanted to park where his pickup wouldn't be obvious from the main road. I suspected the latter.

I pulled the senior center door open and entered the activity room where I was immediately glad-handed by Arlene Koker.

"Charmaine, honey," the activity director said with

a broad smile as she enfolded my hand in hers, "I'm so happy that you could join us."

Arlene looked happy, too. Warm, sincere—no pings in the fake smile department, but I was a little put off by how happy she was to see me. If I'd come to celebrate her daughter's wedding, this measure of sheer joy would be appropriate. For a dance at the senior center? Not so much.

And she didn't let go of my hand.

I didn't know what was up with her, but Arlene was setting off my radar.

"I wouldn't have missed it." Truly. "Not after hearing about all the fun."

She turned to Gladys, one of my grandmother's friends, standing on the opposite side of the receiving line. "Look who's here!"

Gladys squinted at me and shook my hand with her paper dry one. "Hello, dear."

I wasn't sure that she recognized me. "It's Charmaine."

Gladys' squint sharpened. "I'm old, not blind. I know who you are."

Okay. Another blip registered on my weirdometer. I'd either come to the right place or this was going to be a very long, strange night.

"We're very glad you're here," Arlene chirped, whisking me to the other side of the large activity room where half the crowd was sitting in metal folding chairs. "Punch and cookies are over there."

So were Steve and my grandmother, chatting with Nell Neary by the punch bowl. Of the three of them, only Steve glanced my way. Even from thirty feet away I could tell I wasn't going to get anything resembling an Arlene-level reception.

"We're going to get started soon," Arlene said. "Have fun!"

My gaze locked with Steve's. "I intend to."

The gentle sway of my gauze skirt lent a carefree edge to my steps as I crossed the room. At least that's what I hoped, because the man I was approaching looked like a gunslinger itching for a fight, and I needed all the edge I could get.

I cranked up the wattage of my smile. "Fancy meeting you here!"

Steve turned to Gram. "Excuse me for a minute."

She narrowed her gaze at me. No doubt her own internal radar had sensed Steve's tension.

I was going to have to come up with some pretty fancy footwork if she demanded some answers later. But since I had six feet of pissed off male approaching me, that wasn't my immediate concern.

He pushed me by the elbow to an unoccupied corner. "What the hell are you doing here?"

"I'm here with my grandmother, who actually is a registered member of the senior center and enjoys coming to these dance classes." I shrugged out of his grasp and folded my arms across my midsection. "Which senior are you here with?"

"I don't have to explain myself to you."

"That goes both ways, pal."

"Dammit, Char. What are you doing?"

I smiled sweetly. "I'm just here with my grandmother for Tango Tuesday."

He glowered at me.

Just as I was about to suggest we call a truce and get some punch, a screech of feedback pierced my ears. Then, Suzy Harte tapped on the microphone at a raised platform at the opposite end of the floor.

I knew Suzy taught aerobics here at the center, but I hadn't expected to see her at a dance class. Despite what Arlene had said, I hadn't really expected to see Steve here either. It made me wonder what other surprises this night had in store.

"Okay, everyone. Let's get started." Suzy pointed to one of the Gray Ladies sitting next to a CD player, cueing the music. "Take your partners."

I looked for my grandmother where I'd left her by the punchbowl. I saw Nell but no Gram.

Steve grabbed my hand. "Come on," he said with as much enthusiasm as Little Dog when Steve blackmailed him into asking me to dance in the ninth grade.

"But—"

The sensuous rhythm washing over us through the speakers mounted in the corners of the activity room left little doubt about the type of dance featured tonight.

"I don't know how to tango," I said, as he pulled me toward the platform. "I'm just here because—"

"Your grandmother wanted to come. Yeah, tell that story walking."

"For everyone who wasn't here last time," Suzy announced at the microphone, "Jake and I are going to show you the moves, so pay close attention."

The only move I wanted to make was to the nearest exit.

Standing in the small crowd, several feet away from Jayne and Ernie, Steve pulled my hand down to his side, turning me to face him. "Are you paying close attention?" he asked, his eyes dark like pools of molten chocolate.

I was now.

"Men, or ladies," Suzy said, deferring to the female majority of the twenty couples standing in the center of the room, "as you take your partner, remember, the tango is all about the game of seduction."

That elicited some titters from most of the females on the dance floor.

Suzy grinned impishly. "Some of you will just have to use your imagination."

She turned her attention to Jake, the brown-haired, blue-eyed, stud muffin assistant activity director, who taught several exercise classes at the center. From everything Gram had told me about him, attendance had doubled since he joined the staff.

Suzy locked gazes with him, touching his shoulder with the tips of her fingers. Stepping to the strains of the violins carrying the melody, they moved in a circle. "The seduction game begins in the eyes. You want your torso upright and relaxed."

Relaxed, right.

"We don't have to do this," I said, inching away from Steve.

He tightened his grip on my hand. "Trust me, you're doing it."

Suzy stepped so close to Jake they were almost nose to nose. "The man's right hand is placed at the middle of his partner's back." Suzy paused for Jake to demonstrate, then turned to the rest of us. "So, face your partner and *men*, place your hand at the middle of her back."

Fixed on my gaze, Steve seared the center of my back with his palm.

"Now take her right hand with your left."

I lifted my right hand and he pressed his palm to mine.

It felt firm, slightly rough, like a working man's hand. A heady rush reminded me that everything else I felt was strictly off-limits.

"Ladies," Suzy said, "place your left hand on his right shoulder."

My fingertips touched a rope of sinewy muscle in residence under the white cotton of his polo shirt.

"This, ladies and gentlemen, is where the two bodies become one."

Holy cannoli! No wonder Clark's Pharmacy couldn't keep the Viagra in stock.

I swallowed and shifted my gaze to his top button.

"What are you so nervous for?" Steve asked.

"Who said I'm nervous?"

"Your hand is sweaty."

I wiped it on my skirt. "It's hot in here."

"I hadn't noticed." He reclaimed my hand and pulled me closer.

And it was getting hotter.

"Now, we're going to add the steps," Suzy announced. "Watch as Jake moves back with his right foot and I move forward with my left, then he steps left and I step right."

Suzy and the stud muffin twice ran through a full step-by-step demo while she rattled off a string of instructions that made as much sense as fat-free butter to my overheated brain.

She smiled our direction. "See how easy that is?"

"Easy!" I pushed away from Steve. This dance lesson had disaster written all over it. "I don't think so."

He grabbed my hand and pulled me close. "You came here to tango. Let's tango."

"Actually, my grandmother came here to tango. I'm more like her date."

A flicker of a smile betrayed his amusement. "Uh-huh."

"And I promised I'd dance with her."

"Then you'd better learn how first."

Damn. He wasn't giving me an inch toward an escape route.

"Okay, let's try those first basic steps," Suzy announced, stepping into the crowd. "Men, back with your right foot. Ladies, forward with your left."

I stepped on Steve's instep with the toe of my blue canvas espadrille when I noticed Sylvia Jeppesen and Wally Deford dancing near the platform. "Sorry."

"Men, step left, and ladies, step right."

I tried to focus on my feet, but my brain was too busy doing a mental roll call. Ernie, Jayne, Sylvia and Nell—each a surviving family member of a victim on my list—were all present and accounted for. Considering Steve had recently developed an interest in the tango, that couldn't be a coincidence.

"You're supposed to be looking at me, not your feet," Steve muttered.

"Men," Suzy's voice was getting closer, "forward with the right foot. Ladies, step back with your left."

I heard 'right foot' and did a face-plant in his chest. "If I look at you, I swear I'll step on your foot again."

"Men, forward with the left foot, and ladies, back with your right."

I hesitated, my gray matter on overload.

"*Your* right," he said, tapping the toe of my espadrille with his brown leather loafer. "And don't worry about stepping on my foot. You're not that heavy."

My one hundred sixty-four pounds begged to differ. "Gee, thanks."

"I didn't mean it that way."

I met Suzy's gaze as she wove her way to us. She nodded in recognition.

"Now, feet together and let's try that again," she yelled over the music, then placed her hand on my shoulder, beaming like I was her prized pupil. "So glad you can make it. How's it going with you two?"

"Swell," I said flatly.

Steve's lips curled into an easy smile. "She's new."

"So were you last week." Suzy gave me a pat as if to infuse encouragement into me. "Try it again. You'll catch on."

She stepped behind me. "Okay, men, right foot back. Ladies, left foot forward."

I locked onto his gaze. "You were here last week?" Of course, I already knew the answer, but I wanted to watch him dance around the question.

"Good eye contact, Charmaine," Suzy said. "That's key with every step you take."

Yes, it was.

"Men, step left. Ladies, step right."

Steve's pupils constricted as if he were studying me. "You're not looking at your feet."

"And you're not answering the question."

"Men, forward with the right foot. Ladies, back with your left."

His lips compressed for a fraction of a second. "Do you always talk when you dance?"

"Men, forward with the left foot," Suzy shouted like a drill instructor as she stepped to my left. "Ladies, back with the right."

"I do when I'm interested in what the other person has to say."

"Ah." The laugh lines at the corners of his eyes deepened as he held my gaze.

Other than the fact that he found my attempt to read him entertaining, he gave away nothing. Dammit.

"And feet together." Suzy clapped. "You've got it."

Some basic dance steps—not exactly the *it* I'd been going for.

"Okay," Suzy announced in a brisk pace back to the platform, "let's add the rest of the steps."

Let's not.

I was doing little more than running in circles, which might have helped burn off a few bites of pie, but wasn't telling me much that I didn't already know.

I pushed away and fanned myself with my hand. "It's really hot in here."

It wasn't, but making myself a moving target seemed like a good distraction while I searched for my grandmother. I didn't have to look far. "There's Gram," I said when I found her sitting with Arlene in the first row of folding chairs.

Steve grabbed my left hand before I could make a clean getaway. "Where do you think you're going?"

"To get her out here so she can join in on the fun." I tugged at his hand. "Come on, that is the reason I came."

"Sure it is." He glanced back at Suzy and Jake on the platform like I had just colored outside of the lines of his playbook.

Arlene and Gram had identical smiles as we approached, looking like a couple of mother hens with plenty to cackle about.

"Enjoying yourself?" Gram asked, eyeballing Steve's hand in mine.

"Yes, and now it's your turn."

Her eyes widened. "But you two look like you're having so much fun, don't you—"

"No," I blurted out to nip any speculation about our relationship in the bud.

Arlene heaved a sigh.

Sorry to disappoint, Arlene.

I extended my hand to Gram. "It's time to dance."

"Well, if you insist." She smiled at Arlene. "I guess my date's here."

I placed her hand in Steve's. "Yes, he is."

"Oh, a man." Gram beamed. "Even better!"

Steve's grin didn't reach his eyes. He turned to lead Gram to the dance floor and whispered in my ear, "Don't think we're done."

I certainly wasn't done. Not by a long shot.

Chapter Fourteen

I took Gram's seat, next to Arlene. I had questions about the senior center and knew that she'd have some answers.

Arlene patted my knee. "You made a good looking couple out there."

"We're not really a couple. He was just..." Actually, I wasn't sure what he was doing besides screwing with my head. "...helping me with the steps." In his own inimitable way.

"Yes, he's good." Arlene arched her thin eyebrows. "Probably in more ways than one."

We were heading down a path laced with innuendo landmines, and I needed to make a quick course correction before anything exploded onto the gossip circuit.

"So, I noticed Jake out there with Suzy," I said to shift Arlene's attention away from Steve and me. "He's quite the cutie patootie and a good dancer, too."

Arlene folded her hands in her lap and sniffed. "He's all right. Most of the ladies here seem to like him."

What the heck? I thought I'd picked a safe subject. Obviously not.

"He's fairly new, isn't he?" I asked, watching him change partners and take one of the Gray Ladies into his arms.

"Jake Divine has been with us since the first of the year. Ambitious type if you ask me. Ginny recommended him to Monica."

"Who?" *Virginia Straitham?*

"Monica Gerrity."

The corners of Arlene's lips turned down at the mention of Monica's name—clearly not her favorite person.

"You probably haven't met her yet. I doubt she's the Duke's Cafe type. She's from LA," she said as if Monica had smuggled some smog from the Los Angeles basin into the moving van when she headed north. "Took over as director after Ginny."

"Virginia Straitham used to be the director here?"

"Honey, doesn't your granny tell you anything?"

Apparently not nearly enough. "I guess you'll have to fill me in."

"It was an interim position since Ginny was on the board of directors when Nancy got married and moved to Arizona. Lovely man. Divorced twice but an excellent dancer. I hope it works out for her."

Whatever. Nancy's dancing partner wasn't the person I wanted to hear about.

"An interim position for how long?"

"Oh, five, six months," Arlene said, waving to Jayne and Ernie as they passed us on the way to the punchbowl. "They're so cute together. They're dating, you know."

"I've heard." I leaned closer, willing Arlene to focus on one thing at a time so I could connect some dots. "So, Virginia took over this position last year sometime?"

"If memory serves, it was around April."

Jesse Elwood's death had been in April. Not that the two things were connected, but all roads today seemed to be leading me to the senior center.

I stared at Steve while he danced with my grandmother. Based on how he had been spending his Tuesday nights, he'd evidently reached a similar conclusion. "And you say that Virginia Straitham recommended Jake."

"Some friend of her grandson's, I think."

Dancing with Sylvia, a smiling Jake passed in front of us.

"He seems friendly," I said.

Personable eye candy—a perfect dancing partner, especially for the ladies like my granny, who hadn't had a man in their arms for a number of years.

"Oh, he can be quite charming," Arlene said, fixing him with her gaze as if she wanted to squish him like a bug.

We weren't the only women in the room watching Jake. As Suzy walked the dance floor doing her drill instructor routine, her light blue eyes periodically tracked him the way I'd seen Little Dog fixate on Marietta. Only without the drool.

"Suzy and Jake, are they…"

"I actually didn't think Suzy swung that way, if you know what I mean," Arlene said, lowering her voice.

If she didn't, Suzy Harte had been doing a good imitation of a woman who wanted to do a horizontal tango with the best dancer on the floor.

"Never have known her to date," Arlene continued. "Cute enough girl."

"Remember, ladies," Suzy shouted as she moved

between the couples. "Cross and flex, and back with the right foot. Bend your knees."

"Nice figure, too. With that stretching class she teaches, I bet she's plenty bendy." Arlene nudged me with her shoulder. "Can you imagine her in bed?"

Nope. Not an image I wanted in my head, especially when I was already reeling with mental whiplash.

I needed a quick diversion, so I pointed at the gray-haired arrival at the door. "Did someone just come in?"

Arlene sprang up from her seat. "Thanks, hon. Don't want to shirk my welcoming responsibilities."

While Arlene raced to the door, I made my way to the punchbowl. Ordinarily, a concoction of cheap fruit juice concentrate and soda pop wasn't my beverage of choice, but since Nell Neary was serving, a little punch-laced conversation could be mighty tasty. And after the last five minutes with Arlene, I needed a drink.

Nell brightened as I approached. "I didn't expect to see you here tonight. Not too many people our age come to the center."

She'd just aged me a few years, but her point was well-taken. Since we were two of a handful of non-seniors here tonight and I hadn't seen her on the dance floor, I wondered what the attraction was for her.

She handed me a paper cup of punch that looked like Cherry Bliss diluted with ginger ale. "They think coming to the senior center is uncool."

"Maybe nights like Tango Tuesday will help draw more of a crowd." Jake the stud muffin probably didn't hurt, either.

Nell nodded. "I saw you dancing with Steve Sixkiller.

You looked like you were having fun."

That's not exactly what I would have called it.

She lowered her amber-eyed gaze, a hint of a blush tinting her cheeks. "So, are you two…"

"We're just friends."

"Oh. I just thought with the way he was looking at you…"

I almost choked on my punch. "That's part of the dance—the *game of seduction* thing." And he seemed to be a very skilled player. "You know how it is when you've been out there dancing with Thomas."

She shook her head. "Oh, no. I never dance while I'm on duty."

"Ever?" It wasn't like she was the punchbowl watch commander.

Nell's lips curled slightly. "My mom loved to dance when I was little." She blew out a breath as she gazed into the punchbowl. The memories she saw there were obviously strong, bittersweet. "Then she got sick and became confined to a wheelchair. But a couple of years ago, when they started having dance lessons at the center, I thought she'd have fun watching."

"I'm sure she did," I said softly, lapping up every ounce of information Nell was serving me.

"I didn't want her to feel like I was hovering over her, so I stayed over here and took charge of the refreshments. Close enough to be there if she needed me. Far enough away for her to be with her friends." Nell shrugged. "The punchbowl thing sort of stuck. But really, if it hadn't, I never would have met Thomas."

I hadn't seen her boyfriend tonight. "Is he here?"

"His mom hasn't been feeling well, so he's home taking care of her. You know how that goes."

Actually, I didn't. If my mother needed home care, she'd hire a hunky male nurse to tend to her every need.

Nell's eyes widened. "Oh, I guess I lied to you yesterday when I told you how Thomas and I met."

"Really." It had to have been unintentional since nothing registered on my radar.

"He confessed something last night."

I doubted this confession had anything to do with her mother's death, but Nell had my complete attention nonetheless.

"Turns out he'd wanted to talk to me for weeks but couldn't figure out what to say." She smiled sweetly. "He's a little shy."

Nell was more than a little shy, so this probably made them a good match.

"So, Ginny told him to just walk up and compliment me on the punch."

Virginia Straitham was giving him pointers on how to break the ice? She helped get this shy couple together?

Virginia Straitham was the matchmaker.

"Isn't that cute?"

Cute? Not if Warren Straitham was killing his patients so his wife could fix them up on dates!

I nodded like a bobblehead doll.

Keep breathing.

Nell giggled. "I even gave him my secret recipe, like he cared, when he was actually trying to work up the nerve to ask me for a date. Pretty sweet, huh?"

Sweet like rat poison.

"Are you okay?" I heard Nell ask over the clamor of alarm bells going off in my head.

No, I wasn't okay, and neither would she be once she'd learned that Dr. Straitham had killed her mother. "I'm... fine."

"You look a little pale. Let me get you some more punch."

Watching Gram approaching arm in arm with Steve, I locked gazes with him as Nell refilled my cup.

What? he mouthed, his eyes dark with awareness.

"I figured we'd find you over here." Gram frowned as she closed the distance between us. "Honey, you're as white as a sheet! Are you sick?"

She took my cup from me and pressed the back of her hand to my forehead. "You don't feel feverish."

Probably because I wasn't. "Maybe I need some air."

Gram turned to Steve. "Would you mind helping—"

"Let's go." He took my hand and pulled me toward the door while the lilting strains of the next song blasted through the speakers.

I tried to keep up with his long strides as we crossed the length of the floor. "You are *not* going to believe what I just found out!"

The pressure increased on my hand like he'd slapped a warning label on it. "Use your inside voice."

"But—"

"Is something wrong?" Arlene asked as Steve shuttled me past her.

He pushed the glass door and me along with it. "Just getting a little fresh air."

"Holy crap!" I shouted as soon as the door closed

behind us.

He pressed his fingers around my left elbow. "Can you cool it for a minute?" he asked, his nose an inch from mine, his breath warm against my face.

"Hey! I bruise easily."

"You can file a report later. Right now I need you to shut up."

I glared at him while I sucked in oxygen as if I'd finished running a mile.

He loosened his grip and surveyed the dimly lit parking lot. "Where the hell did you park?"

"Down the street."

"Do you have your keys? Where's your bag?"

Standing under a flood light, I pointed to the blue canvas mini-bag that had been hugging my waistband all night. It was a perfect match to my espadrilles—not that I thought this would be the right time to discuss his powers of observation.

"Fine," he said like it was anything but, leading me by the arm down the sidewalk bordering the parking lot.

"Will you stop acting like a cop for a minute?"

"Not gonna happen, Chow Mein."

Once we weren't shielded by the building, a wind gust whipped my skirt around his right leg. I grabbed a handful of blue gauze while I trotted by his side like I was on a very short leash. "But I want to tell you—"

"In the car," Steve said, releasing my arm but not slowing his pace until we reached Gram's Honda.

I unlocked the car and he slid into the passenger seat.

Since my overheated brain felt like it might blow its top and he kept putting a cork in it every time I opened my mouth, I rolled down my window for some cool air.

He pointed at the controls on the side panel. "Window up. If you need air, start the engine."

"Sheesh, is all this cloak and dagger stuff really necessary?"

"You tell me."

I started the engine, rolled up the window, and aimed two of the front vents at my burning cheeks. If Steve needed some air, he could fend for himself.

"So, I'm allowed to speak now?" I asked.

Steve folded his arms across his chest. "Let's have it."

I took a deep breath. "Okay, this is going to sound crazy, but I think Virginia Straitham is up to her eyeballs in this thing with her husband."

"You're right," Steve deadpanned.

I pounded the steering wheel. "I knew it!"

"Not only does that sound crazy, it might qualify as the craziest thing I've ever heard."

"Hey, you weren't there."

Backlit by a streetlight on the corner, his obsidian eyes bore into mine. "Okay, then tell me what I missed."

"Virginia Straitham used to be the senior center director."

"Yeah, so?"

"She took over the position around the same time that Jesse Elwood died."

I waited for a reaction and got nothing but a grimace of irritation as he shifted in his seat and tried to stretch out his right leg.

"Don't you see? It's all connected to the senior center."

Steve's eyebrows arched for a split second, and that

was enough for me.

"That's why you were there," I added to see if he'd deny it.

He blew out a sharp breath. "Stop fishing and get to the point."

"Fine," I said, letting him know that he wasn't the only one experiencing a little irritation. "Virginia coached Nell's new boyfriend on how to strike up a conversation with Nell so that he could work up the nerve to ask her out on a date."

The crease between his brows deepened. "Is that it?"

It wasn't a smoking gun, but what more did he want?

"Thomas and Nell," I said slowly and clearly since he seemed to be having trouble recognizing the significance of what I was telling him, "are now shopping for wedding rings because of Virginia Straitham."

"Because she made a little suggestion."

"Yes! But that's why no one would ever suspect her. She's subtle while she's pulling the strings like a puppet master at the senior center to bring these couples together."

"A puppet master."

I didn't like his tone, but I was willing to overlook it if he'd hear me out.

"Yes! Think about it. First, she tells her husband to kill off Mr. Elwood and Rose and plants a few suggestions in Ernie's ear," I said, making the invisible marionettes hanging from my fingertips dance, "and voila! Jayne and Ernie, a Virginia Stratham love match. Same with Nell and her boyfriend, Thomas, and now Sylvia and Wally. And every one of them was there tonight. Okay, not Thomas but he has a sick mother."

Steve shot me a humorless smile. "Well, I'll give you this much. You came up with an *interesting* theory."

"This is much more than a theory. It makes perfect sense."

"Only if you believe Dr. Straitham's killing his patients."

"Yes," I said with a shiver and shut off the ignition before my teeth started chattering.

"That's where you have a little problem," Steve stated as if he were helping me with my geometry homework, not a murder.

"But—"

"Number one, Trudy Bergeson's death hasn't been ruled a homicide."

"But you think she was murdered or you wouldn't have come tonight. Or last Tuesday," I added to show that I was on to his sudden interest in dance lessons.

"You need to stop jumping to conclusions."

"Are you going to deny it?"

"Char." He turned to face me, the tic above his jaw line counting down the seconds of stony silence between us. "Watch and listen."

"Okay."

"Don't tempt me."

I cocked my head. "So what's the problem, besides you being an obstinate cop who has to do everything by the book?"

His lips curled into a smile that died as quickly as it had appeared. "Unofficially speaking, if Trudy Bergeson's death was suspicious as your whistleblower Cardinale suggests, and something happened early Monday morning..."

My heart pounded with anticipation, like we'd hit top

speed in this roller coaster and were rocketing toward a hairpin turn.

"...the husband of your latest suspect didn't do it."

I knew that Steve believed what he'd just said, but that didn't necessarily mean it was true. "How can you be so sure?"

"Just trust me," he said softly.

I did to a point. But he hadn't exactly been very forthcoming the past week.

"But she has motive, and he has opportunity." What more did Steve want?

He reached for the door handle. "Nice work, Nancy Drew, but that's where you have a problem." He opened the passenger door and climbed out of the Honda.

"Wait a minute!" I scrambled out of my seat, staring at him over the hood of the car. "What's the problem?"

"You said it yourself."

I'd said a lot of stuff today, none of which he appeared to be taking seriously.

He cocked his head. "Your *big news?*"

"About Dr. Straitham having an affair?"

"Do I have to spell it out for you?"

I wished he would. "Uh..."

"Let's just say he was playing doctor somewhere else at the time."

Chapter Fifteen

On our drive home from the senior center, Gram chirped about how much she'd enjoyed our *date* while Steve's revelation about Dr. Straitham reverberated in my brain, and my mood felt as flattened as the dead raccoon we'd passed back on 5th Street.

Within ten minutes of parking Gram in front of her TV, she was snoring. I could either hang around and listen to her snore while I waited for my mother to come home and play kissy-face with Barry Ferris on the front porch...

Shoot me now.

Or, I could wrap my butt around a barstool at Eddie's.

I left Gram a note, grabbed my car keys, and pulled into Eddie's parking lot seven minutes later.

By the number of cars in the front lot, the usual weeknight bowling league crowd had assembled. I was a little disappointed that I didn't see Steve's pickup in the parking lot. It also wasn't in his driveway, despite the fact that he'd left the senior center before me.

The image that Arlene planted in my head two hours earlier flooded back to me, only it wasn't a bendy Suzy doing bedroom gymnastics. Another nimble blonde took center stage in my overheated imagination, bringing the picture of Heather working up a sweat with Steve into sharp focus.

I slapped my head to knock myself back to reality. "Stop it!" What did I care that he'd gone back to his skinny assed, former girlfriend with the perfect hair?

Good for them if they were getting counseling and working things out.

And having great sex in the process.

"Stop it!"

I slammed my car door and headed for the main entrance, the parking lot gravel crunching under my feet.

The side door leading to the kitchen opened, and Rox appeared holding a plastic garbage sack in her hand. She narrowed her eyes at me. "What's your problem?"

"You don't want to know." Not about Heather and Steve. It was high school all over again, and I refused to rekindle any more residual angst than I already had.

Rox tossed the garbage bag into a scarred green dumpster and dropped the lid with a clang. "Come in and tell Roxie all about it." She held the kitchen entrance open for me. A warm wave of yeast, onion, and garlic venting from the pizza oven rolled over me as I stepped through the door.

"You look cute." Her big brown eyes widened. "Been on a date?"

"With my grandmother. It was Tango Tuesday at the senior center."

"Oh. It's Tequila Tuesday here."

Sheesh, couldn't it be plain Tuesday in this town?

A cacophony of bowling balls beating the hell out

of plastic pins in the adjoining building serenaded us as I followed Rox to my usual barstool.

"It's a league playoff night so Eddie's minding the lanes," she said as she stepped behind the bar. "I make better margaritas than him, anyway. Want one?"

"Heck, yeah."

Less than two minutes later, she served me a fishbowl-sized margarita along with a frown chaser. "Okay, so talk to me. What's the problem?"

Where did I start? I had an unofficial murder and a former prime suspect with an official alibi, a mother with the hots for my biology teacher, and a best friend screwing with my head while he screwed around with his hard body ex-girlfriend.

"It's just been a rough night," I said as I stirred the slushy margarita with a flamingo pink plastic straw.

"At the senior center?" Rox chuckled. "Yeah, that's a pretty rough bunch."

"Maybe I'm not a tango kind of girl."

Leaning on her elbows, she watched me sip my margarita. "Seems to be plenty in town who are, especially since Jake showed up there."

"He's very good."

"That's what I hear," Rox said with a sly grin.

The sexual innuendo came through loud and clear. "You know something. Rumor mill or something more substantial?"

"Hey, this is a bar. Get a couple of drinks in some of the ladies on the senior circuit and—"

"What exactly have you heard?"

She eyed a couple of middle-aged men in matching

bowling league shirts entering the bar. "You know, the usual younger man, older woman-type scuttlebutt."

"Oh. You mean Suzy."

Rox stared at me, wide-eyed. "Huh? Is he fooling around with her, too?"

Too? "I don't know. Who are you talking about?"

"I don't have any names." She lowered her voice. "I've just heard some speculation about his *services* there at the center."

"Like *full service* services?"

Rox shushed me. "From what they said about him satisfying his customers, I'd say so."

Maybe that's why Arlene had a burr up her butt. She knew Jake would be more than willing to remove it, for the right price.

So, in addition to dance classes and water aerobics, the senior center now offered matchmaking and escort services? What the heck? And where did Virginia Straitham's involvement begin and end?

If she had her finger on the pulse of the goings on at the center like I believed she did, Virginia would be very aware of Jake's extracurricular activities. From there, it wasn't much of a leap to think that someone who could be bought might take on the occasional job of a more mercenary nature. Especially if that someone were ambitious and had a moral compass that didn't point true.

I took a big gulp from my fishbowl to douse the fire of the Warren Straitham flambé I'd been cooking up the past week. It had seemed like a winning recipe. But flambés can be tricky. Apply heat to the wrong mix of ingredients and the fireball could singe your eyebrows.

Despite what Steve might think, I'd be the first to admit that I'd created a bit of a mess with Dr. Straitham. But I'd only been on the job for a week, so I cut myself a little slack.

Rox reached for a bar towel. "It makes you wonder, doesn't it?"

Lately, everything in my life seemed to be making me wonder.

"I mean, really…" she glanced at me as she wiped away an invisible wet spot on the polished oak separating us. "Who's in charge of this guy?"

I intended to find out.

"What do you actually know about Jake?" I asked.

"Not much. I think he's from Port Townsend. Been living here since last year some time."

If Jake wasn't in town for the first murder, he would have been only a half hour away. Close enough. I made a mental check mark.

It wasn't as if the hospital was locked down much tighter than the courthouse, so someone light on his feet could have danced right into Trudy Bergeson's room, done the deed, then done the boogie before anyone was the wiser. I made another check mark.

Arlene had mentioned that Jake was ambitious. Ambition and success usually went hand in hand. But rarely a day went by when the evening news didn't lead off with a story about how ambition had led someone to make a dangerous and often deadly choice.

Check, check, and check.

I had yet to see anything to indicate that Jake was dangerous, but I'd only seen him on the dance floor. Not exactly a danger zone—at least I hadn't thought so before I tangoed with Steve.

"You have a funny look on your face," Rox said, staring at me.

"Funny ha-ha or odd-looking?"

"Odd." She screwed up her face. "Sorry. I forgot about your diet."

"What diet?"

"Honey, I need to take those guys' order, but did you eat tonight? I bet the tequila is going straight to your head."

I leveled my gaze at her. "Do I look like I've missed a meal?"

"It's just that I heard the news—"

"That Dr. Straitham put me on a diet."

Backing away, Rox shrugged. "It was a slow news day. Maybe I should call Steve to come pick you up."

Hell, no! "I'm fine," I said, waving her off.

I just needed to lose thirty pounds, string more than two hours of sleep together, and figure out if someone was working in a deadly partnership with Virginia Straitham.

Fortunately, Jake taught a midday aerobics class at the senior center. An hour with him might be just what the doctor ordered.

~

I woke up out of a margarita-induced haze to the sound of my mother giggling on the front porch.

Heaven help me. I could hear Barry Ferris' voice like he was in the room with me. No wonder my grandfather had camped out in the den to wait up for me every time I'd had a date.

"Mmmmmm...."

Now, it was kissy face time.

"Do you have any idea what you're doing to me?" he asked when he came up for air.

Yes, and it was way more than I wanted to know.

I glared at the clock. Three-sixteen. I could lie in bed until I couldn't take it anymore, or—since I had crossed that threshold at three-fifteen—I could give up any illusions I had of nightmare-free slumber, make a pot of coffee, and look out the window to see if Steve's truck was in his driveway.

I'm a dessert first kind of girl, so I drew the curtain back and took a bit of twisted consolation when I spotted the Ford pickup parked next to his unmarked, Port Merritt PD Crown Victoria and knew he was sleeping in his own bed.

Now, if I could just purge the sounds of my mother sucking face with Mr. Ferris from my brainpan, I could be a happy, dessert first kind of girl. That was, if it weren't for the fact that this was supposed to be my first day on my new diet. Oh, and I had a noon-hour aerobics class with a potential murder suspect.

Marietta must have tiptoed up the stairs while I made coffee, because when I passed her room to take a shower, I heard giggling. I prayed to God she was alone. If she was screwing Mr. Ferris on my bed, I'd have to set a match to it and bring in a shaman to do a ritual cleansing of my room.

After I showered and dried my hair enough to clip it back, I listened at her door. Nothing but light snoring.

All the Digby women snored.

We tended to have sparse eyelashes, cellulite, and we snored. Marietta never revealed her shortcomings early in her relationships, so I knew she had to be sleeping alone this morning.

Grateful for small mercies, I celebrated with a cup of coffee, then I squeezed into a belted, short-sleeved khaki pantsuit I'd found on a fifty percent off rack in San Francisco. It seemed as lackluster as I felt, so I tied a moss green animal print scarf around my neck to add a little color. Marietta had brought the scarf home with her from shooting a low-budget movie in Thailand the year I'd gotten married. Not my favorite thing, but if she never saw me wear the clothes she bought me, she got a little pissy.

No one wanted to see a pissy Marietta Moreau, least of all me, so the scarf was an easy fashion choice this morning.

I slipped on a pair of butterscotch brown leather sandals, refilled my travel mug with extra strength French roast, and headed for Duke's.

Aunt Alice was standing behind a mixing bowl on the butcher block table when I stepped into the kitchen. She glanced at the clock mounted above a vintage red and white Coca Cola sign. "What the hell are you doing here? It's not even light out."

"I had an early wake up call," I said, omitting any mention of my mother. "Thought I might as well come in and make myself useful."

Scratching the bald spot in the middle of his crew cut, Duke frowned at my khaki pantsuit. "In that? What're you doing? Going on safari?"

"Cute." I set my travel mug on the stainless steel

counter behind me. "What do you want me to get started on?"

"Bake me a couple dozen cinnamon rolls, and I'll consider it a down payment on the patty melt I'll be making you later," he said with a wink.

I knew the wink had nothing to do with the patty melt. Instead it told me that he was grateful to lighten Alice's load.

"I'm on a diet. It'll be a salad." Maybe. If I had time to eat after aerobics class.

Duke chortled. "Okay, a salad. We'll see how long this diet lasts."

I didn't appreciate the sarcasm. "It'll last." At least long enough to convince everyone that I was following Dr. Straitham's advice.

Wincing, Alice eased herself down on her stool. "I can make the damned cinnamon rolls. Go fill up the salt and pepper shakers if you want something to do."

I met Duke's gaze from across the kitchen. His lips flatlined as he shook his head.

Alice gingerly swiveled on her stool to pull a sack of flour from the rack behind her, and I waved Duke away so that I could talk to her alone.

He grabbed his empty cup and reached for hers. "More coffee, dear?"

"No," she barked, short and very unsweet.

After the kitchen door swung shut behind Duke, I took the wooden stool opposite Alice.

She reached for the canister of sugar in the center of the table and glowered at me.

I lowered my head, making myself eye level with her.

"Okay, what's going on with you?"

"Nothing."

"It doesn't look like nothing."

"Says you."

"You look like something hurts."

"At my age something always hurts, but it's nothing to worry about. I'm fine."

"Clearly, you're not. I'm going to make a doctor's appointment for you."

Dr. Straitham wouldn't be too thrilled to see me in his office two days in a row. Maybe I could convince Marietta to tag along as a consolation prize for the old hound dog.

"The hell you are!" Alice said, raising her voice.

"Something's wrong and you need to go to the doctor."

"I'm not going." Her watery hazel eyes narrowed.

"I know what you think, but Dr. Straitham isn't—"

"It's just a little gas. It's nothing."

Lie. Something was very wrong, and she knew it better than I did.

She focused on the egg she had cracked into the mixing bowl and reached for another. "I thought you wanted to make yourself useful."

I was trying. She wouldn't let me.

Duke peeked around the corner and met my gaze. "So, what's the verdict?"

While Alice cracked another egg like she wanted to smash it into Duke's skull, I shrugged at the loaded question that I didn't know how to answer without making the situation worse.

"Tell you what, since I can have bran muffins on my diet…" The size of a pea maybe, not the jumbo muffins

Duke's featured, but it didn't matter. I knew Alice wouldn't fight me over a few lousy muffins.

"…I'm going to make some bran muffins." I reached for a stainless steel mixing bowl. "Maybe some banana nut ones, too. Both have good fiber and I can decide which one I want later."

Alice sniffed and cracked another egg. Her non-response was as good as a green light.

Three hours later, I added a dozen raspberry scones to the bakery shelf, next to Alice's cinnamon rolls, flanked by all the muffins and cookies I'd baked.

The bell over the door jingled and I met Steve's gaze.

His brown eyes shifted to the white apron I had on over my pantsuit. "You're up early."

"It's my curse." Which lately wasn't far from the truth.

He shot me a lopsided smile. "Thought you'd do a little baking before you went out on safari?"

"Everybody's a comedian this morning," I said, heading back into the kitchen.

My great-aunt would snap at me like a turtle defending her nest if I offered to help her with the pie crust she was laboring to roll out, so I decided I might as well join Steve for breakfast.

After hanging up my apron, I stepped around Duke on my way to the tureen of oatmeal he'd made an hour earlier.

"Thanks, kid," he muttered, glancing over his shoulder.

I grabbed a small bowl from the shelf over the stove. "If she gets any worse let me know, and I'll drag her sorry butt to the doctor."

Duke nodded, staring down at the bacon and eggs sputtering on the grill.

As I ladled some oatmeal into my bowl, I met Steve's questioning gaze. I couldn't address any of his concerns about Alice with her sitting behind me in the kitchen, so I took my oatmeal to the counter and sat next to him.

I noticed he didn't have any coffee. Lucille was busy huddling with Suzy and several of the Gray Ladies at the back table, no doubt getting her daily dose from the rumor mill.

"Did you order?" I asked him.

"Never mind that. What's going on with Alice?"

"I don't know." I stepped behind the counter and pulled out two white mugs, filled them from the pot of coffee Lucille had just brewed, and pushed one in front of Steve. "I tried to get her to go to the doctor but she absolutely refuses."

"Not everyone enjoys seeing Dr. Straitham as much as you do," he said, dumping the contents of a creamer into his cup.

I hit Steve with a sideways glance as I took my seat. "Okay, so I was wrong about him. It was an honest mistake."

"It was one step removed from stalking."

Lucille squeaked our direction and reached for the pencil tucked behind her ear. "What will you have, hon?" she asked Steve. "The usual?"

"Fine." He picked up his coffee mug. "Are you going to leave the man alone now?"

Lucille arched her sandy brown eyebrows, her gossip antennae fully extended.

"It's nothing juicy," I said to her between spoonfuls of oatmeal.

She heaved a sigh and squeaked away to tack Steve's breakfast order on the aluminum wheel above the grill.

I turned to Steve. "You told me Dr. Straitham had an alibi."

Staring straight ahead, he drank his coffee.

I leaned on the counter to get a better view of his face. "How did you know that?"

"Knock it off."

"It's a reasonable question."

"Then ask it like a reasonable person, without the stare-down."

"Fine!" I glared at my bowl of congealed oatmeal. "How did you know that he was *indisposed*?"

"Your grandmother told me."

Chapter Sixteen

I gaped at Steve's profile as he calmly sipped his coffee. "My grandmother?"

"She's my snitch."

Big fat lie. "Your snitch. Right."

"She and I prefer the term *informant*," he quipped, the crinkles deepening at the corner of his eye.

"You are so full of shit."

His mouth twisted into an evil grin. "I had you going for a minute."

"Jerk."

Lucille squeaked up with a carafe and refilled our coffee mugs. She looked at me and then at Steve. "Okay, I give. What's up with you two?"

Who knew? Last night we were practically dancing cheek to cheek, and this morning it was like we were back in the fifth grade and he was pulling my ponytail.

"Nothing," I said as I poured two creamers into my coffee. I was blowing my diet but that was the least of my problems.

Ignoring Lucille who watched us like we were the tennis match on center court, I shifted my attention back to Steve. "I take it that means you're not going to tell me?"

"What do you think?" he asked, brushing my fingers as he reached for another creamer.

I wiped my hands with the paper napkin in my lap. I knew I was overreacting to a little incidental contact, but I'd already experienced all the physical contact from Steve Sixkiller that I could handle in a twenty-four hour period.

Lucille sucked in a sharp breath. "Is there new information about Trudy's…?"

I shook my head while Mr. Won't-Answer-Direct-Questions stirred his coffee.

"Damn." Scowling at Steve, she stabbed the air with her index finger. "You should be out there investigating, not in here dilly dallying."

Steve smiled politely. "May I eat my breakfast first?"

"Order up!" Duke announced.

Lucille turned to retrieve Steve's bacon and eggs, then bounced the plate in front of him. "Eat fast."

"I'd do what she says if you want to come back tomorrow," I said, swiveling out of my seat.

Steve poked a runny yolk with the corner of his toast. "Sheesh, the women around here can make it hard on a guy."

"He's just figuring that out now?" Duke muttered as I added my bowl to the plastic tub of dirty dishes under the counter.

I was about to go back and check on Alice when I saw her limping with a pie in her hands. "Need any help with that?"

"Nope," she said, easing past me. "Just stay out of the way."

Since I could see four more pies cooling on the table, I carried them on a tray to the rotating pie display case by the cash register before Alice could snarl at me about helping her.

"I could have done that," she protested.

I slid an apple pie onto the top shelf of the four-tier glass case. "Yeah, you could have agreed to go to the doctor, too."

She huffed as she limped around me. "Leave it alone."

"Do you need to go to the doctor, Alice?" Suzy asked, her pale blue eyes fixed in a piercing stare as she stood at the cash register.

Alice turned toward the kitchen. "No. I just have some family members who like to meddle."

I forced a smile at Suzy. "I think that would be me."

"What's the matter with her?" she whispered.

I knew Alice didn't want anyone else hovering over her, so I opted for an evasive answer. "Just having a bad day." I cranked up the wattage of my smile. "That was a good turnout for your class last night."

"I was happy to see you there. You and Steve make good partners."

I shifted my gaze to the counter and saw Steve staring at us over the rim of his coffee cup. No doubt his male ego sensed we were talking about him.

"Since I kept stepping on his toes, I think he preferred dancing with my grandmother."

Suzy's lips curled in satisfaction. "I sincerely doubt that."

Between this chick's fishing expedition regarding my relationship with Steve and his watchful eyes, I felt like I needed to set sail for calmer waters.

"Speaking of dancing, where did you learn to tango?"

"A dance class a few years ago. I thought it would be a good way to meet people."

"Is that where you met Jake?" I asked, pouncing on the chance to glean a bit of information from someone who appeared to have more than a casual relationship with the guy.

"No, that was back when I lived in Portland." Suzy smiled politely, serving me a skimpy appetizer of cold cuts when I wanted to sink my teeth into the main course of juicy beefsteak.

"You're quite good together. How long has he been your dancing partner?"

She shrugged. "Not long. About a month."

I had expected to see some emotion in her reaction. Instead, Suzy glanced at the clock mounted above the big mouth bass as if I were boring her with news from my grandmother's garden club meeting.

"I have to admit I don't know much about dancing, but he seems like a very good dancer."

"Oh, he is."

"Moves his body *very* well," I said, charging the line with enough innuendo that she'd certainly have some reaction to it.

She nodded. "He's very graceful, very light on his feet."

That was it? We may as well have been talking about Ernie for all the heat this woman was generating.

"Steve moves well, too." Suzy's gaze sharpened as she looked back at him.

I didn't doubt he had lots of moves, none of which I

cared to witness.

Her lips curled, her cheeks dimpling impishly. "I think he shows a lot of potential."

I was pretty sure she wasn't referring to dancing, and we were rapidly getting nowhere I wanted to go, so I pointed at the clock. "Oh, look at the time. Certainly don't want to be late after only one week on the new job."

"I need to get going, too, or I'll be late for my eight o'clock class." Suzy's eyes widened at the collection of baked goodies on the shelves separating us. "Those are some big muffins."

"They're practically fresh out of the oven," I said as an enticement.

She shook her head. "Oh, no, I couldn't. Do you know how much fat is in just one of those muffins?"

Yes, but since I had eaten one seconds after I'd popped it out of the oven, I really didn't want to think about it.

She wrinkled her nose. "Over twenty grams of fat!"

"You don't say." And I wished she hadn't because that forced me to admit that the first day of my new diet was officially screwed, and I hadn't even had lunch yet.

It was a good thing I planned to go to Jake's aerobics class. I could do some damage control in more ways than one.

కా

Forty-five minutes later, I carried a tall mug of freshly brewed coffee to Ben's office and rapped on the open door. I needed information from someone who had worked on some criminal cases with Steve, and I hoped that Ben would be willing to barter.

His gaze tracked the fix of caffeine in my hand so I didn't wait for an invitation. "Good morning," I said, placing the coffee mug on his desk.

"Morning." Ben's eyes zeroed in on my scarf and the corners of his mouth drew back in a tight quirk of amusement.

"What?" I glanced down to see if I had a blob of oatmeal on my scarf.

"The only thing missing is the pith helmet," he deadpanned.

"Sorry I asked." I was never wearing khaki again.

"As a young defense attorney, I was told never to ask a question I didn't already know the answer to."

"Thanks for the advice." Didn't help me a bit since I had no answers and nothing but questions, including my most pressing one: How was I going to dig up more dirt on Virginia and Jake while stuck at the courthouse for most of the day?

"Do you need me to sit in on any witness interviews today?"

"No," he said, rifling through a short stack of papers on his desk. He pulled out a white envelope and handed it to me. "But I do have a subpoena I need delivered."

I glanced at the Port Townsend address on the envelope and recalled Rox telling me that was where Jake was from. I saw a beneficial side trip in my immediate future. "No problem."

Ben took a sip of coffee. "How's your mom?"

"Huh? Oh." He had to have heard about the doctor's

appointment. "She's fine."

"I saw her last night having dinner with Barry Ferris. She looked real fine."

Like the fat grams in my muffin, there was a long list of things I'd rather not hear about, and any attraction Ben Santiago felt for my mother was somewhere near the top of the list.

I squeezed out a smile. "Yeah, she's doing much better."

To steer in our conversation in the direction I wanted to go, I took a seat in the same black captain's chair I'd sat in two weeks earlier. "Could I ask you a couple of questions?"

He leaned back. "Shoot."

"You work closely with law enforcement when prosecuting cases, right?"

"Right."

"So would it be fair to say that you've developed a close working relationship with Detective Sixkiller?"

He grinned.

Not the reaction I was hoping for. "Did I say something funny?"

"No, you just sound like a lawyer."

"I've been paying attention."

Ben gave me a nod. "And where exactly are you going with this line of questioning?"

"You know the Trudy Bergeson case that I've been working on…"

"It's not a—"

"I know it's not an official coroner case, but would you be surprised if you heard that Steve…Detective Sixkiller had launched a police investigation?"

Ben's dark eyes widened for an instant as all traces of his grin disappeared. "That would be unusual for him to do that."

That would be a *yes*.

"But not unheard of," I said, perched at the edge of my seat.

He shrugged. A non-answer that I took as another yes.

"In your experience working with Detective Sixkiller, he wouldn't do this unless he had good reason to believe that the person didn't die from natural causes. Isn't that fair to say?"

Ben's lips compressed as he took a deep breath and slowly released it, which told me he didn't want to answer the question.

"What do you think?" he asked.

That I'd just heard another yes.

I sprung to my feet. "I think I have everything I need. Thanks!"

He leaned back in his creaky chair. "Glad I could help." Pointing at the envelope in my hand, he asked, "Will you be able to deliver that today?"

"Absolutely." Especially if the results of my trip to Port Townsend could make Steve want to work *with* me instead of keeping me on a short leash.

An hour later, Lisa Arbuckle, the assistant prosecutor I'd sat next to in court, stopped me on my way back from starting another pot of coffee.

"Do you have a few minutes?"

Since I had an hour and a half before I needed to leave for the senior center, I nodded.

Lisa was around my age, at least five inches shorter, and sixty pounds lighter. I guessed that her charcoal designer suit, pearls, and pumps ensemble had been selected carefully to elicit confidence from a jury. To help in the stature department, too.

I felt decidedly frumpy by comparison. After she eyed me from head to toe and shot me a fake smile, I didn't feel any better.

"Frankie suggested that I get your opinion on a witness."

That explained the fake smile. This wasn't Lisa's idea.

As we walked toward the conference room, Lisa told me about the witness who claimed to have seen an attack on her boyfriend outside of a club at the south end of Old Town.

"I'm having trouble believing her story," Lisa said, reaching for the doorknob. "So, I'd like to know what you think."

Within a minute of observing Shea, a brassy blonde in her early twenties, tell her account of what happened, I could see why Lisa had her doubts about this witness.

Shea's dramatic palms up plea—the overt desperation to make us believe her felt like she was trying way too hard. Quickly it sealed her deal as a potential witness, at least for me. Something else had to be going on. Something with high enough stakes to wind her up and make her spin this yarn so emphatically.

"What can I say to make you believe me?" she asked,

tears cascading down her cheeks and spilling onto the front of her embroidered peasant shirt.

Absolutely nothing.

Shea wrapped her arms around her midsection and rocked back and forth as if that were all she had to buoy herself while she sat in the eye of a storm.

I glanced at my watch. Thirteen minutes after eleven. I needed this interview to wrap up so I could change into my sweats and head over to Jake's aerobics class, where I intended to be the one asking the questions.

Folding my arms over my belt, I leaned forward to mirror her body language. "I want to believe you," I said while Lisa sat to my left and tapped her pen against the yellow ruled pad she'd been scribbling on for the last half hour.

Lisa set down her pen and handed Shea a small box of tissues. I got the clear impression from Lisa that it was more reflex than sympathy, probably from having witnessed too many crocodile tears in this conference room. But Shea's lower lip wasn't trembling as an accessory to her waterworks. She seemed genuinely afraid.

"I think we have all the information we need from you, Shea, unless you have anything else you'd like to tell us," Lisa said.

Shea wiped her tear-stained cheeks. "If you don't believe me, ask Jake."

My breath caught in my chest. My Jake? "Jake who?"

"Jake Divine. He was there. He can tell you how that lying bitch came after Gabe and me with a knife."

Really.

I scanned the contents of the manila folder at my elbow

while Lisa politely thanked Shea for her time. According to the police report, the incident at the club had taken place just after midnight on the morning of May 19—two hours before Howard Jeppesen's death.

"Well, that was a big waste of time," Lisa said after she closed the conference room door behind Shea.

Not for me. A witness had placed Jake Divine less than ten minutes away from the hospital near the time of a murder.

～

"Good morning!" Marietta chirped, sitting in her robe and sipping coffee at the kitchen table with Gram as I stepped through the back door at eleven forty-two. My mother's puffy, mascara-smudged eyes told me she hadn't been awake long.

"Home a little early for lunch, aren't you?" Gram asked me with a wary glint in her eyes.

I slung my tote over the back of the empty kitchen chair between them. "I'll do lunch later. Just came home to change."

"But you look just..." My mother tucked her chin as her gaze landed on my pantsuit. "Oh, honey, I need to take you shopping, although that is a nice scarf."

"You gave it to me." Sheesh, that's why I was wearing it!

She brightened like she was about to dangle a sparkling new engagement ring in front of my nose. Again. "And doesn't it look lovely on you!" She waggled an index finger at my midsection. "I'd rethink the brown belt. It makes you look like you're going on saf—"

"I know!" I made a break for the stairs before Gram chimed in about my safari suit.

After I changed into a sports bra and the baggy tank top and navy sweatpants I'd found in the bottom drawer in my old room, I laced up my Nikes and met my grandmother on the stairs.

"Where the heck are you off to dressed like that?" Gram asked.

"Aerobics at the senior center."

"You're going there again? What's going on with you?"

"I'm getting healthier, haven't you heard the news?"

Her cheeks flushed. "Well, I might have heard a little something about that from Arlene."

Why was I not surprised?

Since she was dressed in black sweatpants, a long-sleeved T-shirt, and white tennis shoes, I saw an opportunity staring me in the face. "You should come to the class with me."

Gram frowned. "Again? What's in it for me?"

"You'd get away from Mom for an hour, and I'll buy you lunch afterward."

"I'll get my purse."

The parking spots near the door of the senior center were crowded with cars, but I found one at the far end of the lot.

"Now remember," I said as I pulled the key from the

Honda's ignition, "I may want to stay after class for a few minutes to talk to Jake."

Gram unfastened her seatbelt. "No problem. If he's wearing his tight spandex pants, I'll be happy to hang around and watch."

"Gram!"

"What? It doesn't hurt to look."

"See that's all that you do," I muttered under my breath as I got out of the car.

I followed my grandmother through the front door and into the activity room. No reception line this time. Fine by me. I wanted to keep my presence in this class as low profile as possible.

"Oh, goody," Gram said when she spotted Jake chatting with Peggy Como, one of the Gray Ladies, near the raised platform he and Suzy had stood on the night before. "Spandex!"

"Goody," I echoed with considerably less enthusiasm as he flashed his perfect white teeth at us.

The activity room was packed with almost as many bodies as at last night's tango class but with considerably more women. It didn't take a rocket scientist to figure out the reason why. I was looking at him. Five seventy-something women sitting in folding chairs bordering the hardwood floor were staring at Jake like he was a Kahlua cream pie at a Weight Watchers meeting.

One of the women wearing legwarmers I recognized from Dr. Straitham's waiting room. The *Flashdance* wannabe waved at me like we were old friends. Not the first time the Marietta connection had granted me instant acceptance. Today, I was more than willing to take what I could get, especially if it led to some answers about the Jake Divine–Virginia Straitham connection.

A lone man with skinny white legs poking out of baggy purple shorts stood in the back of the activity room. I didn't recognize the chicken legs, but I'd know that full head of steel wool hair anywhere—Wally. Next to him in a sky blue warm-up suit stood Sylvia Jeppesen, who waved Gram and me over. My heart skipped a beat when I spotted the woman standing in the row in front of Sylvia—Virginia Straitham.

Virginia's gaze tightened when it landed on me. Not exactly *stay the hell away from me*, but I got the message loud and clear and took a spot on the floor behind my grandmother. Close enough to observe, far enough away to avoid an ugly scene.

"What are you doing back there?" Gram flicked a wrist at Wally. "Move down. We need to make some room for Char."

"That's okay," I muttered. "I'm fine back here."

"There's lots of room up front," Jake said. "Please, you don't have to hide in the back. There's plenty of space up here."

Up here was right next to Virginia Straitham.

Gram turned with a satisfied smile on her face. "Honey, he's not talking to me."

Taking a deep breath, I skulked to the front row while Virginia glared at me like she wanted to strangle me with the nearest legwarmer.

So much for keeping a low profile.

"Okay, everyone, get to your feet," Jake shouted over the up-tempo music, raising his well-muscled arms to coax the ladies out of their seats. He grinned at me. "Let's get sweaty!"

Oh, brother.

Chapter Seventeen

"Great job, everyone!" Jake said, clapping his hands like a high school cheerleader at the end of the fifty-minute class. He killed the music, then reached for a folded hand towel and wiped the sheen of sweat from his face.

His sexually charged line about getting sweaty hadn't been just innuendo. Unfortunately, I hadn't thought to bring a towel so I used my perspiration-drenched shirt to wipe the drips from my face, making my tank top cling to the roll at my middle—not a good look for me. Also somewhere near the bottom of my list of things to worry about this afternoon.

Expecting to see Gram standing behind me, I met the sharp-eyed gaze of Virginia Straitham, who, unlike me, looked as cool as a cucumber. I would have liked nothing more than to see her sweat, but since I needed to make good on my promise to take Gram to lunch, change my clothes, and head north to Port Townsend, turning some screws on Virginia would have to wait for another day.

Jutting her chin, Virginia acted as if I'd suddenly become invisible, then she waved to Jake and headed for the door behind several other members of the class.

Whatever. Until I had some proof that she was the mastermind pulling the strings around here, I had nothing to say to the woman.

"How'd you like the class?" Jake asked.

I turned to see him smiling down at me.

I raked back the damp bangs clinging to my forehead. "It was a bit more of a workout than I'd expected." And I was a lot more out of shape than I wanted to admit.

He tossed the towel over his shoulder as he stepped off the platform. "Not too much, I hope. I wouldn't want to chase you away after one session."

"It would take more than that to chase me away," I could say honestly to the man who had been in the vicinity of the hospital the early morning of Howard Jeppesen's death.

His gaze swept over me as if he were sizing me up. "Excellent."

As he came closer, I guessed him to be about three inches taller than me. He extended his hand and I breathed in a pleasant musky scent. "We haven't officially met. Jackson Divine, but everyone calls me Jake."

"Charmaine Digby—my friends call me Char."

His handshake was warm and gentle, as if he were used to holding older women's hands. The used car salesman smile that accompanied it oozed charm. "Char it is then."

"I probably should have introduced myself last night. I thought about it," I said, glancing down at the bulge in his spandex to declare some carnal interest, which may have been more effective if I hadn't sweated through all my makeup.

The gleam in his dark blue eyes indicated that I'd scored

some points with his ego. "I thought I recognized you."

"You're a very good dancer."

He bowed slightly. The pleasure signals he sent rang loud and true, but the gesture seemed rehearsed, like he'd been tutored on how to act like a gentleman. Most likely by an older woman who could school him on social niceties.

Given what I'd learned from Arlene, the safe bet would be on Virginia.

"My grandmother has told me how she's enjoyed some of your classes."

Not her exact words. She'd told me she enjoyed *looking* at him teach his classes.

"What else do you teach besides aerobics?" I asked, very conscious of the sweat beading on my upper lip.

"Water aerobics, swimming, stretching, and relaxation therapy. You name it, I do it around here."

I bet he did.

"I imagine that's why Virginia Straitham thought you'd be so perfect for this job."

He blinked, his pupils dilating like I'd struck a nerve.

"If that's the case, I'm grateful," he said with a little flicker of a smile at his lips.

"Have you known her long?"

"A while. She was one of my first clients."

So, the cool cucumber had been getting hot and bothered with this guy. That scored a ten on the yuck factor scale, but it helped make the Virginia-Jake connection that much stronger.

"You may not be interested," he said with a playful cock of his head, "but let me give you my card."

When he turned to grab a day planner from the

platform, I wiped my drippy face with the hem of my shirt.

He pulled out a business card and handed it to me. "I'm also a personal trainer."

I read the card. There was no mention of the Assistant Activity Director position he held at the senior center. Obviously, that wasn't the personal touch type of position he was trying to promote.

"Don't hesitate to contact me if I can offer you any assistance."

Locking gazes, I wanted to slip his card into my cleavage, borrowing a Marietta move from when she played a sultry Russian spy in a Bond spoof movie, but the girls were taking a sauna in my sports bra and I didn't need the ink stains.

He glanced at my grandmother who was sitting in a folding chair in the back of the activity room. "I'm sorry. I'm keeping you."

"No problem. But I probably should get her to lunch. I'm sure she's hungry."

His chiseled lips curled into an easy smile. "So am I, so I understand exactly how she feels."

Sure he did. Although if I hadn't thought he was Virginia's errand boy, I might have wanted to believe him.

"I hope you'll join us again. The next aerobics class is Friday." He pointed at the card in my hand. "But if you're interested in a personalized, one-on-one session, give me a call."

One-on-one sessions—was that what up and coming gigolos were calling their services?

"I'll do that." When they featured ice cream cakes in hell.

I slipped his business card into a pocket of my tote bag and made my way over to Gram.

"Ready for lunch?" I wasn't, but a deal was a deal.

"I'm ready." She looked back at Jake, making his way toward the rear exit. "Did I hear Jake say that he was hungry, too?"

"Something like that."

"Maybe we should ask him to join us and make it a threesome."

"Not a chance."

After grabbing a quick lunch, we rushed home so that I could freshen up and change back into my safari suit. A little worse for wear, but if I was going to be on the hunt this afternoon, I might as well dress the part.

Since this hunter didn't have a great sense of direction, I headed back to the courthouse to get a street map of Port Townsend. As long as I was there, I ran a background check on Jake Divine. Surprisingly, he didn't have a blemish on his record other than a ten-year-old speeding ticket. After I found his last known address in Port Townsend, I went online to print some driving directions. Just in case I happened to find myself in his neighborhood later.

Patsy arched her eyebrows at me as I passed her desk. "Heading out?"

I waited for some safari suit-related snark and got nothing back other than Patsy's usual dose of condescension. At least someone around here didn't feel compelled to take a cheap shot.

"I have subpoena delivery duty, so I'll probably be gone

a couple of hours, depending on how easy it is to find the place." *And what I could find out about Jake Divine.*

She smirked. "Good hunting."

Et tu, Patsy?

Leaving the Prosecutor's office, I noticed Steve sitting alone on a wooden bench outside Judge Navarro's courtroom. He wore his charcoal gray suit so I figured he was scheduled to testify for the prosecution this afternoon.

The eyes of the Chimacam County Sheriff's deputy at the security desk tracked me as I crossed the gold and black checkerboard landing. After a week and a half on the job, he should have recognized me as no threat to anyone on the third floor.

I smiled at the deputy.

His stony expression didn't change.

Leaning forward on the bench, Steve rested his forearms on his thighs and didn't look much more welcoming. "Late lunch or are we off to stalk some unsuspecting doctor's wife?"

I reached into my tote and waved the white envelope with the county seal under his nose. "I'm on official County Prosecutor business."

"Uh-huh. Then where are you going to go?"

"I might go for a latte. Want one?"

"Cut the bullshit," he said, lowering his voice as he pulled me to the railing next to the stairs.

"I don't know what you mean."

With one hand on the railing, Steve edged close, heat radiating from his body. "You know exactly what I mean. Chow Mein, every time I turn around you're looking for trouble, and if you're not careful, it's going to find you."

"Are you trying to scare me?" If he was, he knew exactly what to say.

"I'm trying to tell you that I want you to deliver the subpoena and come right back to the office."

"No mocha latte?"

His gaze softened. "It's not on your diet."

Bastard. "What if I came back with a couple of filets and made you dinner?" With a dollop of conversation for dessert.

He stared at his black oxfords. "Uh—"

The last time I'd heard less enthusiasm about me cooking a meal, I'd been married.

"I want to talk to you about a few things." About a lot of things. I just hoped I wouldn't be the only one doing the talking. "Will you be home later?"

"I have football practice tonight, then..." Watching one of the administrative assistants climb the stairs, he shook his head. "I don't know when I'll be home."

I didn't want to think about who would be keeping him out late tonight.

"Can I get a rain check on those steaks?" Steve asked.

"Sure." I pasted a smile on my face. "No problem. See you later."

Crap! I sounded like I'd be waiting up for him. "Or not."

The corners of his eyes tightened like he was trying to read me. "Is everything okay?"

"Yep. Everything's terrific." I headed for the stairs before I said anything else that I'd regret. "Have a good evening." Or not.

Forty minutes later, I served the subpoena on the owner of Geektek, the Port Townsend computer repair shop where Shea's boyfriend had worked before he was arrested for aggravated assault on May 19th.

Mission accomplished, I stopped for a skinny latte at the Supreme Bean, my favorite espresso stand on the Port Townsend waterfront. Then I followed the directions I'd printed to 1118 Blair Road—Jake Divine's address according to the Washington State Department of Licensing—and parked in front of a sprawling rambler with such an immaculate lawn it could have doubled as a putting green.

As I walked up the concrete paver driveway, I heard barking announcing my arrival and noticed a flutter of curtains at a large picture window. The front door swung open two seconds later.

"Yes?" said a petite woman around my mother's age.

Unlike my mother, she wore Birkenstocks, minimal makeup, and by her shoulder-length salt and pepper waves, I assumed that her locks were chemical-free.

"Mrs. Divine?" I asked.

"Yes?"

"Hi, I'm Stacy," I said, borrowing the name on the tag of the nose-ringed girl who had made my latte. "I went to school with Jackson. Is he home?"

I took a visual inventory of the foyer behind her. Framed family photos hanging next to museum quality prints, a Persian area rug, a brass stand in the corner with an oversized golf umbrella, a BMW in the driveway of a horse acre lot. It all added up to Jackson Divine coming from less than humble roots.

Her mouth puckered. "You know Jack?"

Either that's what they called him at home or he'd changed his name. To reinvent himself in Port Merritt with a sexier persona?

I brightened my smile to counteract the pucker factor. "Is he around?"

"He hasn't lived with us for several years."

"Oh. I'm just here for the day, so I thought I'd look him up."

Jake's mother frowned as she lowered her gaze, assessing me. If I'd known I'd be posing as an old friend of his, I would have lost the safari suit.

"You're a little different from Jack's other friends," she said.

I was sure that was an understatement. I shrugged. "In a good way, I hope."

"Sure, I guess."

Not exactly a ringing endorsement but beggars couldn't be choosers.

"Sorry," Mrs. Divine stepped back, swinging the door open. "Would you like to come in?"

"Thanks." I stepped through the foyer and followed her to a newly remodeled kitchen that was larger than my first apartment.

"Could I offer you some tea? I was about to have some myself."

"Yes, that would be wonderful." Especially if it provided me an opportunity to look around while she fixed the tea.

"Have a seat anywhere," she said, pointing to the adjoining room with a buttercream leather sofa and loveseat, flat screen TV, built-in oak book shelves, and a wood stove in the corner.

"Great room." Except for the Rottweiler barking at me from the other side of a pair of French doors.

"We like it." She rapped on the window. "Bruno, no."

"So, what's Jake…Jack up to these days?" I asked, checking out the collection of photos on the bookcase as Bruno continued to bark at me.

"He's working in Port Merritt and doing very well. Manages a senior center there."

So he told a little fib about the job. There were worse things a son could tell his mother. For instance, that he was a killer for hire.

I studied a holiday picture of the shaggy-haired cutie, standing next to a shiny new bicycle. "I always knew he'd be going places," I said, wishing Bruno would find a nice cat to torment.

"He's a real go getter. Always has been."

He certainly seemed to be, just not in the way that typically made a mother proud.

I held up the photo over Bruno's slobbery protests at every muscle I moved. "He looks like an angel here."

Ignoring Bruno, Mrs. Divine's gaze softened. "He always was a good boy. With a few minor exceptions. Of course, boys will be boys."

She obviously didn't know much, including the company her *good boy* had been keeping.

On the next shelf there was a picture of a man in his forties with two teenagers. The boys looked like they could be brothers. "This is a great picture. When was it taken?"

"That was a fishing trip back when Jack was a senior

in high school. Those boys were inseparable back then—all three of them." She handed me a steaming cup, then turned to the dog. "Bruno, please. Sit," she said as if she were negotiating with a toddler.

"What's his name again—the boy with Jack?" I asked while Bruno ignored her and clawed at the door.

Mrs. Divine knit her brows. "If you were a friend of Jack's you'd know Wesley."

If she moved an inch toward those French doors to sic Bruno on me, I was dropping my Darjeeling on her Indian rug and running to the Jag for my second aerobic workout of the day.

"I was a year ahead of him and didn't spend a lot of time with Wesley." I could probably pass for thirty on a good day, and she was squinting at me without glasses. Something less than 20/20 wouldn't hurt my cause. "I don't think he was in our journalism class. What was his last name?"

"Straitham."

Bingo. "That's right. Wesley Straitham."

"Hmmmm. I don't recall Jack taking journalism in high school."

"Really? I do because I sat right behind him," I said with an innocent shrug. I needed to change the subject and fast. "Is this your husband?"

Frowning at the barking Rottweiler, Mrs. Divine nodded.

"Nice picture." *Please don't sic your dog on me.*

She gave him a hand signal. "Bruno, down!"

The Rottweiler finally sat, strings of drool hanging from his jowls as he gave me the death stare, daring me to make one false move.

I could handle a little drool, especially when the jaws it hung from weren't wrapped around my ankle.

"Good boy!" She turned to me. "We're working on obedience training."

Not hard enough.

I forced a smile and took a sip of bitter tea.

Mrs. Divine took a seat on the love seat opposite me and set her cup on the coffee table between us. "Won't you sit down?"

"I really can't stay." I added my cup to the table. "I just wanted to stop and say hello."

"I don't know why I didn't think of this earlier. I'll call him on his cell," she said, pushing away from the love seat. "Then, you two—"

"Please don't." Really. As I edged my way to the front door, Bruno growled like someone was absconding with his dinner. "I'm heading south for the ferry, so I'll look him up later this afternoon."

She shrugged. "Okay, but—"

"It would be great to get together with Wesley, too. Do you know if he's still living in the area?"

Mrs. Divine pursed her lips. "You have been out of touch. Wesley's in jail."

Chapter Eighteen

From the background check I'd run, Jackson Divine seemed squeaky clean on paper. Stir in the facts that he had changed his name, worked where he could prey on the affections of elderly women, hung out at a knife fight that placed him in the vicinity of a murder, and had a best buddy serving eight months in the county jail for selling anabolic steroids to high school kids, and Jake seemed considerably less than divine.

When I returned to my desk, I ran a records check on Wesley Straitham. The former high school athlete turned steroids dealer had been a houseguest of the county since June. He'd also had prior possession charges that had landed him in jail for several days at a time. None of which overlapped with any date of death for anyone on my victims list.

I leaned back in my chair and reviewed all the notes I'd scribbled for the last two hours. I had five suspicious deaths, four with strong family connections to the senior center where a matchmaking Virginia Straitham and Jake Divine had a personal and professional connection, and both had a personal relationship with Wesley Straitham, who had drug connections.

Since the biggest threat I could pose to anyone was to yell *'Liar, liar, pants on fire!'* I needed a big cop with a big gun.

My favorite cop had already told me that he was otherwise engaged tonight, but he had to come home sometime. Fortunately, my grandfather's den made the perfect stakeout location for Steve's driveway.

Despite a less than stellar first day on my diet, my stomach was growling, and I had a few hours to kill, so I tucked my note pad into my tote and headed for my car with a choice to make. I could go home to the possible fate of having to make polite dinner table conversation with my biology teacher, or I could go to Duke's to glean the latest gossip and get a free meal.

Some decisions aren't that tough.

Five minutes later, I walked in on the big mouth bass serenading a young Japanese tourist with the last tinny chorus of *Don't Worry, Be Happy*. The giggly girl wanted me to take a picture of her with the plastic fish. I didn't mind obliging. It felt like the most normal thing I'd done all day.

Hector, Duke's night cook for the last eleven years, was behind the grill. "Hey, sweet thing," he said, lifting his silver streaked goatee in a chin salute.

Since Hector Avocato was happily married with six granddaughters and I welcomed the distraction of harmless flirtation, I didn't tell him where he could stick his *sweet thing*.

I plopped down on a barstool near the grill. "How's life, Hector?"

"Life is beau-ti-ful," he said, emphasizing every syllable.

"Just like you, *mi querida*."

I blew out a breath, feeling like every ounce of frustration of the last week and a half had burrowed into my aching shoulder muscles. "You're very good for my ego."

He winked. "I know how to treat my women."

Most of his women were under the age of ten.

I stared at the burger patties sizzling on the grill and thought about the grams of fat in each greasy one.

Damn, I hated that I cared.

He flipped one of the patties. "You hungry?"

"I'll make myself a salad in a minute." As soon as I mustered up enough energy to move.

The silver bell over the door jingled, and I peered through the cutout window, half-hoping I'd see Steve. Instead, I met the gaze of Kyle Cardinale.

He arched his eyebrows in surprise and then gave me a little two fingered wave—not exactly an invitation to join him for a cup of coffee, but I'd been flying without a net most of the day. Why stop now?

I grabbed a couple of mugs and carried a carafe to where he sat alone at the counter. "Coffee?"

He nodded. "What are you doing here? Moonlighting?"

"I help Duke out from time to time." And have most of my meals here when my mother was in town.

While I filled our cups, I admired how his black henley showcased the broad shoulders his white lab coat had been hiding. Very fine shoulders.

"What?" he asked with a quizzical smile.

"I haven't seen you out of uniform before."

"Hope I'm not disappointing you." He winked—the

second man who had playfully winked at me tonight.

I was fairly certain that Kyle didn't have six granddaughters, and nothing about the way he'd been looking at me since the day we'd met felt like harmless flirtation. Maybe it was time to lift my ban on Italians.

I rested my elbows on the counter, locking gazes with him. "Trust me, I'm not disappointed."

I'd just lobbed the ball into his court, an easy set up line to gauge his interest.

Instead of keeping the volley going, Kyle's gaze went to the wall clock above the big mouth bass, then he buried his face behind a menu. "I guess I should decide what I want."

Yeah, that would be a good idea. Clearly it wasn't me.

"So," I said after I shifted my libido back into neutral. "What can I get for you?"

"Two turkey hoagies with the works. Better hold the onions. Chips instead of fries, to go."

"Two? They're pretty big."

Nodding, he broke eye contact. "Yeah."

Oh. He had ordered for two.

I had to say something to cut through the wall of tension between us. "Going out on the boat?"

"It's a nice night. Good wind from the Northwest."

Not a bad evasive answer. He skillfully omitted any mention of his sailing partner for the evening, but it told me everything I needed to know. "Enjoy. I'll get your order to the kitchen."

I picked up my coffee mug, tacked Kyle's order to the aluminum wheel, and scampered past Hector like a rabbit beating a retreat to the nearest hole.

"What happened?" Hector asked. "I thought the doctor was a *special* friend."

"Well, you were wrong." Because all my special friends appeared to have other plans with their special friends.

I grabbed a carving knife from the wall rack and blew off some steam on a head of lettuce.

"Ay-yi-yi! Remind me to not piss you off tonight."

It was too late for that.

"You know what? Screw this." I added the chopped lettuce to the plastic bag filled with prepared salad in the refrigerator and pointed my knife at the grill. "Will you throw another burger down for a patty melt? And I'd like extra cheese with that."

His eyes went to the knife. "Maybe this isn't the time to mention it, but I thought you were on a diet."

"Fine! Skip the extra cheese."

"*Mi querida*, that's not what you want."

"You're right. I want that extra cheese."

He gently took the knife from my hand. "You need to get out of the kitchen and do something else for at least an hour."

"Come on, Hector. I'm hungry."

"Since you were just waving a knife around like you're looking for a fight, I'd say you're also ticked off." He pointed the blade at me. "Never eat when you're sad, mad, or glad. That's what I always used to tell my clients when I worked at the health club."

Great. All I needed was another person to help me count my calories.

"That's how I met Sandy." He beamed with pride. "Has maintained her weight for twenty-eight years."

Impressive but depressing. Lately, I didn't seem capable of staying the same weight for twenty-eight hours.

"So, believe me when I tell you—no sad, mad, or glad."

Right. That about covered all my waking hours so I'd be taking off these thirty pounds in no time.

Hector set the knife in the sink. "Go take a walk to work off some of this—"

"Pissiness?"

"You said it, not me. It's a beau-ti-ful evening. Go to the marina and come back when you don't need to hurt my lettuce."

And look like I'm stalking another doctor? "No marina."

He pointed at the back door. "Go somewhere else then. Get your body moving. When you come back, if you still want a patty melt, I'll make you a patty melt."

"You're a good guy, Hector. Although right now, you're really annoying."

"That's my specialty. Annoying my women."

An hour later, the top of my right big toe had a blister from where my sandal had rubbed it raw, and I had at least ten painful blocks ahead of me to get back to Duke's—all downhill. I'd left my tote and cell phone in my kitchen locker, so calling Donna or Rox to beg a ride wasn't an option.

I limped my way toward Broward Park, a tree-lined green space in the residential neighborhood that used to house mill workers and their families but in recent years had given way to pricey bay view condos. The park featured a jungle gym and slide for the kids and, fortunately for me, wooden benches for the adults too tired to stand and watch them. It was after seven so the dogs in the park outnumbered the kids. I was in no mood to get chummy with any of Bruno's cousins, so I sat my sorry ass down on a bench under the canopy of a massive Douglas fir, took off my sandals, and inspected the damage.

After a few minutes of the sun on my face, a warm breeze fluttering through my hair, and the sound of children's laughter in my ears, I no longer cared that one of the boats I saw sailing on Merritt Bay was Dr. Cardinale enjoying his evening away from the hospital with someone other than me.

Maybe the reinstatement of my ban on Italians was just as well. I already had a pesky matter of five murders on my mind, and my mother didn't seem to be leaving town anytime soon. I really didn't need to pile on the additional aggravation of dating someone prettier than me.

I breathed in the scent of burgers barbequing in the picnic area and my stomach growled in response. I was ten blocks away from a salad with fat-free dressing or a grilled chicken breast sandwich with no mayo. Just ten blocks and one stupid blister that impaired my sustained effort at tranquility, not to mention my ability to walk without cursing in the vicinity of small children.

Rubbing my big toe, I stared at the street and watched an old Camaro rumble by.

Damn! That was Little Dog's car. I could have hitched a ride to Duke's.

Since George was an assistant peewee football coach

with Steve, that signaled the end of practice. I fastened
my sandals to be ready to stick my thumb out at the next
Duke's regular who drove by.

I didn't have to wait long. In the distance I saw Steve's
F150 gleaming like gun metal under the slowly setting sun.
I stepped to the curb, and a nanosecond later I could see
that Steve had a blonde next to him in the passenger seat.

"Great." I started walking. With any luck he was gazing
into Heather's baby blues and didn't notice me.

I hadn't taken ten steps before Steve pulled up to the
curb, pacing me. "Need a lift?" he asked.

I painted a smile on my face and kept moving. "No,
thanks."

"Are you sure? You're walking funny."

"Really, I'm fine." And might have felt even better if
Heather's son, Robby, hadn't been craning his neck at me
from the crew cab like they had slowed to watch a train
wreck.

Move on. Nothing to see here.

"Where's your car?" Steve asked.

"Duke's," I said, trying to ignore my blister.

"So, you walked up here?"

Some detective. I stopped in my tracks and looked past
a clearly annoyed Heather to lock gazes with Steve. "Yes, I
went for a walk. Is that okay with you?"

"Those aren't exactly walking shoes."

"They're very comfortable." At least that had been true
an hour ago.

Steve narrowed his eyes at me. "Are you sure you don't
want a ride?"

I'd take a bullet first. "Absolutely."

I stepped back to the sidewalk. Hoping that he'd get a clue and spare me from looking any more lame than I already did, I picked up my pace. After several painful seconds, I watched Steve turn right at the corner of the next block. Going to Heather's house for a nice family dinner? How cozy.

A half hour of cursing and two benches later, Duke's kitchen screen door banged shut behind me.

"*Querida*, you had a good, long walk," Hector said with a nod of approval. "How do you feel?"

"I'll have my patty melt now."

❧

The second I stepped through my grandmother's back door, my mother pounced on me like a pit bull on a pork chop. "If you have any plans for Saturday, cancel them."

Given how today had gone, it was a safe bet that a hot date with Kyle Cardinale wasn't in my immediate future. "What's Saturday?"

She blinked at me. "Your grandmother's eightieth birthday."

What kind of granddaughter was I? I'd forgotten all about it. "Are we going out to celebrate?"

"Something much better." She spread her arms as if she were about to break into song. "We're having a dinner party here!"

Since it had been over thirty years since my mother had risked losing a manicured fingernail in a kitchen, there was no doubt who would be doing the cooking.

"Mom, I have no time to prepare for a big dinner party."

"It's not going to be a big elaborate thing. Your grandmother made it very clear that she doesn't want that. We're going to have a barbeque."

"We?"

Her mouth split into a dazzling smile. "You and me and Barry!"

Criminy. Searing flesh with Barry Ferris and my mother. Not at the top of my list of fun party ideas.

I slipped the handle of my tote over the back of a kitchen chair, my mind racing for an escape route out of this culinary disaster zone. "It might rain. Let's just go out to a restaurant."

"Nonsense, it's supposed to be beautiful all weekend, and a private dinner party here will be much more fun."

"For whom?" I mumbled under my breath.

"We can have all sorts of wonderful barbeque-y things. Some nice salmon, maybe some oysters on the half shell."

"Oysters? I thought you said Gram didn't want anything elaborate."

Marietta's smile vanished without a trace. "Okay. So, no oysters." She picked up a notepad and pen from the kitchen table. "There are plenty of other yummy things we can have."

Looking over her shoulder, I scanned her list of yummy things, and it read like we'd be hosting a wedding reception—and it had better not be another one of hers. "How many people are coming to this soiree?"

"I thought twelve was a perfect number," she said, flipping the page to a short list of names—mainly family and my grandmother's close friends. Of course, Barry Ferris was numero uno.

"Fewer would be okay, too," I said, reading Steve's name at the bottom of the page. "Like eleven."

"Oh, no. There's no symmetry with eleven."

A barbeque without symmetry. What was I thinking?

"Besides," she added. "I've already prepared the invitations."

I watched as my mother rifled through a stack of white embossed envelopes and set aside the one addressed to Barry Ferris. She handed me the rest. "If you wouldn't mind delivering these tomorrow since we're a little short on time."

I didn't have the energy to remind Marietta that she could borrow Gram's car and deliver her invitations herself, so I chose the path of least resistance. "Fine."

"One last thing. Let me give you this." She tore out a page from her notepad and handed it to me. "It's really just a few ideas for the menu, but that should get you started."

Either the fat from my patty melt had clogged the arteries to my brain or I'd lost the ability to understand my mother without the Southern accent. "Started with what?"

"Your shopping list for the party, silly."

Chapter Nineteen

Planning Gram's birthday party with Marietta was making my molars hurt, so after I changed into a pair of faded blue jeans and a navy slouch shirt, I grabbed my car keys and drove to the Red Apple Market to find my happy place with a candy bar—just a small one since I was on a diet. I also grabbed a loaf of whole wheat bread. I didn't want to look like a fat chick desperate for a chocolate fix.

"That's not dinner, is it?" Steve said, standing in line behind me.

Shit. "No." I glanced down at the box of Cap'n Crunch and the six-pack of Coronas in his hands. "Is that yours?"

I regretted the question as soon as it popped out of my mouth, especially since he was probably on his way home from Heather's.

A smile played at his lips. "It's more like dessert."

Knowing Heather hadn't served him dessert registered a blip on my joy meter, not that I should care.

After an uncomfortable silence, I carried my groceries to the door and waited to find out if Steve was heading home. I needed an opportunity to tell him everything I'd learned about Jake Divine and this was as good as any.

"How are you doing?" Steve asked as he approached, glancing down at the raw skin on my big toe.

I should have hidden the evidence and not worn my flip flops. "It's nothing."

The automatic door swung open and he followed me to the parking lot. "Doesn't look like nothing. Would it feel better with a beer?"

That sounded like an opportunity to me. "It wouldn't feel any worse."

After I followed Steve home, I parked the Jag in Gram's driveway and met him at his front door.

I hadn't been inside his house since before his mother had remarried two years ago and moved to New Mexico. It seemed like déjà vu following him to the same sunny yellow kitchen with gingham curtains and white appliances, only this time for a beer instead of his mother's oatmeal cookies.

I noticed that the hardwood floors still needed refinishing and the solid oak dining room table hadn't moved more than an inch since the last time I'd seen it, but that's where the familiarity ended. Gone was the damask pattern wallpaper behind the table. Instead, a solid brick red accent wall extended from the dining room to the living room where a nubby area rug in bold earth tones separated a chocolate brown leather sectional from an overstuffed chair and ottoman the color of cherry cola. Woven wood blinds replaced his mother's pleated curtains, leaving little doubt of the masculine taste of the new owner.

Steve set the grocery bag with the Coronas on the white tile counter, and I glanced up at the chicken-themed French country wallpaper bordering the kitchen. "You don't really strike me as a chicken kind of guy."

"Their days are numbered," he said, handing me a beer. "I'm just a little busy right now."

I had some strong opinions about how he'd been spending his time, but given why I was about to suck down one of his Coronas, it wasn't in my best interest to appear critical of my host.

Wandering into the living room, I noticed that other than an antique kerosene lamp on one of the old cherry wood end tables and a set of soapstone coasters, there wasn't a knickknack in sight. It was clean, uncluttered, unlike my grandmother's front room—a dust magnet with her collection of blue Depression glass.

"I like what you've done in here," I said. "It suits you."

He took a seat on the far end of the leather sectional and rested his beer bottle on his knee. "It's okay, for now."

I wasn't sure what that meant. Since my thoughts went to a woman in his life who might have some different decorating ideas, I directed my attention to the framed black and white photos on the wall. "These are nice." I recognized the barn from the old Hansen farm where Gram used to buy her eggs. "Local artist?"

"Yeah. Me."

I turned, facing him. "Since when are you a photographer?"

"There's a lot you don't know about me."

True. We had history, but we'd barely scratched the surface of the past sixteen years of our lives. I didn't know why he'd left Seattle Homicide to come back to Port Merritt. I also didn't know why he'd broken up with his old girlfriend. Last I'd heard from Rox, they were talking about getting married, then I came back home and it seemed he had started up again with Heather.

"I have no doubt of that," I admitted.

His eyes darkened as his gaze locked on mine. "What do you want to know?"

Everything.

I sat in the overstuffed chair while a revolving door of questions I dared not ask swung through the recesses of my mind.

I considered my options. Yes, Steve had presented me with an open invitation to satisfy my curiosity, but there had always been a line in our relationship I knew I mustn't cross. It could make things between us complicated, and the last thing I needed was another complication.

Focusing on the label of my beer bottle, I beat a quick retreat from that line. "You know, the meaning of life. Why nice people are dying at the hospital. Little stuff like that."

He blew out a deep breath. "Char—"

"Don't *Char* me. We need to talk about this."

Steve drained his beer bottle and pushed out of his seat. "We have talked about it, but one of us appears to have selective hearing." He tipped his bottle toward me. "Want another one?"

I shook my head. "I need to tell you something."

"As a friend or a cop?"

"Both."

His jaw tightened. "Is this going to piss me off?"

"Not if you keep an open mind."

"Shit," Steve muttered, stalking to the kitchen. "I don't like the sound of this already."

"I haven't even said anything yet!"

"Then get on with it."

"Fine! I discovered something today."

He fired a squinty-eyed glare at me from the kitchen.

"While I was in Port Townsend to serve that subpoena, I stopped at Jake Divine's parents' house and spoke with his mother."

"Dammit, Char!" Steve barked, crossing the room. "What part of 'stay out of this' do you not understand?"

"I understand plenty, including the fact that you're more pissed off than surprised that I talked to her."

Glowering, he sat back down and twisted off the bottle cap like he wanted to wring someone's neck. I didn't have to guess whose.

I sighed. "Okay, so you're not happy that I took a side trip after I got that latte."

"This isn't funny."

"I know." I leaned closer. "There's something going on at the senior center."

I studied Steve's face for a reaction, but the tic above his jaw line only confirmed what I already knew. I needed to tread lightly if I didn't want to witness a major explosion.

Even at my pre-divorce weight I wasn't very light on my feet, so I braced myself. "And I think Jake Divine is right in the middle of it."

No explosion. Instead, Steve blinked. "What makes you say that?"

"For one, he's going by a different name. It's like he's trying to reinvent himself here in Port Merritt."

"Since you recently changed *your* name, I don't think you should make too much of that."

Okay, he had a point. I had dumped Christopher

Scolari's last name the day my divorce was final. "But unlike Jake or Jack—as everyone *used* to call him—a guy who appears to depend upon the generosity of older women, I didn't attend the knife fight that placed him five blocks away the night of Howard Jeppensen's death."

Steve's dark gaze sharpened. "How do you know about the knife fight?"

"Shea, the girlfriend of the defendant in that case, placed him there."

Steve slowly nodded. I didn't know if it was because of what I knew or what he had just found out.

"It seems awfully convenient that Virginia Straitham got Jake Divine that job at the senior center," I said, watching Steve, "and when you add in the fact that his buddy Wesley has access to prescription drugs to do Grandma's bidding…"

I spotted a flicker of a frown but nothing to indicate surprise. I wasn't telling him anything he didn't already know.

"…the three of them are probably up to their eyeballs in these murders," I added, anticipating a reminder that this wasn't an official murder investigation.

Nothing. Instead, he took a pull off his beer bottle.

After several exasperating seconds ticked by, I couldn't take any more of the silent treatment. "Well? Aren't you going to say anything like stop jumping to conclusions, and Howard's death doesn't necessarily have anything to do with Trudy's?"

His jaw tightened. "I'd say you pretty much covered it."

Lie. He was holding something back, the poker face firmly in place while he played his cards close to the vest.

I leaned back in my chair and folded my arms. "In other words, you aren't going to say anything on this subject."

"I can tell you this much. *If* you're right, and *if* Trudy's death becomes a coroner's case, there will be an official investigation."

Duh.

"In the meantime," he said, sounding like he was conducting a lecture, "you don't want to force anybody's hand by trying to flush them out like a bird dog, or by speaking to their mothers. Mothers tend to call their sons when a strange girl shows up on their doorstep."

"I didn't use my real name."

"Like his mother wouldn't be able to describe you with that big game hunting outfit you were wearing today."

"So, stay out of this, Char," I said, mimicking him. "You don't want me to get hurt. That's what you're saying, right?"

The corners of his lips curled into a humorless smile. "You have been listening."

"I wish you'd take this more seriously. At least five people have been killed."

The frown line between his brows deepened. "I never said I wasn't taking this seriously."

True. And he made no effort to deny the fact that Trudy's murder was the tip of this iceberg.

I sucked in a breath. "That's why you were there Tuesday. You've been investigating this all along!"

"Walk away from this, Char."

"But I can help. I'm going to his aerobics class now and—"

"Are you fuckin' kidding me? Find something else to

do for a couple of weeks and stay away from the senior center."

"But—"

"And that includes Tango Tuesday!"

"But if you're—"

"Chow Mein, trust me on this," he said, his voice low, calm.

"What are you going to do?"

"Trust me and let it go."

Not the answer I wanted to hear. "I trust you." I picked up my beer and headed for the door.

"I mean it. You need to let this go," he called after me.

Right.

∽

Steve fixed me with a molten chocolate gaze as he held me tight on the dance floor. "Let go, Char."

"You're not exactly making it easy," I said, the skirt of my little black dress swaying in rhythm to Hernando's Hideaway.

He guided me back, step by seductive step. "It's easier than you think. Trust me." He cradled me in his arms, his lips closing in on mine.

Suddenly, I was staring into eyes as cold as death, and the music stopped.

Leaning over my hospital bed, Jake kissed me lightly on the lips. "Goodbye."

Goodbye?

"Steve!" I screamed, searching the room for him.

While Jake stroked my hair with one hand, he reached for a hypodermic needle with the other. "Shhhh. Relax. It will be over soon."

"No!"

Wake up. Wake up. Wake up.

Jolting awake, I pushed back the covers and bolted out of the hide-a-bed.

Sucking down oxygen like I'd run all the way home from the hospital, I stood at the foot of the Crippler and stared at the only thing that had been hovering over my bed—the orange and white tail of my grandmother's tabby.

A bead of cold sweat trickled down my back. "Dammit, Myron!"

Myron responded by jumping down and claiming my pillow.

"You can have it." After that nightmare I couldn't have been more done with it.

My flesh prickly with goosebumps, I raced upstairs to the bathroom to shake off what had to be the result of a beer-infused, hyperactive subconscious. Either that or a sadistic one. Although I had looked damned good in that black dress.

After a long, hot shower I was finally able to wash away my fear of dancing boogeymen with hypodermic needles. I took the easy route with my hair and pulled it back into my tortoiseshell clip, and then swiped on a layer of mascara and some lip gloss. Finally, I pulled on a pair of navy slacks and an oversized navy and white polka dotted tunic—Patsy attire, nothing that would turn heads. After the dream I'd had, perfect.

Fifteen minutes later, Aunt Alice frowned at me as

I tied the strings of a white apron around my waist and joined her at her work table. "You're making a bad habit out of these early mornings," she said sharply.

"I'll sleep when I'm dead or when Marietta leaves, whichever happens first."

My great-aunt grimaced as she flattened piecrust dough with her rolling pin. "Why is she still here?"

The reasons why my mother blew in and out of my life always had everything to do with when she was needed in front of a camera or the latest man in her life.

"I'm sure she'll leave next week some time." When her presence was required in Los Angeles to shoot her next infomercial.

My more immediate concern was Alice, standing statue still with her eyes squeezed shut.

"Aunt Alice, are you okay?"

"I'm fine. I just have a little hitch in my giddy-up is all."

Lie. A whopper of a lie that didn't begin to explain the pasty pallor of her skin.

Duke stood by the fryer and met my gaze while he dipped a couple of sour cream old-fashioneds into chocolate glaze. He slowly shook his head, concern etched into every line of his grizzled face.

"You've had this 'hitch' for days. Let me take you to the doctor," I said to Alice.

She eased herself down onto her wooden stool. "Don't be ridiculous. You don't run to the doctor because of a little bit of gas."

Whatever this was, it wasn't a little bit of gas, but she was stubbornly sticking to the same lame story.

I grabbed a bowl and reached for the bag of flour.

She scowled at me. "What are you doing?"

"I need a bran muffin...for my diet." If she could stick to her lame story, so could I.

Almost three hours later, I'd stocked the bakery shelves with very little protest from Alice and the last of the pies were in the oven. I'd expected her to take a break and have something to eat. Instead, I saw her wincing as she measured flour into a stainless steel mixing bowl. "I thought we were done with the baking."

"This is for Norm," she said, reaching for the salt. "Sour cream apple. His favorite pie."

Norm Bergeson had rarely come to Duke's pie happy hour even before Trudy's death. That meant that Alice planned to make a house call. Not only did I smell the heavenly aroma of pie crust venting from the oven, I sniffed some luck wafting my way.

"He barely ate anything last week," Alice added.

Last Saturday we'd left the man with a month's worth of cake and casseroles. If he was going hungry, it wasn't because he had an empty refrigerator.

Alice sliced a stick of butter into her bowl. "I'm just going to see how he's doing. I owe that much to Trudy."

"You know, I'm planning on taking an early lunch today." I wasn't until a minute ago. "I could stop by before noon, then drive you over to Norm's." And on the way back, drag her into Dr. Straitham's office.

She pursed her lips. "I'm perfectly capable—"

"Sounds like a perfect plan," Duke said as he grabbed a flat of eggs from the refrigerator behind me.

"I don't need to be babied," Alice grumbled. "I'm fine."

I smiled at her. "You know I don't believe you."

She scoffed. "That lie-dar of yours isn't infallible."

"True." I reached into my tote and pulled out the invitation addressed to Duke and Alice. "But if you don't feel better by tomorrow, you might not be able to come to the party."

Alice frowned at the white envelope. "What party?"

"Your sister's eightieth birthday party," I said.

Lucille squeaked our direction with a coffee carafe, her eyes widening at the envelope in my hand. "Did I hear something about a party?"

Yes, and I didn't have an invitation with her name on it.

"Eleanor's eightieth birthday," Alice said to Lucille. "I forgot all about it. Can you imagine that?"

Lucille refilled Alice's cup. "You've been a little under the weather. You're entitled to forget a couple of things."

She turned to me expectantly, waiting. I knew it wasn't to see if I wanted a coffee refill.

"It's just a barbeque," I said. "Family and a few friends." I hoped she would get the hint.

She did, loud and clear. And by Lucille's pained expression I might as well have backed over her with my car.

Good grief. I reached into my tote for the envelope addressed to Gladys, pulled out the embossed invitation and handed it to Lucille.

Sorry, Gladys. "I hope you'll be able to make it."

Lucille beamed and slipped the invitation into her front pocket. "I wouldn't miss it!"

"Good save," Duke whispered in my ear as Lucille squeaked away. "We never would have heard the end of that one."

And he would have never let me forget it. No, thank you.

Duke ambled toward the grill. "Mornin', Steve."

My heartbeat quickened at the mention of Steve's name. Stupid dream.

Now was as good a time as ever to complete my delivery service duty, so I slid the white envelope addressed to him onto the counter, next to his coffee cup. "With compliments from my mother."

Steve glared at it like it was an invitation to a baby shower.

"She's throwing a birthday party for Gram," I said.

He folded the invitation into his back pocket. "You couldn't just tell me about it?"

"Hey, don't shoot the messenger."

The silver bell over the door jingled as Jake Divine walked in. He gave me a friendly wave, kicking my pulse into hyperdrive.

I locked onto Steve's gaze. "Jake's here."

"And probably not to see you. I know I'm wasting my breath, but try to act normally."

Act normally. Sure, I could do that.

Maybe.

Steve drained his coffee mug. "I could use some more coffee."

"Uh-huh," I muttered, staring at Jake as he swung a leg around the barstool two down from Steve.

Jake smiled as bright and sunny as the summer morning. "Good morning!"

His cheerful demeanor didn't set off any warning signs to suggest that he was doing anything more than stopping in for some breakfast before work. But since I had just paid a visit to his mother yesterday, I doubted that he had a sudden hankering for bacon and eggs.

"Morning," I said, suddenly spitless.

He cocked his head. "Do you work here?"

"Uh...I help out some."

"Lucky me," he said with a predatory smile.

And unlucky me.

Since Lucille was busy giving the Gray Ladies their checks, I plopped a menu and a white mug in front of Jake and reached for the carafe. "Coffee?"

"Never touch the stuff."

Steve pushed his mug at me. "I do."

My hand shook as I filled Steve's coffee mug.

"Relax," Steve whispered.

Like that could happen.

Jake's gaze tracked me as I returned the carafe to the warmer. "Will I see you in class tomorrow?" he asked.

Heck no. "Maybe. If I can get away."

Jake nodded, assessing, appraising. He raised his water glass to me. "I'll look forward to tomorrow then."

Wow, this guy was good. I had a feeling that the petite blonde closing in on us like a buff swat team of one thought so, too.

"Fancy meeting you here." Suzy possessively placed a hand on Jake's shoulder and leveled her ice blue gaze at me. She smiled, a thin veil over the stormy flash of anger I'd just witnessed.

She waved a green order ticket at me. "Would you mind ringing me up? I'm in a bit of a hurry." She turned to Jake. "See you later."

"Later," he said, winking at me.

Criminy! Did he have to act so cavalier in front of his girlfriend?

I followed Suzy to the cash register. With a frosty glare, she handed me the order ticket and a crisp ten dollar bill. "What are you doing?"

Huh? "Making change."

"You know what I mean."

"Just now, with Jake?"

She squinted at me with the same look of disdain as the master chef who had once referred to my pumpkin banana mousse as "barfait." He was right, of course. I should have rethought the pumpkin.

I didn't need to rethink anything having to do with Jake. I needed to get away from him—his crazy girlfriend, too.

"Steve and I were just talking with Jake," I said.

"Steve and you…." The tension in Suzy's thin lips eased into a cool smile. "Good, because Jake isn't for you."

It didn't look like Jake would be the one for her, either, but I couldn't exactly inform her that it was because her boyfriend was destined for some big, hairy dude in cell block D.

Suzy slipped her change into her wallet and smiled sweet as one of my grandmother's sugar cookies. "Have a great day."

The odds of that happening were only slightly better than me being able to fit into my little black dress in the harsh light of day.

As Suzy started for the door, I raced to the kitchen to make a getaway to the courthouse, but before I had a chance to pull off my apron, Lucille rounded the corner.

"Did you hear the news?" she asked, her face flushed.

Duke and Alice turned to face Lucille.

"Peggy was rushed to the hospital this morning. The girls were just telling me that she felt tingling in her left arm, so Carmen took her to the ER. They're running tests, but it looks like she had a heart attack."

Alice took a sharp breath. "Oh dear."

Lucille nodded. "If I were her husband, I'd be standing vigil over my wife the next couple of nights," she announced, ladling Steve's oatmeal into a bowl.

I hated agreeing with the resident conspiracy theorist, but since all the murders had taken place after midnight, an all-night vigil seemed like a good precaution.

"Here we go again," Duke said with a groan as he plated a stack of pancakes.

Not if I could help it.

I glanced through the cutout window in front of Duke and met the inquiring eyes of Jake Divine. He crooked his finger at me.

I swallowed the growing lump in my throat and took the bowl of oatmeal from Lucille. "I'm heading that way." And I didn't want her to. The last thing we needed was for Peggy to be offered up as the killer's next victim because of Lucille's loose lips.

Steve sipped his coffee as he watched me round the corner.

I set the bowl in front of Steve and turned to Jake. "I have to go to work, but I'm sure your order will be up in a couple of minutes."

"Never mind that. Did I just hear that Peggy had a heart attack?" Jake asked without an iota of emotion.

Shit. And Steve thought I had a loud *inside voice.*

"I really don't know," I said in little more than a whisper, my chest fluttering with butterflies ready to take flight to the nearest exit. "Lucille doesn't always get her facts straight, so I wouldn't make too much out of anything you might have heard."

"I'll call the hospital when I get to work. If it was a heart attack, I'm sure Arlene will want to send flowers." He punctuated the statement with a charmer's smile, but his dark eyes held as much warmth as my ex-husband's when he handed me the keys to his Jaguar.

"Flowers are nice." But a bodyguard would make a more useful gift.

I locked eyes with Steve as Lucille delivered Jake's breakfast order.

Steve shook his head.

Walk away, Char.

I excused myself, grabbed my tote and sprinted to the parking lot, where I promptly threw up.

Chapter Twenty

Wanda McCormick did a double take when I stood at the police station counter a half hour later. "You look a little green around the gills. Are you okay, hon?"

I was a lot better than Peggy was going to be if Steve didn't put a 24-hour watch on Jake Divine.

"I'm fine. I just need to speak with Steve for a few minutes."

A few seconds after Wanda relayed the message, he opened the security door. "It didn't take long for you to get here."

I stepped past him, inhaling a note of menthol from his aftershave. "What are we going to do about Peggy?" I asked on the way down the hall to the Investigation Division.

Steve closed his office door and took a seat behind his uncluttered metal desk. "*We* aren't going to do anything."

"Fine. Then at least tell me that you'll put a tail on Jake Divine."

"You watch too much TV."

"Okay, then do whatever you need to so that if he makes a move on Peggy, you can arrest him."

"I don't think you need to worry about Peggy."

She was over seventy, had connections to the senior center, and her husband was in the same bowling league as Norm and Ernie. Not that I was all that crazy about Lucille's bowling league theory, but given everything I'd learned since the morning Trudy had died, I didn't want to take any chances.

"You were there," I reminded Steve. "Jake heard everything Lucille said. What if Peggy becomes his next target?"

Steve glanced at his Timex and pushed out of his chair. "I have a meeting in a few minutes, but I can tell you that you're making too much out of this."

As usual, he was telling me the truth, just not the whole truth.

"I'm making too much out of the fact that Peggy's going to be a sitting duck in the hospital?"

He blew out a breath. "Have you seen her recently?"

"She was at Jake's aerobics class yesterday."

"An aerobic workout—so, until this morning, she seemed pretty healthy. Could you have said the same for Trudy?"

"No, but—"

"Then don't worry about Peggy Como. I'm sure she's in good hands at the hospital."

That made intellectual sense, but I worked more from gut instinct, and my instincts told me to be wary of anything Jake Divine might say or do. And since he seemed very interested in Peggy's condition, I couldn't help but worry about where that interest might lead.

"I have to go," Steve said, shrugging his shoulders into

a midnight blue blazer.

I followed him out of his office.

"Be good," he said as he held the security door open for me. "And promise me that you'll stay away from Jake Divine and the senior center."

I raised my right hand. "I swear I won't go to the senior center." Fortunately, he didn't mention the hospital.

∽

After spending the rest of the morning sitting in on Lisa's interviews with two additional less than reliable witnesses to the aggravated assault case, we broke for lunch and I made tracks to Duke's.

Aunt Alice pulled off her apron the instant I stepped through the kitchen door. "Good. I want to get to Norm's before the macaroni and cheese gets cold."

"You made mac and cheese?" I loved my great-aunt's mac and cheese. All the carbs and every bit of the fat. Definitely not heart-healthy diet food, and I didn't care. Especially now that I knew I didn't have to worry about Warren Straitham administering some vigilante justice on me for not following his dietary advice.

"It's for Norm," she admonished, pointing at a blue and white insulated cooler on the table. "You're on a diet, remember?"

Like my growling stomach needed the reminder.

I set the plastic cooler with the mac and cheese and the apple pie in the back seat of the Jag and held the passenger door open for Alice.

With her eyes squeezed shut, my great-aunt held her breath as she eased herself into the bucket seat.

"The 'hitch in your giddy-up' looks like it's getting worse," I said.

Alice glared at me as she reached for the seatbelt. "It'll go away. I just need to get off my feet for a little while."

Right. That was wishful thinking at best.

"I know you don't want to see Dr. Straitham," I said as I slid into the driver's seat, "but we could swing by the clinic across the street from the hospital and—"

"No! I'm fine."

"Uh-huh. And people think I'm a bad liar."

Closing her eyes, Alice leaned back against the headrest. "I'm just fine," she muttered as I pulled out of the parking lot.

I had the distinct impression that I wasn't the one in the car she was trying to convince.

After a silent five-minute drive up the hill past the hospital and a right on J Street, I parked in front of the Bergeson's modest rambler.

Alice frowned at the Buick sedan parked in the driveway.

I didn't recognize the car. "Belong to someone you know?"

"Bonnie Haney. Damned vulture. Swooping in the second Trudy's out of the picture."

"Maybe she's being neighborly and is checking in on him. Like you are."

Alice scowled.

Yeah, I didn't believe it, either.

I pulled the cooler from the back seat and opened the passenger door.

Staring out the windshield, Alice hugged her arms to her chest. "I'll wait here...and stay off my feet."

Fine by me. If she was right about Norm's visitor, it would be easier for me to talk to Mrs. Haney without my great-aunt getting huffy and accusing her of staking a claim on Norm.

Seconds after I rang the doorbell, Norm Bergeson swung the front door open.

He stood a little taller than a week ago Saturday, like a weight on his shoulders had been lifted. His light blue eyes, magnified by his thick glasses, looked bloodshot—I suspected from a lack of sleep.

"Well, at least my visitors are starting to get a little younger," he said with a brittle smile.

"Hi, Mr. Bergeson. My Aunt Alice wasn't quite up to coming in, but she thought you might enjoy the sour cream apple pie and mac and cheese she baked for you."

He stood on the front step and gave Alice a wave. "Don't tell her that I've already got a refrigerator full of macaroni. I'll be happy to take the pie off your hands, though."

After Norm ushered me in, I locked gazes with a less than pleased Virginia Straitham sitting in his living room.

Holy cannoli! I'd just caught the self-appointed matchmaker in the act.

Bonnie Haney waved to me from the loveseat opposite Virginia's chair. It was a good thing that Aunt Alice was out in the car because she would have combusted at the sight of Trudy's silver-plated tea service sitting on the coffee table in front of Bonnie.

"Sorry to interrupt," I said, my heart racing as Virginia

frowned at me like I was a pesky wasp buzzing her silver-streaked beehive.

Norm led the way to the kitchen. "You're not interrupting. We were just talking about old times."

On legs rubbery with adrenaline, I carried the cooler to the kitchen counter and breathed in the familiar aroma of vanilla and brown sugar. Someone had been baking—Alice's apple pie had competition.

"Old times?" I asked. With Bonnie Haney?

Unlike Ernie, Norm didn't hang out at the senior center, and as far as I knew, Bonnie and Trudy weren't close friends. Other than an acquaintance with Virginia Straitham, I itched to learn what Norm and Bonnie had in common.

I set the pie tin next to a cooling coffee cake on the tile counter, and Norm pulled a fork out of a drawer.

"Ancient times, back in my twenties when I worked in the maintenance department at the hospital in Port Townsend." He scooped out a forkful of apple pie and shut his eyes as he chewed. "Tell Alice she hasn't lost her touch," he said, stabbing another bite.

I was more interested in where he was going with his story about working at the hospital. "So, you knew Mrs. Haney back then?"

He nodded. "Her husband, Buck, was my boss for a couple of years until he went into business for himself. Shortly after that I became head of the department."

"I didn't realize you two went back that far."

"We all did."

"Who all?"

He smiled, bittersweet. "Buck and Bonnie, Ginny and

Warren, me and Trudy. We all met there."

What? "Virginia Straitham worked at that hospital?"

"Fresh out of nursing school, I think."

"She's a nurse?" A nurse—someone who would have lots of experience administering injections.

Norm looked past me. "Isn't that right, Ginny? Wasn't PT General your first job out of nursing school?"

I froze, my pulse pounding in my ears, as Virginia sauntered into the kitchen with the silver tea pot. For a big woman, she moved quietly.

"That's right." She filled an electric kettle from the tap. "Seems like a million years ago."

Norm's eyes misted. "Seems like yesterday."

I only cared about the here and now, especially since I suddenly had a suspect who probably knew a dozen ways to kill a patient without leaving a trace.

Bonnie entered the kitchen and made a beeline to the apple pie. "Oh, doesn't that look delicious." She patted Norm on the hand. "We should probably use a plate, though. Don't you think?"

With a sigh punctuating his thoughts, Norm walked around to the other side of the counter, hunkered down on one of the barstools, and cupped his chin with his palm.

Oblivious to the annoyance radiating from Norm, Bonnie smiled at me as she reached for the plates. "Will you be joining us for tea?"

I'd seen all I wanted to see, so I took that as my cue to leave. "Alice is outside, waiting in the car, so I need to get going."

Bonnie's eyes brightened as if a fluorescent bulb had clicked on in her head. "You and Alice wouldn't be heading to the hospital from here, would you?"

I would be later, but I had no intention of tipping off Virginia Straitham to that fact. "We hadn't planned to. Why?"

"I have a get well gift for Peggy in the car." Bonnie's thin lips flattened. "Of course, you've heard about her heart attack."

Virginia clucked her tongue. "I kept telling Peggy that she needed to pay more attention to her diet. All that cheese. Warren warned her that with her high cholesterol she needed to change her ways, but did she listen?"

I shut the lid of the cooler so she couldn't see the macaroni and cheese I planned to scarf down for lunch.

Bonnie pressed her hand on Virginia's shoulder. "I'm sure she'll be okay. Maybe this will serve as a warning— something that will encourage her to make a few lifestyle changes."

"Maybe," Virginia said, solemnly staring out the kitchen window. "But not all of us listen to warnings."

My gut told me she wasn't referring to Peggy's last checkup.

With Norm sitting at the counter, I couldn't very well ask Virginia any leading questions about what warning signs Trudy might have received, so I grabbed my lunch box, said my goodbyes, and hightailed it to the front door.

"Thank you so much for coming," Bonnie said, acting the part of the perfect hostess as she opened the door for me.

I felt like telling her to not get too cozy in that role. Once Norm learned the truth about Trudy's death, it wouldn't matter what old times he, Bonnie, and Virginia

had shared. That tie would no longer be binding, and he'd
be telling them to get the hell out of his kitchen.

Back in the Jag, I tried to convince Aunt Alice to let
me take her to the clinic across from Chimacam Memorial.
Since she stubbornly insisted that she just needed to stay
off her feet for a little while, I drove her home. After fixing
her a cup of tea and making her promise to call me if
she changed her mind, I went back to Duke's to fill my
stomach with mac and cheese and my head with the latest
scuttlebutt from the hospital.

Lucille frowned when she saw me pull the untouched
casserole dish from the cooler. "I thought Alice baked that
for Norm."

"She did, but his refrigerator was full so he bequeathed
it to me." I grabbed two white bowls and pulled out a
couple of forks from the utensil drawer. "We just won't
tell her."

Lucille shot me a conspiratorial grin as she joined me
at the table.

Duke glanced back over his shoulder. "Did you take
Alice home?"

"Yep. She said she was going to rest, but you and I
both know that she needs to see a doctor."

He nodded. "Try telling her that."

I had. Several times.

"You know why she won't go," Lucille said with her
mouth full. "She's still convinced that Doc Straitham killed
Rose and Trudy. And that alibi his *girlfriend* gave him? She
doesn't buy it. I'm not so sure that I do, either."

"How do you know about him having an alibi?" There
was no way that Steve would have fed that tasty morsel to

Gossip Central.

Lucille's coral painted lips curled into a satisfied smile. "I have my sources."

Not always reliable, but if one of the Straithams was killing the doctor's patients, I couldn't afford to be picky about where her information came from.

"What else do your sources tell you?"

"Nothing substantial about his lady friend, but Cindy made it sound like it's somebody at the hospital."

When I'd spoken to Cindy Tobias on Monday, she had been willing only to mention seeing Dr. Straitham's car. Because she didn't want to get anyone in trouble, or because she was covering for a coworker?

"Did she mention any names?"

Lucille shook her head. "No names, but I think it's a nurse. It would be typical of the doc. Always getting a new car every couple of years. I wouldn't be a bit surprised to find out that Warren wanted to trade Ginny in on a newer model."

I stabbed a crusty bit of cheese with my fork. "What else have you heard? Anything new on Peggy's condition?"

"Cindy was here for lunch a half hour ago. Said it didn't look serious, but it sounded like they were going to keep Peggy overnight for observation."

I could only hope that Steve was right—that Peggy would be in good hands at the hospital.

Lucille blanched as if she had read my mind. "That'll make her a sitting duck."

I know. "Not if her husband is with her."

"Sylvia was by Howard's side that entire night. Look what happened to him!"

I dropped my fork, my appetite gone.

Duke scowled at us. "How many lunch breaks are we taking today?"

Rolling her eyes, Lucille leaned closer. "I'll be dipped if I'm going to let anyone get to Peggy tonight."

I pushed away my bowl. "If you take the first shift, I'll take the second. Try to keep a low profile, though. And no weapons."

"Damn," Lucille grumbled.

"It won't help Peggy if someone calls security about a crazy woman waving a gun around and you're escorted out of the hospital."

Lucille shrugged. "Whatever."

"No one will try anything in front of a witness. All we have to do is stay awake." I yawned. I'd have a much better chance of staying awake if I could squeeze in a two-hour power nap after dinner.

Lucille nodded. "Sounds like a plan. I can't stay awake much past ten, though." She downed the last of her coffee. "Even on this swill."

It sounded like a plan to me, too. Not much of one, but if Peggy were still alive in the morning, it was good enough.

Chapter Twenty-One

After I climbed the courthouse steps to the third floor, I saw Jake Divine sitting alone on a yellow chair in the hall across from the County Prosecutor's office door.

Tendrils of his hair looked slightly damp like he'd showered before he changed into a pair of black jeans and a white oxford shirt.

His eyes widened in recognition. "You were the one."

"Excuse me?" I asked, my heart thudding as if I'd just finished running up the stairs.

"My mother called me. You talked to her yesterday."

Guilty as charged.

I met the gaze of the Sheriff's Deputy staring at us from twenty feet away. He seemed even less impressed with me than usual, but I took some comfort in the knowledge that backup was seconds away if I needed it.

"Who the hell are you?" There was no trace of the charmer left in Jake's voice. Instead, he sounded like a recalcitrant adolescent. "And where do you get off asking my mother a bunch of questions about me?"

"I was simply doing a background check," I said, trying to maintain what little composure I still possessed. "It's part of my job here." Sort of.

Jake leaned toward me, tension coiled in him like a cobra, ready to strike at the slightest provocation. "If you want to know anything, you ask me and leave my family out of it."

Since he was sitting in the hallway like the two witnesses I had interviewed with Lisa Arbuckle earlier this morning, I had a feeling I'd be doing exactly that and a lot sooner than he thought.

Lisa stepped to the office doorway. "Mr. Divine, sorry to keep you waiting."

Jake stood, towering over the petite Deputy Prosecutor as she introduced herself.

Lisa turned to me. "Do you have time to sit in on this?"

I wouldn't have missed it. "All the time you need."

I followed Lisa and Jake to the conference room opposite Ben's office and took a seat next to Lisa.

Like with all the other witness interviews she'd conducted in the last few days, Lisa poured Jake a glass of water from a plastic carafe at the center of the table and tried to make him comfortable with some preliminary chitchat.

He folded his arms over his chest and sat sullenly, making it abundantly clear she was wasting her time.

"Mr. Divine," Lisa said. "I've read the statement you gave to the police and have a few more questions for you."

He slanted an angry glare my way. "Does she have to be here?"

Lisa and I exchanged glances.

"Do you know one another?" she asked me.

"A little," I said. "I've taken a couple of his classes

at the senior center." I left out the part about visiting his mother to dig up some dirt on him and hoped that Jake would do the same.

Lisa smiled politely across the table at Jake. "I can't see how that should present much of a problem, can you, Mr. Divine?"

Jake shrugged a shoulder. "Can we just get on with it?"

"Fine." Lisa opened the manila file folder on the table in front of her and flipped to a page of handwritten notes. "Now, let's go over the early morning events of May 19th. You'd said that you went to the club with a few of your friends. Is that correct?"

"Not exactly," Jake said. "I worked that night, had dinner with a girl I know, then I met up with some of my friends there."

A girl—did he mean Suzy? It seemed strange that someone his age would refer to her as a girl. Then again, from where I sat there wasn't much about Jake Divine that seemed all that typical.

"It says here that you're a personal trainer in addition to being the Assistant Activity Director at the senior center," Lisa said.

Jake sat up a little straighter. "That's right."

"Who were you working with that night?" I asked.

His jaw tightened. "A client."

That narrowed it down. "Someone you know from your job at the senior center?"

"Yeah."

"Your client's name, please?"

Lisa's eyebrows arched—a little warning sign that I was taking us down a road she hadn't planned to travel. But this could be an avenue to the truth about what was going on at the senior center, so she might as well come along for the ride.

Jake blew out a breath. "Peggy Como."

Peggy. Where Jake went, trouble seemed to follow.

"And where do you work with your clients for these one-on-one sessions?" I asked.

"Usually, their home. If they have a gym membership, we go there."

Peggy didn't look like someone who had ever seen the inside of an athletic club. "Where did you work with Peggy Como?"

"Her home."

"What time were you there?"

"We started around seven and I left a few minutes after eight."

"Was her husband there?" I asked, nodding as I got the wrap it up signal from Lisa.

Jake frowned. "I think he was bowling."

How convenient. "What is the nature of your relationship with Peggy Como?"

"My relationship? I'm her trainer."

"Is that the full extent of your relationship?" I tried to keep the innuendo out of my voice.

"She's old enough to be my grandmother! What the hell kind of question is that?"

It was the kind of question to get an emotional read on him, and I'd just hit pay dirt.

I smiled politely. "Would you please answer the question?"

He took a deep breath. "I have a working relationship

with Peggy Como. She's a nice lady who wanted to lose a few pounds, and she hired me to help her."

True.

I had a sinking feeling that his *special* services might not be as special as I'd been led to believe.

"And what about your relationship with Virginia Straitham?" I sensed anger, tension at the mention of her name. "How would you characterize that?"

"What's that got to do with anything?" he demanded, raising his voice.

Lisa shifted her gaze to me like I'd better come up with a good answer and fast.

"It's just that you seem to be a jack-of-all-trades at the senior center, and since Mrs. Straitham recommended you for that job, I was wondering if she ever asks you to do the occasional odd job for her?"

His eyes narrowed to dark slits. "Like what?"

"Like a job within a few blocks of the club," I said to Jake. "Around two a.m. on the 19th."

"A job?" he repeated, a sneer of contempt tugging at his lips. "I don't know what you mean."

"Did she give you an errand or ask you to do anything after you left the club?"

"No. Why the hell would she?"

Ever since Norm had told me that Virginia Straitham had been a nurse, I'd been asking the same question. Why would she need Jake? He'd be a loose end—a liability she couldn't afford in the dangerous game she was playing.

Jake raked his fingers through his hair. "After Gabe and that crazy chick got into it in front of the club, I didn't want to stick around, so I headed home."

I believed him. The services Jake offered might be a little questionable, but he was no killer for hire.

Lisa clicked her pen, signaling that my time at the wheel had just run out. "Mr. Divine, let's talk about what you saw at the club that night, shall we?"

Jake spent the next few minutes giving her a blow-by-blow account that generally supported Shea's story.

After a couple of follow up questions, Lisa turned to me. "Anything else?"

Since Jake might have witnessed more than just a knife fight that night, "Actually, yes." But what I wanted to know concerned my case, not hers. "If you have some place you need to be, you probably don't need to need to stay for this."

The tight quirk at a corner of the Deputy Prosecutor's mouth told me I'd taken a flying leap beyond my role as a departmental assistant.

Lisa stood and slipped the folder under her arm. "Thank you, Mr. Divine." She turned and pointed her jaw at me. "See me when you're done here."

Swell. I already knew that I'd ticked her off. With any luck, not enough for her to complain to Frankie about me.

After Lisa shut the conference room door behind her, I smiled across the table at Jake. "I have a couple of things I'd like to go over with you."

Jake slumped in his seat. "What else can I tell you? I've already gone over everything."

"I know, but something else happened that night, so I'm hoping you can help us connect a few dots."

Jake stared longingly at the door like a child given a timeout.

"So, after you went out to dinner with your girlfriend…"
I waited for him to give me a name.

"Kim."

I stared at him in disbelief. "Kim from the cafe?"

"Yeah?"

"Are you still going out with her?" And if Suzy knew,
why was she telling *me* to stay away from her man?

"Are you trying to tell me that you care?" Jake asked
smugly, his mouth curling into a tight smirk.

"How about if you just answer the question."

"We're not exactly going steady if that's what you're
trying to find out."

Jerk. If I hadn't seen him on the dance floor with Suzy,
I would never have believed there was anything between
them.

"So, you and Kim were on a date, then you took her
home and went on to the club around midnight."

"Right."

"Did you see anybody in the area who didn't look like
they belonged there? Anything unusual?"

"Besides a knife fight?"

I forced a smile. "Besides the knife fight."

He shook his head. "When I was heading home, I
thought I saw Mrs. Straitham's car go by, but other than
that, the streets were pretty dead."

"When was that?"

"Around twelve forty-five." Jake rubbed his forehead,
and frowned at me like I was giving him a headache. "You
know, I already told the detective all this shit. Aren't you
guys all on the same side?"

Apparently not.

After showing Jake the door, I made a quick side trip to Lisa's office to do some damage control. Since she looked like she'd been sucking on a lemon for the last ten minutes, I knew that hijacking her interview with Jake Divine hadn't helped my chances of seeing day thirty of my thirty-day trial.

"Would you care to explain what happened in there?" she asked.

To avoid yet another reminder that Trudy's case wasn't official, I tiptoed around the truth. "I needed to gather some information for an unrelated coroner case." I hoped she wouldn't ask which one. "Sorry if I overstepped."

"See that it doesn't happen again," Lisa said, sounding as frosty as my ex-mother-in-law. "And shut the door on your way out."

Okay, I had a wedge of condescension pie coming. But a little dressing down was a price I'd willingly pay for a witness who might have seen Virginia Straitham's car in the vicinity of the hospital on the night Howard Jeppeson died.

I skulked back to my desk and called Steve's cell phone.

"I'm a little busy here," he said. "Let me call you back."

"Well, I'm busy, too, and you could have saved me a lot of time if you had told me that Jake wasn't a suspect."

"It's not my job to keep you informed, Chow Mein."

"Obviously. Just remember, pal, that can work both ways."

"Meaning what?"

"Meaning that I don't have to share what I find out with you."

"Char, considering what you've found out so far, that

wouldn't be a great loss."

"Thanks a lot!" I disconnected and slumped back in my desk chair.

Irritating man. Heather deserved him. They could irritate the hell out of one another for eternity for all I cared.

So, I was wrong about Jake and Dr. Straitham. Like the hotshot detective had never arrested the wrong suspect before.

Couldn't he just take Virginia Straitham in for questioning? If Jake was right and he had seen Virginia's car that night....

"Shit." I redialed Steve's number.

"You know how I told you I was busy," he said after one ring.

"Yeah?"

"I'm still busy."

"This will only take a minute."

He blew out a breath. "Then start talking."

"I'm concerned that Virginia Straitham might make a move on Peggy tonight—"

"I don't think that's something you need to worry about."

"But—"

"It's not going to happen."

I lowered my voice. "Nothing will happen to Peggy or it's not Virginia Straitham?"

"I have to go."

"Steve." Silence. "Steve...?" More silence.

I stared down at my cell phone. *Call ended.* "Shit!"

∽

After three hours of dreamless sleep in my grandmother's bed, I put on an old sweatshirt over my tank and pulled my hair back into a ponytail. Faint smears of black mascara accentuated the circles under my eyes, making me look like an extra from *Night of the Living Dead*. I swiped them away and added a swish of my mother's bronzer. Slightly ghoulish with sun-kissed cheeks—not the look I'd ordinarily go for, but good enough for guard dog duty.

By the time I'd wolfed down the roast chicken and gravy dinner Gram had kept warm in the oven for me and drunk half a pot of coffee, I felt locked and loaded for the night ahead.

All I had to do was sit outside Peggy's hospital room and stay awake. I might not have the world's greatest detecting skills, but I'd worked the graveyard shift as a pastry chef plenty of times and had years of experience with staying awake while the rest of the world slept.

I grabbed my denim jacket out of the hall closet.

My mother looked up from the fashion magazine she'd been reading while Gram snored in her recliner. "Where are you going?"

The less I said about going to the hospital in the middle of the night, the better. "Out."

She glanced at the clock. "It's almost ten. Kind of late to go out when you have to get up early for work tomorrow, isn't it?"

Since when did my mother pay attention to the hours I kept?

"It's not a date. It's just something I have to do for work."

"Dressed like that?" She tossed aside her reading glasses. "Are you're going on some sort of stakeout?"

"It's not a stakeout."

Marietta sat at the edge of the sofa. "But this has to do with Trudy's death, doesn't it?"

I didn't have time to play *Twenty Questions.* "I have to go." I grabbed my car keys from the kitchen table and headed for the door.

"Is this something dangerous?" she asked, closing the distance between us.

I sure hoped not. "I'll be fine."

I slid behind the wheel of the Jag and was about to shift into reverse when my mother climbed into the passenger seat.

"What are you doing?" I asked her.

"Riding shotgun."

"I'm going to be gone all night."

Her eyes widened. "*All* night? Seriously?"

"If you get sleepy or bored or have some sort of midnight rendezvous planned with Barry Ferris, I'm not bringing you home. And I don't have time to talk anymore about this."

Marietta fastened her seat belt. "Then we'd better get going."

I backed out of the driveway and glimpsed the light glowing in Steve's living room. Part of me wanted to pull over, pound on his front door and refuse to leave until he convinced me that I didn't need to worry about Peggy Como becoming Virginia's next victim. But I knew that would be a waste of time. He wasn't going to tell me anything and I was going to suffer Lucille's wrath if I didn't show up in the next five minutes, so I hit the accelerator to put any hesitation I felt in my rearview mirror.

"Oh, I almost forgot. I'm packin'," Marietta said, patting her Louis Vuitton tote bag.

I had a very bad feeling that she wasn't talking about a midnight snack. "Packing what?"

"Just a Taser, but it's better than nothing."

Lord help me. "Says you."

After all the coffee I'd sucked down, the last thing I needed was to come back from the bathroom and get tased by a mother with an itchy trigger finger. "Do you actually know how to use a Taser?"

"I had a training class a couple of years ago," she said, looking at her reflection in the visor mirror as she fluffed her cropped hair. "Where are we going anyway?"

"The hospital. Keep that thing in your bag. We don't want to have any accidents."

"Sugah, I've never shot anyone accidentally in my life. Well, I did hit the instructor in the ass, but he was a jerk and had it coming."

Criminy, it was going to be a long night.

Chapter Twenty-Two

"About damned time," Lucille grumbled when Marietta and I found her sitting outside of Peggy's hospital room. "I gotta pee."

Marietta sniffed, scanning the speckled blue-gray vinyl. "It smells like someone else did, too."

Lucille pushed herself out of her chair. "You get used to it."

"I seriously doubt that," my mother said under her breath.

"Just be grateful you were spared the play-by-play about Luther Purdy's prostate." Lucille scowled at the doorway across the hall. "I got to hear about his plumbing problems for two hours. Thank God Tina medicated him. At least the snoring helped keep me awake."

"Tina?" As in Tina Norton?

Lucille jabbed her thumb toward the nurses' station. "The little brunette down there."

I glanced at the petite woman in blue who had been on duty just hours before Rose Kozarek and Jesse Elwood died. I hoped Tina didn't have anywhere to run off to because she and I needed to take a stroll down memory lane.

"You brought your mom?" Lucille smirked. "What for, back up?"

"She wanted to help." And I couldn't get her out of my car.

"We're tag-teaming on this one," Marietta said, like it was a line from her old show. "And if there's any sign of trouble, I'm packin'."

Lucille's eyes widened. "Me, too. Whatcha got?"

Marietta fished a black leather case out of her bag. It looked innocuous enough until she unsnapped the cover. "Fifty thousand volts, six ounces, laser sight, stun feature. It's got it all."

"Sweet!" Lucille said, nodding with approval at the metallic pink Taser aimed at my belly button.

"Whoa!" I ducked into Peggy's doorway. "Careful where you point that thing."

"Don't be a wuss. Just look at what this baby can do." Marietta took a shooter's stance and shined a LED light into Luther's room. "It doubles as a flashlight. Cute, huh?"

Anything that could fire fifty thousand volts at Luther Purdy wasn't cute.

"I've got its daddy." Lucille pulled out a heftier black Taser from her patent leather handbag. "I call it the Intimidator. Not quite as stylish, but pretty dang effective as a motivator."

"The Intimidator—I like it," Marietta said, giving Lucille a fist bump.

The sight of Marietta and Lucille bonding over fifty thousand volts gave me the willies.

"I don't, and you need to put those things away before

we get tossed out of here." I peered over at the nurse's station and saw that Tina Norton had a telephone receiver to her ear, no doubt with security on speed dial. "Now!"

Lucille waved the Intimidator Tina's direction. "Hell, you don't have to worry about Tina. Her ex was the one who sold it to me. Said it used to be hers. He got it back in the settlement."

Which showed how boring I was. The only weapon my ex ever got from me was a can of mace I'd been too afraid to carry in my tote bag. "Just because she used to be a member of your Taser packin' mama club doesn't mean she wants anyone taking target practice in the hallway."

Lucille holstered her Taser and dropped it in her handbag. "Will you relax? She's good people, and she knows we're here to get Peggy through the night."

"You told her that?"

"Well, I've been sitting out here for the last four hours. I had to tell her something."

"What did she say when you told her?"

"Nothin' much. Said it made sense given everything that's been going on lately."

All the more reason for me to talk to Tina Norton as soon as possible, but first, I needed to complete tonight's changing of the guard. "Other than that, how did it go?"

"Aside from Luther, it's been real quiet the last couple of hours," Lucille said.

I glanced into Peggy's room. Illuminated only by the light from the hallway, it contained two beds, two chairs, and no husband—just a slumbering Peggy hooked up to a monitor silently displaying numbers and a steady, pulsing bright red heart. "How's Peggy doing?"

Lucille shrugged. "Must be doing okay. They're sending her home tomorrow."

"Peggy Como?" Marietta whispered, leaning into my shoulder as she slipped her holstered Taser back into her tote. "I don't understand. Why would anyone want to hurt Peggy?"

"Or Trudy or Rose," Lucille added.

My mother's face screwed into a Botox-resistant frown. "It doesn't make any sense."

Unless Virginia Straitham was responsible for five deaths in this hospital, and in the world according to Virginia, Bert Como deserved a wife who would follow doctor's orders.

"A lot of things don't make sense right now." Trudy, Rose, Howard, Bernadette, Mr. Elwood, my mother dating Barry Ferris.

Marietta patted my back, like that would make it feel better. Maybe it did. A little.

"What's the game plan?" she asked.

"I'll tell you what my plan is," Lucille said, pulling on a white cable knit sweater. "I'm gonna go home and catch the last half of *Law and Order*, but first I gotta hit the head."

I sat in one of the two chairs outside Peggy's room and watched Lucille wave at Tina as she squeaked her way down the hall. With Tina alone at the nurses' station and off the phone, it seemed like a perfect chance for me to take her pulse on what she thought was going on in her hospital.

My mother sat in the chair next to me. "Stay here," I told her. "Watch anyone who goes into Peggy's room. Any doctor, any nurse, any anybody."

She patted the bulge in her tote bag and saluted.

"Please don't shoot anybody until I get back," I said, heading for the nurses' station.

Tina looked up from the computer monitor she was sitting behind. The overhead florescent light didn't do the little bags under her eyes any favors. I shuddered to think about what it was doing to mine.

She squeezed out a shy smile as she looked past me. "I'm sorry. I have to ask. Was that Marietta Moreau with you?"

"Yep."

"I knew it."

"Would you like her autograph?" I wasn't above selling out my mother for some information. "When you have a couple of minutes, come on over and I'll introduce you."

"Oh, I wouldn't want to impose."

The wide-eyed spark of joy in her eyes told me Tina wouldn't need much arm-twisting.

"She enjoys meeting fans." Understatement of the year. "And we'll be here for a while, so you might as well say hello to her."

I leaned on the counter separating us. "My name is Charmaine by the way."

"Tina Norton," she said with a pleasant smile.

"Could I ask you a couple of questions?"

The smile disappeared and she broke eye contact. "I suppose."

"You worked the nights Rose Kozarek and Jesse Elwood died."

"How do you know—"

"I'm a Deputy Coroner and I've been looking into the

death of Trudy Bergeson. I'm concerned that the three deaths might be related."

She pressed her lips together as if she dared not say what she was thinking.

"You also were here the night of Trudy's death, weren't you?" I asked.

Tina squinted at her computer monitor like she wanted to jump inside it and disappear. "I've already told the police everything I know about that night."

It figured that Steve would have already talked to her. "I'm sure you have." And Steve won't share. "But if I could ask just a couple more questions it would really help with our investigation." I tossed in an earnest smile for good measure.

"If this is about Dr. Straitham, I'm quite sure he didn't have anything to do with those deaths," Tina said with a flush creeping into her cheeks.

She was very quick to jump to the conclusion that I wanted to talk about Dr. Straitham. "Why do you say that?"

"He wasn't here," she said softly.

"Neither were you unless you worked a very long shift."

"My shift ends at midnight." Eyes downcast, Tina pressed her palms together as if she were offering up a prayer. "Neither one of us was here."

The other woman. A small piece of this deadly puzzle clicked into place.

"I understand, but you may have seen something before you left."

"I don't remember seeing anything unusual," she said.

"Your initials are on a log that indicates that you were one of the last members of the staff here to see Rose

Kozarek and Jesse Elwood alive. Do you remember seeing anyone hanging around their rooms those nights?"

She shook her head. "We lock the main entrance at nine, so typically, aside from the staff, no one but immediate family is here that late."

Marietta and I had no trouble getting in through the emergency entrance. A nurse even held the door open for us. There's no way that Virginia would view a locked door as much of a deterrent.

"Did you happen to see Mrs. Straitham that night?"

"No, I'd remember that."

I didn't doubt for a second that Tina was telling the truth.

A light flashed on her computer monitor and she pushed out of her chair. "I'm needed by a patient. You'll have to excuse me."

I watched Dr. Straitham's lover pass another nurse as she walked down the other end of the hall. Tina moved quickly, with quiet, compact steps—the kind of silent footfalls that would be perfect for darting in and out of a room without disturbing the patient. Especially useful in the wee hours of the morning if the situation warranted some stealth.

Virginia Straitham was a much bigger woman. In a pair of flats with crepe soles was she capable of stealth mode? Maybe. She had certainly snuck up on me at Norm Bergeson's house. Add in the fact that there could easily be times when there was no one at the nurses' station with line of sight to a patient's room, and the killer didn't need to be extraordinarily sneaky. She just needed the opportunity to get in and get out unobserved. And with the elevator just thirty feet away, she could probably slip in and out of any one of these rooms, administer a deadly injection, and be off the second floor in less than a minute.

I pulled out my cell phone as I walked toward Peggy's room.

"Are you calling for backup?" my mother asked.

And Steve thought I watched too much TV. "No." I looked to see if the coast was still clear, then I punched a button to start the stopwatch feature on my phone.

I didn't want to give poor Peggy another heart attack, so I hesitated at the doorway for a moment to make sure that she was still asleep before moving closer to stand by her bedside. After waiting ten seconds I looked up and down the hallway from her doorway.

Marietta frowned at me. "What the heck are you doing?"

"Give me a minute." Even less if my theory proved true.

I walked to the elevator and pressed the *down* button. When the door opened I checked the elapsed time on my cell phone. Forty-one seconds.

I looked up, expecting to see an empty elevator. Instead, I locked eyes with Virginia Straitham. The air vacated my lungs as if I'd just been punched in the solar plexus.

Stepping around me like I was no more significant than an ant invading her picnic, she surveyed the hallway with a determined set to her jaw. Her emotions seemed to be on lockdown, giving her the appearance of a matronly Marine on a reconnaissance mission. After her gaze landed on Marietta, Virginia returned to the elevator.

Mission over or aborted? I couldn't read her.

She held the elevator door open. "Going down?"

"No, I...forgot something," I croaked, my throat wound tight with adrenaline.

With a dismissive glance, Virginia pressed a button and the elevator door closed.

Holy crap!

No need to panic. Nothing happened. Breathe.

My heart pounding, I slumped in the chair next to my mother.

"What's the matter with you?" she asked. "You look like you've seen a ghost."

"No ghost." But I may have just seen a murderer.

My grandmother was standing next to her gurgling coffeemaker when Marietta and I stepped through the kitchen door around six the next morning.

"Thank God!" Gram said, slapping her palm to the collar of her pink chenille robe. "Where have you two been? I hardly slept a wink last night, I was so worried."

I forced a smile. "If it's any consolation, we didn't get much sleep either."

"Where'd you go?"

"The hospital," my mother said, heading for the stairs.

Gram sharply inhaled. "Who died?"

"No one died." Since I hadn't been to work yet, at least no one that I knew of.

"We made sure of that," Marietta called out from the top of the staircase. "And now I'm going to bed."

Gram scowled at me. "This is about Trudy, isn't it?"

And Bernadette, Jesse, Rose and Howard. "Sort of."

Gram pointed an arthritic finger at my chest. "You need to let go of this thing about Warren Straitham. I don't care what you and Alice think you saw at the funeral, he couldn't have had anything to do with Trudy's death."

"I think you're absolutely right."

"Then what were you two doing at the hospital all night?"

"Lucille and I thought—"

"Lucille's involved in this caper?" Gram rolled her eyes. "Did you know that crazy woman carries a Taser in her handbag?"

I didn't have the heart to tell my grandmother that her daughter had just schlepped one upstairs.

"No one was tased last night, and we're all perfectly safe and sound."

"Thank the good Lord for small favors. Promise me that you'll never do anything like that again."

"Sorry to worry you, Gram." But until Virginia Straitham was arrested, I couldn't make any promises.

"I'm going back to bed." My grandmother shuffled to the stairs in her pink fuzzy slippers. "You should try to get some sleep, too."

I should also try to stick to my diet, but that wasn't going to happen either.

Since I had to be at work in less than two hours, I poured myself a cup of coffee and took it upstairs. After a fifteen minute shower, I dried my hair and did the flat iron thing, then crammed myself into a pair of control top pantyhose. I felt like a pork link sausage, but at least I could fasten the waistband button of the black pantsuit I'd worn to Trudy's funeral. I wanted Steve to take me seriously today and that required pants that weren't held together by a safety pin.

I stepped through Duke's kitchen door around seven-thirty.

Aunt Alice sat on her wooden stool and frowned at my pantsuit. "Who died?" she asked, sounding just like Gram.

"No one died. Can't a girl dress for work?"

She grunted. "You must want something."

Dang. Was I that obvious?

I grabbed an oatmeal raisin cookie from a cooling rack. "How do you feel?"

"Better," she said without looking up from fluting the edge of the marionberry pie on the table in front of her.

I wanted to believe my great-aunt, but she looked as pale as the flour dusting her worktable.

Lucille rounded the corner and grabbed a bowl. "Hey," she said, "anything happen after I left?"

I didn't want to light a match under Lucille by mentioning Virginia Straitham's appearance at the hospital, so I shook my head. "It was a pretty quiet night. We left around six."

"One of the girls told me Peggy will get discharged in an hour or two, so it looks like she's out of the woods." Lucille gave me a thumbs up sign, then squeaked away with a bowl of oatmeal. Since I could see Steve through the window over the grill, I had a good guess about that bowl's destination.

That meant that I needed to lose the cookie. No one takes anybody seriously when they're eating a cookie.

Duke turned to me as I reached for the plastic wrap

he kept on a shelf across from the grill. I braced for a wisecrack about my breakfast choice, a Free Lunch remark, something. Instead, he glanced back at Alice, deep furrows carved into in his forehead.

"How's she doing this morning?" I asked.

He shrugged. "She seems a little better. We got her something at Clark's to help her sleep last night."

Then, maybe she wasn't lying. My brain was so weary of chasing red herrings that I was more than happy to trust Duke's judgment when it came to my great-aunt.

I just wished that I could get Steve to trust mine where Virginia Straitham was concerned.

"I was thinking about making chili for tomorrow," Duke said, watching me as I covered the rest of my breakfast in plastic wrap.

He made chili every day. I felt like I was missing something. "Okay."

"Unless you want something else for the party."

The party! I'd forgotten all about it. "No, chili's terrific. Gram loves your chili."

That meant I needed to bake a cake tomorrow. And before that I needed to get paid, go shopping, and convince Steve that Virginia Straitham was a serial killer.

Good thing I was wearing my power suit. I had a feeling I was going to need it. Probably another cookie or three and a mocha latte, too.

At the moment I'd settle for a cup of Duke's coffee, especially since it gave me an excuse to sit down with Steve.

I took a deep breath, brushed the cookie crumbs from my lapels, and stepped around the corner. "Good morning," I said to Steve.

His gaze dropped to the suit, a smile playing at the corners of his mouth. "You look pretty good, all things considered."

I pulled a coffee cup from the rack. If I hadn't known that Duke would make me pay for breaking it against Steve's thick skull, I would have been tempted. "What's that supposed to mean?"

"I don't imagine you got much sleep last night."

"Since you didn't bother to stop by the hospital, I can't imagine how you could presume to know how much sleep I got."

"I was just finishing my morning run when you pulled into your grandmother's driveway."

Oh. Sometimes it was very unhandy to have him living across the street.

While I grabbed the coffee carafe and filled my cup, he pushed his empty one toward me.

"And Lucille mentioned your girl's night out," he said as I gave him a refill.

I didn't like his tone. "It wasn't like we were having fun."

"You could have listened to me and gotten a little more sleep."

"I might have if you'd done a little more talking."

Irritating man.

I came around the counter and took the seat next to him. "Peggy's supposed to go home in a couple of hours," I said, using his spoon to stir creamer into my coffee. "But that might not have been the case if we hadn't been there."

Steve turned to face me. "What's that supposed to mean?"

"I saw Virginia Straitham on the elevator."

"When was this?"

"A little before eleven."

"Huh," Steve grunted, his mouth full with oatmeal.

"If we hadn't been there…"

He swallowed. "Peggy would still be going home in a couple of hours."

"You didn't see Virginia on the elevator. She wasn't there in the middle of the night to deliver flowers."

"Maybe she was just looking for someone," he said, working on his oatmeal.

"Well, she found me, and clearly she wasn't happy about it because I foiled her plans."

"Chow Mein, I know you have a hard time believing this, but not everything is as it appears."

"I know what I saw."

"More like what you think you saw."

"Steve, she—"

"If you needed to see a certain doctor in the middle of the night, where would you go?"

"Well, if she had been looking for her husband, he wasn't there. And why would he be there around eleven? Tina Norton doesn't get off shift until midnight."

Steve reached for his wallet. "Then that would probably narrow down who Mrs. Straitham came to see."

"Shit." I had just saved the other woman from an angry encounter with the wife.

He patted me on the top of my head. "Have a nice day."

Chapter Twenty-Three

After I got off work, I spent two hours with my mother force-marching me into every grocery store in town before I dropped her off at a four-star marina restaurant for her dinner date with Barry Ferris. With Gram at her Friday night mahjong game, that gave me the house to myself.

Sleep beckoned, but since I knew I'd be counting murder victims of Virginia Stratham instead of sheep, I put away the groceries, changed into a tank top and my gauze skirt, and then called Donna to meet me at Eddie's for a drink.

"You should thank me," she said, resting her head on my shoulder as I sat next to her at the bar an hour later. "I saved you from a complete and utter dud."

"Who? Justin?"

Donna straightened and heaved a sigh. "Nice package but not much staying power if you know what I mean."

Eddie refilled my empty wine glass. "Some guys got it, some don't."

She waved him off when he offered her a refill. "And those who got it usually don't have to brag about it."

"Ouch!" Eddie winced. "Have you been talking to my

wife again?"

Donna smiled. "We do like to share some little secrets,"

"Sweetheart, it's not that little," he said with an evil grin.

When Eddie crossed the room to clear a table, Donna reached for her wallet. "I hate to drink and run but I told the girls at the salon that I'd meet them at the new club in Port Townsend by nine. Wanna come with and make a night of it?"

"I made a night of it last night," I said, fighting off a yawn. Once I got a couple of glasses of wine in me, all I wanted tonight was a date with the Sandman. "Have fun."

After saying goodbye to Eddie, Donna waved at me as she headed for the door.

I waved back and a dark-haired body builder type with bowling ball-sized biceps smiled at me a split-second before his eyes shifted to my boobs.

Averting my gaze, I sipped my wine. Despite the physical inventory the guy had just taken, I doubted Mr. Muscles would make a move on me. Donna was probably more his type.

"Can I buy you a drink?" he asked over Tom Petty and the Heartbreakers wailing through the overhead speakers.

Then again, Donna wasn't here.

I held up my wineglass. "Got one, thanks."

He picked up his beer bottle and slid onto the seat next to me. "I'm Jimmy. What's your name?"

"Char."

"Like Charlene?"

Close enough. "Sure."

He leaned an elbow against the bar. "Cute name for a

cute girl."

Was this guy for real?

There was definite male interest with the dilated pupils and the way he squared himself up to me, but a few beers could probably make Lucille look good to Jimmy.

He raised his bottle to Eddie to signal for another one. "Are you sure I can't buy you a drink?" Jimmy asked, smiling down at the girls under my lacey tank top.

What the heck. Another glass of wine would guarantee that I'd fall asleep the second I made contact with my pillow. "Maybe just one."

"Sorry I'm late, honey," Steve said, standing behind me, squeezing my shoulders.

I stiffened as he kissed me on the cheek and tightened his embrace. He angled against the bar, looking past me at Jimmy. "Who's your friend?"

I sighed. "This is Jimmy. He *was* keeping me company. Pretty good company, too."

"Thanks, Jimmy," Steve said. "I've got it from here."

"Sorry, man." Jimmy scooped up his beer bottle and scurried away like a wolf who had no intention of challenging this pack's alpha male.

I wriggled out of Steve's grasp. "That was completely uncalled for."

"Uh-huh." He threw a twenty on the counter. "Let's go."

I scowled at him. "I'm not done with my drink and after spending most of the last twenty-four hours with my mother, not to mention all your lack of assistance, I need it."

"I told you everything I could."

"Well, you could have been a little more specific."

"You want specific?" He emptied my wineglass in two gulps, then clasped his hand around my flabby bicep. "Come on."

Eddie picked up my empty glass. "You kids aren't having a fight in my bar, are you?"

"We are if he doesn't let go," I said, glaring at Steve.

He released my arm. "Happy?"

"Delirious!" I grabbed my tote and stormed toward the door. "What the hell is wrong with you?"

"Me! What was that back there?" Steve asked, hot on my heels.

I pushed the door open. "I could ask you the same thing!"

"Y'all come back now," Eddie called after us.

A light breeze cooled my overheated cheeks as I stalked to the side lot where I'd parked the Jag. "Go away, Steve."

His oxfords crunched on the loose gravel behind me. "Don't act like you're mad."

I spun on my heel to face him. "This isn't an act."

"You weren't interested in *Jimmy*."

"I could have been!"

"He wasn't your type."

I stabbed an index finger at his chest. "You don't get to decide who's my type!"

"If you want specifics then know that *Jimmy* only wanted one thing."

Like that was something that had escaped my notice.

Running his thumb over the strap of my tank top, Steve's gaze darkened.

If he was trying to get me even more hot and bothered,

he was doing a good job. "That guy had just sat down. You don't know…"

Steve's eyes shifted lower, surveying my breasts. "Trust me, any guy who sees you in this wants to see what's under the lace."

My mouth went dry. "You don't get to say that to me."

"Char—"

"You don't get to show up and pull my hair at Trudy's funeral when Heather is sitting right next to you, or offer me a ride in your truck when you're acting like one big happy family, or tell me which men I can have a drink with."

His gaze softened like a block of chocolate over a flame. Since I was a sucker for chocolate fondue, I felt my resolve melting and that scared the bejesus out of me.

"It's crossing the line." And I desperately needed him to stay on his side if I was going to have a prayer of staying on mine.

"Are you done?" he asked.

I took a shaky breath. "No."

"Too bad." He hooked his finger under the strap of my tank and pulled me close. His lips touched mine, feather-light, testing.

My brain screamed at me. *Mistake!*

He tried to deepen the kiss, but I pressed a palm to his chest to put some distance between us before I combusted. "What the hell are you doing?"

Steve raked his fingers through his hair. "Char—"

"You're one of my best friends, and you're screwing with my head when I haven't had any sleep! I don't want to sound whiny," and I knew that's exactly how I sounded, "but that's really unfair."

He blew out a wine-scented breath. "Right. We should continue this conversation after you've had some sleep."

Huh? The talking part or the other stuff? I felt like I'd been caught up in a whirlwind and my brain couldn't keep pace. All I knew was that chocolate fondue couldn't be on my diet.

He slipped his arm around my shoulder and led me to my car. "Let's get you home."

He held the driver's side door open for me as I slid behind the wheel. "I'll follow you."

I tightened my grip on the steering wheel. "That's really not necessary," I said, trying to sound casual. "Thanks to you I barely touched that second drink, so you don't have to see me home."

"Yeah, I sort of do. I live there."

∽

After tossing and turning half the night, I poured myself a glass of Chardonnay, put on my denim jacket over my nightshirt and went out the front door to sit on the porch swing. While I stared across the street at Steve's house as a cool breeze fluttered over me, a dog barked in the distance. At least I wasn't the only one awake in the neighborhood.

I heard the front door open and looked back to see my mother, barefoot and wearing one of my hooded sweatshirts over her satin negligee.

As if echoing my thoughts, the porch swing squealed in protest when she sat down next to me. "Can't sleep?"

I shook my head. "Too many things to think about."

She reached for my wineglass. "Me too." She took a sip and handed the glass back to me—the second time tonight someone had cut into my alcohol consumption. "How's Peggy?"

"She went home, so she's probably doing fine." And sleeping contentedly, unlike the two of us.

My mother nodded. "Our mission was accomplished then."

"Right."

Nothing was accomplished other than me discovering where Dr. Straitham's alibi came from. The rest of the *mission* had been a complete waste of time, like most everything I'd done the past week.

The porch swing squeaked as we swayed back and forth and shared the wine.

"What did you do tonight?" she asked.

"Nothing much." Had a fight with Steve, then kissed and sort of made up. "How 'bout you? How was dinner?"

"Fine." Hugging her legs to her chest, she huddled next to me for several silent seconds like Gram's tabby cat, only without the flicking tail to torment me. "Barry wants to get married."

"What? You've known him for less than two weeks."

"Actually, we met when you were in high school."

"So you saw him once for five minutes! That doesn't count."

Marietta sniffed. "Well, if you're gonna split hairs, I also bumped into him at your graduation."

"Okay, ten minutes. Mother, this is crazy. You just got divorced."

"I know."

"You don't need to get involved with anyone right now."

"I know."

"He's a nice guy and he's screwing with you." Just like Steve was screwing with me, making me second guess everything I thought I knew to be true.

She heaved a sigh. "Yes, he is, and he's good at it too."

Okay, maybe not screwing with her in exactly the same way.

Marietta took the wineglass from my hand and drained it. "I think I'm going to need more of this stuff if I'm going to get any sleep tonight."

I pushed off the porch swing. "I'll get the bottle."

Six hours later, Gram walked into the kitchen with Steve while I stood at the counter, whipping the vanilla buttercream frosting for her birthday cake.

Steve and I locked gazes, and he shot me an easy smile. Other than the fact that I felt like all the air had been sucked out of the room, it was as if last night had never happened.

"Help yourself to coffee, Stevie," Gram said.

"Thanks." He handed her a sparkly, rainbow-striped gift bag. "Happy birthday, Eleanor."

Gram beamed. "Should I open it now, or wait until later?"

"I'd open it now," he said, giving my ponytail a tug on his way to the coffeepot.

What the hell? Were we just buddies again?

Gram squealed with delight at the Port Merritt Police Department cap and coffee mug he'd given her. While she smashed down her peach gelato curls with the cap, Steve grabbed a ceramic cup and filled it from the second pot of French roast I'd brewed that morning.

"I feel like I need to eat a doughnut!" Gram announced, the apples of her cheeks glowing. "Then, maybe later, arrest somebody."

"If I were you, I'd start by rousting the vagrant you've got sleeping on the front porch," Steve said, stirring some milk into his coffee.

Gram blinked. "What vagrant?"

"Mom's out on the porch swing," I said.

"For pity's sake!" Gram rushed to the front door. "What's she doing out there?"

Last I looked she was snoring.

Setting his coffee down, Steve leaned against the counter and dipped a finger into the bowl of frosting. "I didn't have any time to do real shopping," he said apologetically.

I couldn't look at him. "She's happy."

He licked the buttercream from his finger. "Mmm, it's good."

"Don't sound so surprised," I muttered, spreading frosting over the first layer of Gram's cake. "I can do some things well."

"I never said you couldn't."

"Right. You only insinuated."

"What's your problem?"

I glared at him. Aside from having a wine hangover, my former biology teacher as a potential daddy, and a murderer on the loose, I was looking at it. "Absolutely nothing. I'm perfectly fine."

"Sure."

He brushed my cheek with the pad of his thumb and I stiffened.

"What are you doing?" I asked, my face aflame like he'd just flipped the *on* switch of my schoolgirl crush. Again.

"Relax. It was just a little bit of flour." The laugh lines etched at the corners of his eyes deepened as his gaze swept my face. Unfortunately, I didn't have an ounce of makeup on.

When Steve reached for his coffee cup, I turned my focus back to the birthday cake. "Have a seat," I said, trying to exercise some self-control instead of staring at the lips that had kissed mine last night. "Unless you need to get going." Which would really help in the self-control department.

"I'm in no hurry. And I'd like to finish my coffee first."

If he cared about me at all, he needed to drink faster.

The front door clicked shut. I hoped that meant I'd have the birthday girl back in the kitchen to divert Steve's attention. Instead, seconds later, I heard the water running. No doubt that was Gram's doing since we both knew it was Marietta's cure for a hangover—a long hot bath, preferably with a bloody Mary.

My body ached to disappear in a bath. The bloody Mary, not so much. Although after a couple of those I might not care about Steve seeing me without my makeup.

Steve dipped his finger back into the frosting, and I lost my capacity to breathe as I watched him lick it off. Dammit.

"Why are you over here so early?" Eating my buttercream, seeing me at my worst, and making me crazy.

"I wanted to give your grandmother her present and see if you needed anything for later. More wine maybe?"

That meant he saw the empty bottle by the porch swing. Always the cop, always observing, and yet so clueless about what he was doing to my libido.

"I'm heading to football practice, but I can swing by a store on the way back."

"Sure, another bottle of Chardonnay or whatever you want," I said, spreading frosting with a shaky hand. "Say hi to Heather."

He took a deep breath. I didn't have to look at him to sense the slow burn in how he released it. "What makes you say that?"

"You'll be seeing her at practice, right?"

"Probably."

"Seems like the friendly thing to say then."

He tilted my chin, forcing me to face him, but the intensity of his dark eyes overloaded my senses, and I stared down at the ribbed collar of his faded Police Academy T-shirt.

"Look at me," he demanded.

Reluctantly, I dropped the spatula into the mixing bowl and gazed up at him.

"I'm not back together with Heather. I'm not seeing her other than at her son's football practices. We're just friends." He waited, giving me an open invitation to search his face. "Did any of that register as the truth?"

"Yes," I said, my voice mainly breath. He hadn't lied. But we were just friends, too. At least that's what I'd thought until he kissed me stupid last night.

"Good, because the kid is having a hard time since his dad walked out of his life. Heather, too. Even sought some professional advice about it."

That explained the appointment with the psychologist. I cringed at the memory of following her, of intruding on someone's pain. Even if it was Heather.

He gripped me by the shoulders. "So, are you done being a jackass about this?"

I pushed him away. "How am I supposed to answer that? If I say yes, I'm a jackass!"

His lips curled into a killer smile as he dipped the tip of his index finger into the frosting and held it in front of my nose. "Say yes, Chow Mein."

I knew that look. I'd seen it last night. My breath caught in my throat. "What are you doing?"

"Trust me," he said, lightly touching the frosting to my lips.

Feeling like I might start sizzling on the spot, I licked off the dab of buttercream. "This is crazy. We're friends. I can't—"

"Why?"

"Because... this will change everything."

"I know." He leaned closer, tempting me with more frosting. "About time, don't you think?"

"Is this a trick question?"

"Say yes, dammit."

Yes.

Closing my eyes, I sucked the buttercream from his fingertip, savoring the sensuous explosion of sweet vanilla and the slightly rough texture of his skin that made the sizzle at my core flare like a grease fire. Just when I thought my hair might burst into flames, he pressed his lips against mine, seeking, tentatively tasting, cranking my blood pressure to the boiling point.

Danger signs flashed in my head. *You're just friends. You're not his type. You don't have any makeup on!*

Steve cupped my face and deepened the kiss, consuming me and my capacity for rational thought. Wrapping my arms around him, I relished the taste of him, a yummy blend of buttercream, coffee, and...Steve.

I heard the water turn off upstairs, and since that meant that my grandmother could walk in on us at any moment, that put a fizzle in my sizzle and I broke off the kiss. "Okay. Yes! But you're one of my best friends."

"There's no reason that has to change." He glanced down at the telltale bulge in his jeans. "Well, maybe some things might change."

"You sound like you want dessert and you haven't even asked me to dinner yet."

He grinned. "Would you like to have dinner later?"

"You're already coming here for dinner."

"Then, how about a late night supper at my place?"

"And compare notes about the case?"

He tucked back a lock of hair that had fallen loose from my ponytail. "No shop talk during dates, Deputy."

I sighed, but the thirteen-year-old girl inside me was giddy to hear him call this supper a *date*. "Dang."

"When I stop at the store, I'll grab an extra bottle of wine."

I heard Gram's footfalls on the stairs. Stepping out of Steve's reach, I picked up the package of chocolate chips

I'd set out to make a ganache glaze. "I'll bring dessert." Chocolate ganache fondue came to mind.

His gaze darkened. "Chow Mein, you'll be the dessert."

∽

By five o'clock, my mother and I had platters of shrimp, potato salad, and bowtie pasta with artichoke hearts neatly laid out on Gram's dining room table. Once Lucille arrived with her scalloped potato casserole, it looked like we were setting the stage for another funeral reception, so for Alice's sake, I placed the birthday cake in the middle of the table and shoved Lucille's casserole into the oven to keep it warm and out of sight.

Since I knew Duke would be bringing chili, I'd baked cornbread, and Steve put a case of beer into a bucket of ice.

Barry had fired up the charcoal briquettes and had a dozen seasoned beef patties and shish kabob skewers at the ready, awaiting the arrival of Duke and Alice—the only guests on Marietta's invitation list who had yet to make an appearance.

By five-fifteen, Gram and I were exchanging nervous glances when I called Duke and Alice's home phone number and there was no answer.

"Duke has never been late a day in his life," Gram said, perched on the edge of a kitchen chair.

I leaned against the tile counter. "Maybe there was a problem at the cafe and they're on the way."

Lucille scowled at me from the dining room. "All this

food is going to spoil if we don't eat soon."

She was just hungry. We all were.

I met Gram's gaze. "The briquettes are ready. It's your birthday. What do you want to do?"

With worry lining her brow she blew out a sigh. "Let's fire up the burgers and maybe they'll get here by the time they're done."

Almost an hour later, Steve kept me company in the kitchen while I ground the beans for coffee to serve with the black and white fudge cake I'd baked for Gram's birthday.

I reached for a paper filter and felt his eyes tracking me.

"Stop it," I said, feeling the flame of a blush crawling into my cheeks.

He folded his arms as he leaned against the counter. "Stop what?"

"Stop looking at me like it's time for dessert."

"Hey, if you can't stand the heat, get out of the kitchen."

"Speaking of getting out of the kitchen, while the coffee's brewing, I'm going to drive over to Duke and Alice's house to make sure they're okay."

Steve pulled a ring of keys out of his pocket. "I'll drive."

Just as we started for the door, the telephone rang. Steve answered and immediately averted his gaze.

My heart stopped. "Duke?" I whispered.

Steve nodded. "We'll be right there." He hung up the phone. "Alice is in the hospital."

Chapter Twenty-Four

By the time Gram, Steve, my mother and I stepped through the emergency entrance of Chimacam Memorial Hospital, they had taken Aunt Alice to the third floor for surgery.

"Shit!" I knew better than to believe my great-aunt when her every action told me that something was very wrong.

Steve pressed his hand in mine as if he could hear my thoughts.

I leaned into his warmth as we waited for the elevator. "I should have brought her here days ago."

"You and what army?" he whispered.

I could have done something. Should have done something.

When we arrived at the third floor, we made our way to the end of the hallway, where Duke was sitting alone in a row of five uncomfortable-looking, hard back chairs.

"Her appendix burst," he said as Gram took the seat next to him. "Probably this morning according to the ER doc. Damn fool woman. Refused to get in the car until I told her it was time to go to your birthday party." He shook his head, his expression grim. "Sorry to spoil the festivities."

Gram patted his hand. "Don't be silly. At this age birthdays aren't nearly as fun as they used to be."

Duke squinted down the hall at a nurse in green surgical scrubs pushing a gurney. "Still beats the alternative."

Seconds later, he brightened at the steady stream of swear words coming from the gurney and pushed up from his seat. "I'd recognize that mouth anywhere."

"Oh, mah," my mother said. "I had no idea Aunt Alice had such a unique vocabulary."

Gram's cheeks flushed. "Neither did I."

Me either. I suspected some drug they gave her was doing most of the talking.

The nurse slowed to a stop in front of Duke. "Here she is. And not very happy about it either."

"No! I know what goes on here!" Alice cried, her wrists in restraints, her short hair tucked into a light blue shower cap. "I want to go home!"

"I know, honey," Duke said, leaning over the gurney. "But your appendix burst and they have to go in and fix you up."

Alice's eyes shimmered with unshed tears as we gathered around her. "Please don't let them touch me."

"Alley cat, you're gonna come through this just fine." Duke squeezed her hand. "They'll take real good care of you." He looked back at the nurse. "Won't you?"

"We sure will." She patted my great-aunt's shoulder.

Alice's face glistened with sweat as she struggled against the restraints. "Keep away from me," she growled. "Don't think that I don't know what you've been doing!"

The nurse rolled her eyes. "They told me she's been making accusations like that ever since she came into the ER. They gave her something to help her relax, but it doesn't seem to have kicked in yet."

Probably because Alice was kicking back.

I reached for my great-aunt's hand and she gripped onto me like I was a lifeline.

"She's here," Alice said, her nails digging into my palm. "You believe me, don't you?"

"I believe you." I also believed that she was scared of her own shadow right now, but I couldn't take the chance and not ask. "Who's here?"

"You should probably say good-bye now," the nurse said.

Not so fast. "Aunt Alice, who's here?"

She shook her head, a tear running down her cheek. "Don't leave me alone with her."

Her who? This nurse? "Who—"

"For heaven's sake, don't carry on so. It's not forever." Gram gently wiped her sister's tear away. "We'll be waiting for you when you get out of surgery."

Alice stared at me with glassy eyes. "You promise you'll be here?"

I squeezed her hand. "I promise we won't leave you alone for a minute."

After Duke gave Alice a kiss, we all watched as she was wheeled through a secured doorway.

The second the door shut behind her, I pulled Steve aside. "You heard that, right? *She's* in the building."

He shrugged. "Said by a woman on some good drugs."

"But if Alice is right…." Her big mouth could have just

made her the next target. "Did you run a background check on *all* the doctors and nurses working at the hospital?"

"Yeah."

"And?"

He shot me a sideways glance. "And nothing."

"Nothing turned up or there's nothing that you're willing to tell me?"

Wordlessly, he walked back and sat next to Gram.

Damn. I should have made our dessert plans contingent on full disclosure.

Almost three hours later, after a surgical nurse escorted Duke and Gram through a set of double doors to see Alice in recovery, my mother turned to me and heaved a sigh of relief. "Thank God she's out of the woods." She grabbed her tote and pulled out her cell phone. "I'll call Barry and let him know." She cast a quizzical look at me. "Should I also ask him to take me home?"

I turned to Steve. "I won't be leaving anytime soon. Would you mind?"

"If you want to go outside and make that call," he said to Marietta, "I'll be there in a minute."

After she disappeared into an elevator, Steve squeezed my hand. "Sorry about supper. I'd like a rain check on that dessert."

Me too, especially since I'd been having chocolate fondue fantasies all afternoon.

"We'll do it another time," I quipped, trying to act casual instead of sounding like a sex-starved female.

He grinned, setting a torch to my cheeks.

Crap. "I meant that figuratively, not literally."

"You're blushing."

"I know."

"It's cute."

"Yeah, well, I'm a cute girl. Just ask Jimmy."

"I don't need to ask Jimmy. I already know that."

I walked Steve to the elevator. I had hoped for a kiss goodbye. Instead, his lips flatlined as the doors opened.

"What?" I asked.

The crease between his brows deepened. "It's going to be a while before they move her to a room. And you're practically dead on your feet."

"I'm perfectly fine."

"Yeah, I've heard that before."

I leveled my gaze at him. "Really. I'm okay."

"Uh-huh. I'll come back with a couple of coffees. Maybe even a mocha latte."

"That's sweet." Really sweet. "But—"

"Caffeine will help, but there's no way you can pull another all-nighter."

He'd just watered down all that sugar with an icy stare, sending a chilling ripple down my spine. "Are you saying that Alice really could be in danger?"

Steve stepped into the elevator. "Not on my watch."

～

Shortly after midnight, Alice settled into her room on the second floor. Since Steve and I planned to stay with her through the night, we managed to convince Duke and Gram to go home and get some sleep so that they could spell us in the morning.

With Steve in the room, I knew Alice was safe, despite the fact that a murderer could be roaming the halls of the hospital.

He and I locked gazes for several silent seconds.

I smiled, drinking in the way his eyes gleamed like onyx in the soft light bathing the room.

"You look tired," he said.

I felt like an emotional and physical wreck, so there was no point in denying it. "Probably because I am."

"There's an empty bed there," he said, cocking his head at the unoccupied twin bed closest to the door.

My brain slammed on the brakes. "*That* is not going to happen. Not here, not tonight!"

"You're right, so maybe you'd like to get a couple hours of shut-eye while I'm on watch."

Oh.

And snore in front of him before we'd even had a first date? That wasn't going to happen either. "I'm fine."

He blew out a breath. "That's what you keep saying. It would be more believable if you actually got some sleep now and then."

I'd sleep when this was all over. Tonight, I just wanted to keep my promise and see Alice safely through the next few hours.

"I'm okay. I had a double mocha latte, so I'm good to go."

"Sure you are," he said, folding his arms over his chest.

I stood and pressed my fingertips to the growing ache

in the small of my back, thanks to all the long nights I'd spent thrashing around in the Crippler. "Really, I'm good. I just need to get up and move. Work out the kinks." And the nervous knots he and Alice had tied me into the last two days.

He pushed out of his chair. "I could help with those kinks."

I froze, hesitant to ask what he had in mind, but exhilarated down to my toenails when he pulled me close.

"Wrap your arms around my neck," he said.

His warmth felt too good to offer up any resistance. Locking my hands at the base of his neck, I nestled closer, flattening my breasts against his ribcage.

He pulled up my cotton shirt and ran his palms up and down my back.

"Trying to cop a feel?" I asked.

"Not yet, but the night's young."

I tried to not moan as he worked his magic fingers into the knot at the small of my back. "Oh, yes…. There. That's wonderful."

"What the hell are you two doing?" the raspy voice behind me demanded.

I turned and saw Aunt Alice squinting back at me from her hospital bed.

"We're not doing anything." I pulled away from Steve as if she'd just caught us making out in the back of Duke's delivery van. "Steve's here, keeping me company."

She aimed a parental scowl at him. "Looked to me like he was copping a feel."

"Well, he wasn't." But he may have worked his way up to it if she hadn't woken up.

She squinted at the wall clock. "What time is it?"

"One-twenty-five," Steve said. "Do you need anything?"

Alice reached out to me. "You're not leaving, are you?"

I gave her hand a squeeze. "We're both going to be here all night."

Her eyelids fluttered shut. "You're a good girl. Just don't be such a noisy one." She opened an eye. "And Stevie."

He stepped to the foot of her bed. "Ma'am?"

She stabbed the air with a bony index finger. "Watch where you put your hands because I could wake up at any minute."

Criminy. Who was watching who?

A few minutes before two, Steve's cell phone rang. He stepped into Alice's bathroom to take the call. Seconds later, I heard a loud expletive, then the door swung open and we locked gazes.

"What's wrong?" I asked.

Shadows played in the contours of his face, accentuating his cheekbones. "Another stabbing outside of that nightclub."

There was only one nightclub in town, where Jake Divine had witnessed the knife fight back in May.

"I've got to go." Steve touched my hand. "You okay?"

I forced a smile and nodded. I hated the idea of him leaving me alone, but I understood that he had to do his job.

He stared at me, the tic in his cheek counting off several silent seconds. "The hell you are," he muttered, punching numbers on his cell phone.

I must not have looked very convincing.

Twenty minutes later, I was pacing the hallway outside Alice's room when my mother stepped off the elevator.

Wearing formfitting black denim jeans, my hooded sweatshirt from last night, black suede boots, and Gram's Port Merritt PD cap, she headed my direction with a canvas knapsack slung over her shoulder. All she needed was a bandolier of shotgun shells strapped over the other shoulder to look like a cover model for *Guns and Ammo*.

"What are you doing here?" I asked.

Marietta sashayed past me, her chunky boot heels thunking against the linoleum. "Steve called me for backup."

And here I thought he and I were getting along so well.

I followed her into Alice's room. "You probably don't need to stay. No point in both of us—"

"I wouldn't hear of it. Besides…" She patted the pink Taser holstered to her black leather belt. "…I brought protection."

The last time someone said that to me, he was talking about condoms. I didn't feel any safer then than I did now.

"I also brought reinforcements." My mother unzipped the knapsack. "Steve told me you might be hungry, so I cut you a slice of birthday cake." She handed me a clear plastic container and a dessert fork. "Your grandmother loved it, by the way."

"Great." I stared at the plastic container in my hand. Steve was wrong. I was too tied up in nervous knots to be hungry.

Marietta unscrewed an aluminum thermos and filled

the lid with coffee. "I made it as soon as Steve called. Just guessed when I dumped the beans in. Hope it's okay."

I sipped the steaming inky brew. If Duke's was industrial strength, my mother's coffee could double for jet fuel. "Holy moly!" I was going to be awake until Christmas.

She winced. "Too strong?"

I set down the cup and forked some birthday cake into my mouth to neutralize the acid threatening to dissolve my stomach lining. "Good and strong. Thanks."

Beaming, she peeked around the curtain separating the two beds. "How's the patient?"

"Sleepy!" Alice grumbled from the next bed.

Marietta pulled back the ringed cotton room divider. "You're awake."

Good. I wanted to ask my great-aunt a few questions.

Alice blinked at the plastic container on my lap. "Is that birthday cake?" she asked, slurring her words.

I put the cake down on the table next to me. "Yes, and since the doctor said that you're going to be on a liquid diet for a little while, we'll save you some."

Alice heaved a sigh. "Party pooper."

I held her plastic cup so that she could take a sip of water. "Aunt Alice, earlier tonight you said that you knew what was going on here."

She waved the cup away. "Uh-huh."

"What did you mean by that?"

Alice yawned, her pupils dilated, her gaze unfocused.

I pressed closer. "Did it have something to do with someone you saw downstairs?"

Her eyelids fluttered shut. "What?"

"Oh, no you don't. Stay awake for a few more minutes

and talk to me."

"Hmmmmm?"

I touched her hand. "Remember how afraid you were before they wheeled you into surgery?"

"Yessss...." Her breathing slowed as sleep took hold, thanks to the narcotics being pumped into her bloodstream.

"She's out," Marietta announced.

"Damn."

"What do we do now?"

I reached for the thermos. "We stay awake."

Chapter Twenty-Five

Pacing the length of Aunt Alice's room while she and my mother snored like dueling buzz saws, I glanced at a wall clock. Three fifty-four. Considering the time and my sleep-deprived brain, I was doing okay. But after sucking down all that coffee and the bottle of water I found in the knapsack, I needed to use the bathroom and soon or I'd be doing the potty dance instead of pacing.

I stood over the spare bed where Marietta was curled up next to the Taser she'd unhooked from her belt. "Mom?"

She stirred. "Hmmmmm?"

"I have to go to the bathroom."

She rolled onto her back. "So go."

Entering the bathroom in Alice's room, I left the door ajar so that I could see the nurse if she came in to check on Alice while I was on the toilet.

Just as I dropped trou, I saw a shadow cross the doorway and my heart almost jumped out of my throat.

I told my sphincter to hold tight for a few minutes, pulled up my pants, and crept to the door to listen for movement. Other than the roar of my pulse pounding in my ears, I heard nothing but some unladylike snoring.

Pushing the door open, I stepped out of the bathroom and saw Suzy standing next to the bed, smiling down at Alice like an adoring mother beholding her newborn.

"What are you doing?" I demanded, the hair on my arms standing at high alert.

Suzy sucked in a breath and tucked her right hand into the front pocket of her light blue tunic. "You startled me." She aimed a cool smile at me. "I just wanted to see how Alice was doing."

Lie.

She wanted something more, and I knew it had everything to do with what was in her pocket.

"Her color has certainly improved since she came into the ER," she added, as if sugar-coating the lie would make it easier for me to swallow.

"You were working in the ER when Alice arrived?" Where she would have heard my great-aunt's accusations, maybe more than one of them aimed directly at Suzy.

She nodded, fingering the IV tubing connected to Alice's arm just like the nurse who had come into the room almost an hour earlier. "I'm on a break, but I thought I'd check in on our patient for a few minutes."

My mother sat up, blinking at Suzy. "What's she doing here?"

I inched closer, my focus on Suzy's hands—empty—but I wasn't taking any chances. "Step away from Alice, now."

Alice snorted awake. "What?"

Suzy tilted her head at me. In the low light her pale blue eyes looked glassy, like lifeless doll's eyes. "I'm just here to help."

I didn't doubt she had told the truth, but I couldn't imagine who she thought she was helping.

"What's going on?" Alice asked, her voice groggy with sleep.

I patted her ankle. "Don't worry. I'm here, so is Mom."

I kept my gaze fixed on Suzy. "If you want to help, why don't you start by telling us what's in your pocket."

"It's nothing. Just some medication I'm taking," she said in a melodic, singsong voice as if she had taken over Trudy's old role of *Story Lady*.

Lie.

"Mom, go to the nurses' station and tell them to call security."

Marietta ran out the door.

"And call Steve," I yelled after her.

"This is silly." Suzy pointed at the empty coffee thermos as she stepped toward the door. "If you drank less of that stuff you wouldn't be so nervous and leap to all these crazy conclusions."

Or need to pee.

I stepped in front of her, blocking her escape route.

The planes of her pixie face hardened as she narrowed her gaze. "If you'll excuse me, I have to get back to work."

"I'm sure they can spare you for a few more minutes."

Suzy's eyes widened. "I have patients who need me."

I had the sick feeling that her patients would rest much easier if I kept Suzy occupied. "I'm sure you do."

"And not just patients, family members. I'm sure you saw it tonight in your own family, when a loved one is suffering, everyone suffers. Truly, they need all the comfort they can find during these difficult times."

"Is that what the syringe in your pocket is about? Ending suffering?"

She eased closer to the door. "I already told you that's my medication."

"I don't believe you. I think that's something you injected into Trudy and several other patients in this hospital."

"You're delusional," she said, trying to push past me.

"One of us certainly is."

I grabbed Suzy's arm to throw her to the spare bed and pin her there until security arrived, but she had leverage on me, forcing me down spread-eagle, my chin landing hard on my mother's Taser.

Suzy made a break for the door. Since she'd been working out forever and I'd taken one aerobics class in the last ten years, I knew there was no way I could outrun her. But I did have one thing in my favor—Marietta's Taser.

I rolled off the bed and ran into the hallway, fumbling with the Taser in my hand.

Standing at the nurses' station, my mother dropped the phone that had been to her ear and stood in front of the elevator like a linebacker, ready to take Suzy down if she made a break for that escape route.

Suzy hesitated, and I took the shooter's stance I saw Marietta use Thursday night, pushed a button and fired...a flashlight beam at Suzy's back. "Shit!"

"You need to activate it!" my mother yelled.

That little detail hadn't been mentioned during Thursday's demo. "How do you do that?"

"Give it to me!"

With a shaky hand I slid the Taser across the linoleum

to her.

"What's going on?" A nurse in pink scrubs demanded, stepping out of a patient's room and colliding with Suzy.

"Stop her!" I shouted, running as fast as I could.

Suzy stumbled down to one knee. As she scampered back to her feet, I lunged at her, knocking her facedown to the floor.

She bucked and kicked as Marietta circled with the Taser. "Let go!" Suzy cried. "You're making a big mistake."

Not this time.

Grabbing Suzy's wrists, I straddled her, bearing down with the full force of my hundred and sixty-four pounds. Probably the one and only time I was grateful to outweigh someone.

She squirmed, twisting, cursing. Then, Marietta pressed the Taser against Suzy's neck, and I felt the body underneath me go rigid.

Rolling off of Suzy's back, my chest heaved to suck down oxygen as I shuddered at the sight of her convulsing body. She moaned, mewing in pain—pain that my mother and I had caused.

I'd never wanted to cause anyone physical pain before. Of course, this bitch had tried to kill my aunt Alice and had been responsible for at least five other deaths.

I could easily make an exception for Suzy.

"Are you crazy?" yelled the nurse in pink scrubs as she ran to Suzy's side.

"No." I pointed at the serial killer next to me. "But she is."

The nurse glared at me as she checked Suzy's pulse. "Security's on the way."

Good. Hopefully with a pair of handcuffs. And if the
security guy didn't have any, I knew a detective who would.

"Are you okay, honey?" my mother asked, squatting
beside me as I sat on my butt, my rubbery legs splayed like
a rag doll. "Your nose is bleeding."

I used the sleeve of my sweatshirt to swipe at my
oozing nose. "I'm okay." Which was more than I could say
for Suzy, who was still twitching.

Another nurse handed me a tissue. "Oh my God,
what'd you do to her?"

"Nothing that she didn't deserve." My mother stood,
pointing at Suzy with the Taser. "You don't mess with me
and mine."

I had a hunch that Marietta was quoting from one
of her old space cowboy movies, but I didn't care. I just
wanted someone from security to arrive so that I could
haul ass to the nearest bathroom before I peed my pants.

As I pushed myself to my knees, the elevator doors
opened and I looked up to see Kyle Cardinale staring at the
pink Taser in my mother's hand. "What the hell is going
on here?"

Not a guy with handcuffs, but close enough.

"I don't have time to explain because I *really* have to
pee. Just keep an eye on Suzy. I think she's the one who
killed Trudy."

∽

I woke up to the heavenly aroma of the mocha latte
Steve had in his hand.

"You know that isn't on my diet," I told him.

He smiled and sat on the edge of the double bed in his guest room. "I think you're entitled this afternoon."

"Afternoon?" I read the clock on the nightstand. It was almost one o'clock—over seven hours since Steve tucked me into his spare bed. "I should go." Take a shower, brush my teeth, put on some makeup.

"Maybe you could drink your coffee before you run off. I was also thinking you might be hungry. You missed lunch."

Breakfast, too. Birthday cake before three a.m. didn't really count.

I propped myself up with a couple of extra pillows and sipped my latte. "Are you done at the station?"

When Steve had brought me home to his house from the hospital, he said it would take a while. He'd never booked a serial killer before.

"Done for a while," he said, brushing back a strand of hair from my face. "She didn't have much to say other than to protest that we were keeping her from her work."

"Killing people?"

"She prefers to call it *alleviating their suffering*."

"So I heard from the Angel of Mercy herself when she went after Aunt Alice to shut her drug-induced big mouth."

Steve shook his head. "There was nothing angelic about the vial we found in her pocket."

"What was it?"

"Something I can't pronounce. According to Dr. Cardinale, it's a paralytic drug used in anesthesia. A hefty enough dose…instant cardiac arrest."

Which explained why pulmonary failure was the cause of death for most of the names on my victims list—all of them with family members who attended Suzy's dance class.

With the one exception of Norm Bergeson. "But why kill Trudy?" I asked.

"I know Norm brought her to the ER three times in the last seven months, so Suzy didn't need a class at the senior center to get to know Norm and develop a relationship with him. And when the opportunity presented itself a couple of weeks ago...."

"Suzy made a decision that both Norm and Trudy had suffered enough and made her move," I said. "Then, after the funeral, Virginia Stratham would enter the picture to play Cupid with the suddenly single family member—"

Steve blew out a breath. "You're not going to let go of that matchmaking thing, are you?"

"Because it makes perfect sense. And it gave Suzy even more satisfaction because she got to see the fruits of her labor blossom at the senior center." Like at the dance class, she saw Jayne, Ernie, Sylvia, and Nell—all smiling and happy, probably for the first time in years. "Crazy satisfaction."

I shivered. "Makes me wonder how long she's been in the *mercy* business."

Steve nodded. "The FBI's been called in since this has a lot in common with a string of suspicious deaths—mercy killings—four years ago in Portland."

"Suzy told me she used to live in Portland. That's where she took dance lessons."

Steve nodded. "They'll want to talk to you. Your

mother, too."

No doubt Marietta would make sure plenty of local media were on hand to conduct follow-up interviews. That meant that my grudge match with the Crippler wouldn't be ending any time soon.

I gulped down some more coffee, willing the chocolate to transport me to my happy place. "So, what happens until the FBI gets here?"

He blew out a breath. "We wait."

"Again? I swear, you do more waiting than anyone I know."

A smile teased at the corners of his mouth. "It comes with the territory. But while we're waiting, how about some lunch?"

"What's on the menu? I'm on a diet, you know."

He shot me an evil grin. "I thought we'd start with dessert."

THE END

About the Author

Wendy Delaney writes fun-filled cozy mysteries and is the award-winning author of the Working Stiffs Mystery series. A long-time member of Sisters in Crime, Mystery Writers of America, and Romance Writers of America, she's a Food Network addict and pastry chef wannabe. When she's not killing off story people she can be found on her treadmill, working off the calories from her latest culinary adventure. Wendy makes her home in the Seattle area with the love of her life and has two grown sons.

You can visit her website at www.wendydelaney.com, email her at wendy@wendydelaney.com, and connect with her on Facebook at www.facebook.com/wendy.delaney.908.